DEATH BY ARMOIRE

DEATH BY ARMOIRE

A Palmetto Antiques Mystery

by

Albert A. Bell, Jr.

Claystone Books
http://www.albertbell.com/

2017© Albert A. Bell, Jr

Book design by Luci Mott (Fosterbooks)
Armoire image courtesy of:
Schwartz Woodworking
The Amish Furniture Gallery
of Lockport, Illinois

ISBN-13: 978-1545320235

ISBN-10: 1545320233

AUTHOR'S NOTE

My grandparents lived in a small town in upstate South Carolina. That's where I was born, but the town in this book is not meant to be that town. It inspired me, but I haven't tried to depict it down to the last detail.

My grandfather owned an antique store in that small town. It wasn't on the town square and looked nothing like the store in this book, but it inspired me. My grandparents owned a big, beautiful old house on the south side of town, and it inspired me.

No person or place in this book is meant to portray a real person or place. Any similarities are the result of inspiration.

Albert Bell

DEATH BY ARMOIRE

CHAPTER 1

I love everything about my house, but the one part that I would never give up is the front porch. The builders of big old Southern houses like mine, which goes back to 1887, understood the importance of a porch. My house, a joyously gaudy Queen Anne, faces east, with a huge magnolia tree and an ancient oak—and thus very little grass—in the yard, and the porch runs across the front and halfway back along both sides. On the south side there's a large swing mounted from the ceiling.

At the northeast corner the porch bulges out to create a circular area where I have a table and chairs, the same table and chairs my mother had when I was a little girl growing up here. Because of the conical shape of the roof over this area and the black shingles, I dubbed it the Witch's Hat when I was a child, and the name stuck. It's the perfect place to eat breakfast on a summer morning, as I did so many times as a child, as I did with my children, and as I was about to do now.

But now everything's different. My children are grown, my mother died eight years ago, my father a year after that, and my cheating ex-husband Troy died a week ago.

As I arranged my breakfast on the table, Troy's companion dog Pepper trotted up the steps and plopped down on his haunches next to me. I gave him the extra slices of bacon I had fixed, and they disappeared in two gulps. Pepper is a five-year-old Gordon Setter. Everybody thinks he's named Pepper because of his color—the black that's typical for a Gordon—but his name is actually short for Sgt. Pepper, after Troy's favorite Beatles' album.

Neither of my children can have a dog in their apartments—and Pepper's too large for their apartments anyway—so I had to take him in. Gordon Setters are known for their loyalty and good nature. Pepper actually excels Troy in both those categories, but we're still trying to figure out our relationship. I've never been a pet person.

My cell phone rang and I cursed myself for putting the thing on the tray when I came out here. Force of habit. It was my agent, Dave Siegler. I wasn't sure whether he was calling about the book I was supposed to have finished this week or about the proposal he emailed to me on the day Troy died. We had talked once earlier in the week, when I called to tell him about Troy's death, but we hadn't discussed business, of course. I guessed he had waited as long as a New York agent could contain himself.

"Good morning, Dave," I said.

"Good morning, Maureen." His voice took on the somber, consoling tone of a funeral director which I had heard so often, from so many people, in the last few days. "How are you doing?"

"I'm managing. It's been three days since the funeral. Your flowers were beautiful. Thank you." Even though I had requested donations to the Wounded Warrior Project in lieu of flowers.

"It's the least I could do. I'm sorry I couldn't get down there."

"I wouldn't expect you to make that trip. I appreciate your thoughtfulness. Thank the girls in your office for the card."

"I'll do that. So ... how are ... things with you?"

"Beginning to get back to normal ... the new normal. It's a beautiful morning. Life will go on. It has to, doesn't it?" I dropped half a biscuit on the floor for Pepper. He had already had his nutritionally balanced breakfast and had joined me on a thirty-minute run-walk. "I'll send you the final version of the Mudcat Jones book today."

Mudcat Jones is a reclusive folk musician who lives in the mountains near Asheville. I had spent three days up there going over what I hoped was the last revision of the book I had ghost-written for him. We couldn't do it by email because he lives off the grid. He doesn't want anything to do with "that interweb thang." I was on my way back to Lawrenceville the day Troy died.

"Good, good," Dave said. "I wasn't worried about it. I guess I can let you in on a little secret. I always set deadlines earlier than I actually need the work done."

"I figured that out a long time ago. All of your clients have."

Dave paused, so I took a bite of my eggs.

"I don't mean to push you, Maureen," he finally said, "but could we talk a little new business? And if you're not ready," he added in a rush, "just say so."

"Is this about that proposal you sent me the day Troy died?"

"Yeah. Sorry about the timing, but—"

"There was no way you could know, Dave."

"No, of course not. Well, have you ... had a chance to look at it?" He sounded as diffident as a fifteen-year-old boy asking a girl out for the first time.

"No."

"Oh." Rejection, total fail. "Well, I'm working on a deal to have somebody ghost-write an autobiography of Artemisia."

"The painter? That's a new direction for you."

"What? No." Total confusion. "She's a singer. Wait, there's a paint-er named Artemisia?" He was already thinking about trademark problems, protecting the brand, avoiding buyers' confusion—a mar-keter's worst nightmare.

"Yes. Artemisia Gentileschi. She lived in the 1600s."

He gave a huge sigh of relief. "No kidding. She would definitely need somebody to *ghost*-write her autobiography, wouldn't she?"

That would be an assignment I'd love to have. In the fifteen years I've been ghost-writing books for celebrities—tell-alls, autobiogra-phies, memoirs, cookbooks—I'd never worked with anybody as in-teresting as a brilliant female Renaissance painter who was raped by her teacher and brought him to trial and got him convicted. Four hundred years from now none of the people I've written about, or with, will be remembered. I've made a comfortable living and writ-ing is the only career I've ever wanted, but I turned forty-seven this spring and the man I spent twenty-three years with just died. In the last week I'd spent a lot of time on this porch with Pepper, under the Witch's Hat or in the swing, wondering what it all meant.

"So, what Artemisia are you talking about?" I asked.

"The singer."

"Sorry, that doesn't tell me anything. Does she have a last name?"

"She does, but she doesn't use it. You know, like Cher and Adele."

"With a name like Artemisia I guess you only need one. You say she's a singer?"

"She won 'America's Icon' last year, when she was fifteen. I thought maybe you had Googled her after you got my email."

"Dave, I've spent the last week dealing with Troy's death and the funeral. I haven't looked at any messages or returned any calls that didn't have to do with that." I took a sip of my orange juice. "That's behind me now, and I'm going to finish the Mudcat book by tonight. I promise. I think you'll be pleased with it. Even Mudcat was, and that's saying something."

"I'm sure I will be, and I'm sorry I have to call you now." He sounded like he really was sorry, not just funeral-director sorry. He's been my agent for sixteen years—I was his second client—and I've always respected his sincerity. "I thought maybe, you know, since he was your ex ... ."

"And since he cheated on me, I could just shrug it off. Is that what you're thinking?" Even to myself I sounded harsh.

"I'm sorry, Maureen. This was a bad idea." The fifteen-year-old boy was in full retreat, palms sweating and zits throbbing. "I'll ... I'll get back to you."

"No. We might as well talk about it. We have to sometime." I tried to shift into business mode. "You say this girl won something?"

He sighed in relief, taking a metaphorical step back in my direction. "Yeah. She won 'America's Icon' last year, like I said, when she was just fifteen."

My neighbor across the street, seventy-year-old Suellen Gillespie, stepped out on her porch to pick up her paper. She waved and looked like she was thinking about coming over. I made sure she saw that I was on the phone. Suellen, in the fine tradition of a small town in South Carolina, had "called on" me twice in the past week with food in hand. My introvert soul couldn't stand any more such courtesy right now, and my body didn't need the calories.

"So, 'America's Icon.' Is that one of those contest shows where everybody tries to see how loud they can sing?"

Dave gave his signature half-snort, half-laugh. "That's one way of describing it, I guess. I gather you haven't watched it. It's been on for six or seven years."

"My, where does the time go? No, I've never seen it. Barely even heard of it. I'm not their target audience, I'm sure. Wrong demographic." Some people get depressed on the decade birthdays. Forty-seven, earlier this year, had sent me into a spin. Nobody in my family has made it to 93, so I figure I'm over the halfway point. It's all downhill from here. And now Troy ... .

"Well, that doesn't matter," Dave said. "This girl's really talented and she's got a back story that will leave you choked up, even if you don't have any more semblance of a heart than a New York agent."

"Dave, I do have a heart, and right now it's still struggling with what I've just lost." I was surprised at how hard Troy's death had hit me. Even with what he had done to me, I cared for him, and I knew he was hurt. For the past week I'd felt like one big, raw nerve.

"I know, Maureen, and again I'm sorry I have to call you. I've put it off longer than I should have. I'm meeting with Artemisia and her mother this morning, and I've got to get this project going."

"Because next week nobody will remember who this girl is?" I was surprised to hear myself sounding so bitchy. I like Dave and appreciate everything he's done for me.

"No, because I think she's going to be a real star and I want to get on the bandwagon early. This could be the start of a long-term relationship, for me and for whoever writes this book." The take-charge agent began to emerge. "I can't wait for you, Maureen. If you don't take the assignment, I'll give it to Cassondra. She's meeting with us."

"Cassondra? Be sure you pronounce it correctly." I knew the woman, another client of Dave's, was just waiting to climb over me, like Dante clambering over Satan on his way out of hell. In general I can work with anyone, but the couple of times I'd met Cassondra face-to-face, I had had to fall back heavily on my inbred Southern gentility. Hearing her name stirred up resentment that had been simmering all week, just waiting for a target. "That little back-stabber's half my age. What has she written?"

"You mean aside from stuff for fan sites about Artemisia and other contestants on 'America's Icon'? Not much, I guess."

"Well, maybe you should just let her do this book. You said this girl is fifteen—"

"Sixteen now. She was fifteen when she won last year."

"Okay. Even at sixteen, it shouldn't take more than a weekend to write her life story. Why publish it? Just post it on Facebook."

From the change in his voice, Dave must have leaned back in his chair, something he typically does when a conversation gets unpleasant. It's his way of withdrawing as much as he can while still being in the room. "Come on, Maureen. This isn't like you."

The bitterness and despair—the way I felt torn between the memory of Troy and the memory of his cheating on me—that had been building up all week burst out. "Hey, maybe she can put it all in a text message—144 characters should be enough. Oh, wait, I know, she could tweet it. Artemisia's fans might have that long an attention span. Make it #flashinthepan."

"Now you're just being snarky, Maureen. Artemisia has actually done some pretty incredible stuff for somebody her age."

"Unless she's walked on water, I'm not interested."

"I haven't heard about that, but she does charity work. For example, she works with Wounded Warriors. You know about Wounded Warriors, don't you? By the way, I made a donation to them, in addition to the flowers. I just thought there ought to be flowers."

I didn't respond. I was too choked up to respond.

"Her dad lost both legs in Afghanistan," Dave said reverently. "His vehicle hit an IED."

I closed my eyes, trying to keep the tears from running down my cheeks. "Damn you, Dave. That's not fair." Troy, a colonel in the National Guard, had come back from his second tour in Afghanistan in one piece physically but as broken in spirit as this girl's father was in body. I petted Pepper, lying at my feet now. As a companion dog, he had meant so much to Troy in his struggle with PTSD. He sat up and laid his head on my knee.

"I'm just asking you to give her a chance, Maureen. You're the best at what you do. I think you could write a terrific book with this girl. She's a real sweetheart."

"Dave, any other time I would probably grit my teeth and say yes. But please hear me. I need a little time off. I just finished a book, and I've got so much to deal with after Troy's death. Give me the next assignment, maybe in a couple of months."

Dave paused and I could picture him twisting his mouth, pursing his lips as though he'd bitten into something sour, the way he usually did when we discussed my fee. Finally he said, "Maureen, have you ever heard of Wally Pipp?"

"Who is he?" I sat up straight, startling Pepper, who had always been keyed in to Troy's mood swings. "Some rapper? I will not write about a rapper. I've told you that."

"No. Wally Pipp played first base for the New York Yankees back in the 1920s. He was damned good, too. If you'll pardon an awful pun, you could say he 'rapped' a few home runs before they got Babe Ruth. Led the American League twice, in fact. Then he batted clean-up behind Ruth. But one day in mid-season he had a headache and asked to sit out a game. They put in this kid named Lou Gehrig, who played in—"

"Yeah, I know, I know. Over two thousand consecutive games." Troy and our son Robert used to be huge baseball fans. Although not a big fan myself, I knew enough of the basics to follow their conversations and I had certainly been aware of Cal Ripkin breaking Gehrig's record.

"To be exact, 2,130 games." Dave is a nut not just for statistics but for precise statistics and all kinds of details. It makes him a tough editor but a good one. "And do you know what happened to Wally Pipp?"

"Well, since I never heard of him, I guess I don't." I took a sip of my coffee, which was getting cold.

"He was put on waivers at the end of the season. He ended up in Cincinnati." Dave pronounced the name of the Ohio city like it tasted bad: "Cincin*n*ati."

I got up and started to pace the porch, with Pepper at my heels. "Are you threatening me, Dave? If I don't do this book, are you going to ship me off to some literary equivalent of Cincinnati?"

"No, not at all. I'm just saying—"

"Look, I know I'm being difficult, but my husband died a week ago. Okay, my cheating *ex*-husband. We were married for twenty-three years. We still had a connection, through our kids. This has hit me a lot harder than I could have expected." I felt myself tearing up again. I'd been doing that a lot these last few days. I stopped on the north side of the house, trying to stay out of sight of my neighbors. The trees between my house and the Monroes' to the north provided some cover.

"Maureen, are you okay?" Dave asked.

"More or less." I leaned against the porch railing and pulled myself together enough to finish the conversation. "It's just that, I'm realizing I still had more feelings for Troy than I would let myself admit, and now I've got to start settling his estate and decide what to do with his store. That's the first item on my agenda today."

"What *can* you do with that place? The guy was a hoarder." I had taken Dave by Troy's antique store when he came down to Lawrenceville a few years ago to finalize a particularly complicated deal with me.

I started to walk back toward the Witch's Hat. "Not a hoarder in the technical sense. He sold enough pieces to keep the store going, but it wasn't always easy for him to let go of things, I'll admit that. His father was definitely a hoarder before him. Letting them have that store was the only way my mother-in-law and I could keep the stuff out of our houses. Now I've got to concentrate on sorting it out."

"Are you going to be okay with going back in there?" Dave asked. "I mean, since Troy, you know, died there ... ."

"I guess I'll find out this morning." I hadn't been back in the store since Troy's accident, but I was determined to cross that bridge today. I had to, or be stuck on this side of a huge chasm for the rest of my life.

"Have you considered burning the place for the insurance?" Dave asked, a little too jovially.

"That would be pretty obvious, don't you think?"

"Yeah, especially when you're going steady with a cop now."

I thought "going steady" was too juvenile a term, but I let the comment slide by. "Besides, I'm not sure Troy had any insurance. I haven't found a policy yet." My son and daughter had brought all of Troy's papers from the store over to my house, to spare me the pain of going in there until absolutely necessary. I had spent hours sorting them in the family room on the third floor of my house.

"Are you going to take one out then?"

"That's another item on my very long to-do list. I've just got too much on my mind right now. I do not want to write about some teenaged flavor of the week, no matter how sympathetic a person she is. All I would be capable of is some slap-dash, half-ass book."

"You could never do that sort of work, Maureen."

"Well, thanks for the vote of confidence."

Dave gave a heavy sigh, with a sort of groan to it, his version of an audible white flag. "Okay. Give me a call when you're ready to go back to work."

"Thanks for understanding, Dave. And thanks again for the flowers. And for the donation. I'll talk to you soon."

❖❖❖

CHAPTER 2

From my house on South Arbor Street, the heart of Lawrenceville's historic district, it's only a five-minute walk to the town square and Troy's store. This morning I managed to make the trip take ten minutes. Pepper walked and trotted the distance several times, coming back to see why I wasn't moving any faster.

"Sorry, guy. This isn't going to be easy."

Troy's store is called The Palmetto Antiques Gallery. The building was originally a department store, what retailers today would call an anchor store. It sits on the southeast corner of the town square. Lawrenceville is one of those old, old towns built around a square with the county courthouse—an 1870s monstrosity built to replace the one burned in the Civil War—in the center. The modern courthouse and judicial facilities have been moved to the edge of town, near Walmart, so the original courthouse has only a few minor offices still in it. My grandmother used to tell me how, on Friday nights, people would drive into town, park around the square and give the kids fifty cents while the adults went from car to car visiting. She regaled me with tales of how much she could buy with that fifty cents.

In the 1960s Lawrenceville, like a lot of small towns in the South, fell on hard times as the textile industry declined. Half the stores around the square were shuttered. Troy's grandfather—already in his fifties by then—bought this building for practically nothing. He meant it to be a legitimate used furniture and antique store, something to keep him busy after he retired from teaching, which was mandatory at 65 in those days. Since there is a palmetto tree in front of the store—not a common sight in upstate South Carolina, even though it is the state tree and appears on the flag—and since the top two floors were configured as galleries, with an atrium effect open to the top of the building, the name seemed an obvious choice.

Troy's father, Wyatt, began buying up whole households of furniture, much faster than he sold anything. Troy added to the amalgam by going to estate sales and garage sales at the end of the day and buying whatever was left.

I do have to give them credit for arranging things in a semi-logical fashion. The really nice pieces are on the first floor, near the front, where people can see them through the large plate glass windows on two sides. With the economic recovery of this area in the last ten years and a determined tourism campaign, there are potential customers. Toward the back of the first floor are display cases containing jewelry, coins, books, and other possibly collectible items. The furniture is grouped by types—sofas, beds, tables and chairs. Used appliances are all in one place, on the third floor. To get the place up to code, Troy's father installed new restrooms and a small elevator for customers. At the back of the building, which goes all the way through the block, is a large freight elevator.

That's where they found Troy.

Actually his girlfriend found him. The coroner's verdict was "Death by Misadventure." Apparently Troy had been trying to move a tall, heavy armoire from the most recent batch of furniture he'd bought. For some reason he hadn't waited for his part-time employee, a muscular young African American man named Joseph Hughes, to help him. The armoire tipped over, crushing Troy. His head was caught between the armoire and the concrete floor.

I delayed the inevitable for a few more minutes by getting a coffee across the street from the store. Pepper sat down on the sidewalk, as he was accustomed to do when Troy stopped here, I guess. The owner, Pam, whom I've known since junior high, came out from behind the counter to hug me and tell me that my order was on the house.

"*So* sorry about Troy, Maureen," she said. "It was a beautiful funeral—the honor guard and the salute. I was in tears." She held the door for me and knelt to pet Pepper. "You miss him too, don't you, buddy? We all do. He was a great guy. You know, half the furniture in my house came from his store." She looked back up at me. "It was a shame that he had such a difficult time these last few years."

"Thank you, Pam. That means a lot. It really does." But the private, introvert part of me wished that everybody in town didn't know about Troy's struggle.

Crossing the street, I read the sign in the front window announcing that the store was closed for a few days. Troy and I had been co-owners of the building and the business. I thought, when we got divorced, that he would take me off the deeds, but he never would talk about buying me out or making any other changes. I urged him to put our daughter Rebecca's name on things. The antiquing gene seems to have skipped her older brother, Robert, and landed squarely in her double helix. Robert is establishing himself as an attorney in Greenville, thirty miles from here. He and his partner, Derrick, don't find Lawrenceville a particularly welcoming place.

Rebecca has worked in the store since she was in high school and got a college degree in business specifically so she could take over the place someday. She and I ran it, with help from Troy's dad, while Troy did his tours in Afghanistan. I assumed she would inherit the business.

But, as I went through Troy's papers from the store over the last couple of days, I discovered that he had made no changes since our divorce. I am now the owner of this dinosaur of a building and the sole proprietor of The Palmetto Antiques Gallery, and Rebecca isn't at all happy about it. She helped Wyatt and me in planning the funeral, but she's been quite frosty toward me in the few contacts we've had since then. It's as though something is eating at her.

I suspect it has to do with one piece of paper I found among Troy's effects—a recent offer from a realtor who wants to convert the building into upscale shops on the first floor and condos on the upper floors, filling in the galleries. When I saw the amount he was offering, I had to sit down. Rebecca probably suspects I'll sell the building.

I went around to the rear of the building to the door where we enter the store. Troy's big panel truck—a full-sized Ford Transit, like the guys on "American Pickers" drive—was still parked there, next to the overhead door that's used for moving furniture in and out. The only key I had to the truck was the one in Troy's set. He never gave me one of my own.

I was surprised to see the store's door partly open—ajar, as my crossword puzzles always say. Was Rebecca already here? She hadn't told me she was coming in today.

I paused just inside the door, flipped on the lights, and called out. "Rebecca? Are you here, hon? Joseph?" We had told Joseph we would call him when we were ready to reopen and would pay him during the interval, but I thought he might have stopped by to check on things. He's good about stuff like that.

Pepper advanced cautiously into the building, then stopped, ears up.

"What is it, boy?" I came up beside him.

That's when I saw the armoire that had fallen on Troy. After he was found and the police were finished with the scene, my friend, Detective Scott Kelly, whom I have been dating—but not going steady with—for about six months, made sure it was cleaned up and turned to face the wall. I had not been in here to see Troy lying dead. Because I wasn't his wife anymore and because I'd been out of town that day, they hadn't called me until they had taken him to the morgue. Since his girlfriend found him, I guess they thought it would be awkward to have me on the scene. They called Rebecca and she told me what they had done.

Now the armoire—a large, heavy Arts and Crafts piece—had been turned back around. The doors on the top part were hanging open and the drawers on the bottom had been pulled out and dropped on the floor. Someone had also rummaged through the matching dresser and the chest of drawers that Troy bought in the same lot. Other pieces sitting near them had not been bothered, as far as I could tell.

As I was calling 9-1-1 the thought flashed through my mind that there was something familiar about this furniture, but I didn't have time to pursue the idea before the operator answered. When I told her where I was and what had happened, she asked, "Are you still in the store, ma'am?"

"Yes, at the back door."

"You need to get out, ma'am, and wait for the officers to get there. And stay on the line until they arrive."

She was right, of course. For all I knew, whoever had broken in could still be in the store.

"Pepper, let's go."

Just to be on the safe side, Pepper and I crossed the street and stood on the sidewalk. I kept the phone to my ear until a police car pulled up, lights on but no sirens. Right behind it was Scott's car. "They're here," I told the operator. "Thanks for your help."

The two uniformed officers were barely out of their car, putting on their hats and adjusting their belts, when Scott crossed over to me and touched my arm. "Are you all right?"

"Yeah, I'm fine. What are you doing here?" I've known Scott for about two years. He's loving and attentive but always seems to know what's going on in my life.

"I heard the call on my scanner. Did you see anybody?"

"No, but somebody has pulled out drawers and thrown things around."

"Wait here. I'll go with the uniforms to check the place and make sure it's empty. It'll take a few minutes." He started back across the street.

By now Pam and a couple of her customers had come out of the coffee shop, the only place on this side of the square that was open before nine.

"What's going on, Maureen?" Pam asked, stroking Pepper's head absent-mindedly.

"I think somebody broke into the store. The police are checking to see if they're still in there."

"Oh, my gosh! Do you want to come in and sit down?"

"Thanks, no. I'll just wait here." There's nothing I dislike more than being the center of attention. I am an introvert. That's why ghost-writing is perfect for me. I have the pleasure of writing and spending a lot of time by myself, but I don't have to do book-signings or publicity appearances. And I make a decent, steady income.

"Do you need a refill on that coffee?"

"I'm good." *Hurry up, Scott.*

As though in a telepathic answer to my plea, Scott emerged from the building and waved for me to come over.

"Take care," Pam said. "And don't hesitate to call me if you need anything."

The two uniformed officers came out of the building as an evidence technician's van pulled up and the techs got out their boxes of equipment and cameras.

"There's nobody in there," Scott said, "but one of the display cases toward the back was smashed. We're going to dust for fingerprints and check for any other forensic evidence. It probably won't tell us anything, though. Who knows how many people have touched those things over the years?"

"Okay. Thanks, and thanks for getting here so quickly."

"Just servin' and protectin', ma'am," he said in what was supposed to be a Jimmy Stewart imitation, I think. Or maybe it was Barney Fife. His ability to do impressions is not one of the things that attract me to him. "That's what we do. You have a key to the front door, don't you?"

"Yes. The same key unlocks the back and the front. We just don't use the front door much."

"Let's go in that way so we won't interfere with the techs. It doesn't look like anything has been disturbed in the rest of the building, just at the rear. There was no sign of forced entry. Somebody had a key or picked your lock, which would have been very easy to do."

With Pepper between us we walked around to the front of the store, and Scott shook his head as I unlocked the door. As far as I know, the locks are the originals, the kind that can click shut behind you. Troy had locked himself out a couple of times and had to call me for my spare set of keys.

"You know," Scott harrumphed, "the locks on this building are so old they're practically worthless. My ten-year-old nephew could pick them." Scott has never married, but his sister and her husband have two kids who adore him. "I know this is an antique store, but you don't have to have antique locks. You need to install deadbolts. And alarms. If you put in deadbolts and alarms, it would probably lower your insurance premium."

If we have any insurance. "We've never had any problem." I knew I sounded too defensive. The bell over the door jingled as we entered.

"Maureen, somebody broke in. That means you have a problem. I know you don't have security cameras in the loading area, but what about up front here? Maybe whoever broke in came far enough into this part of the store that we could see them, even if they didn't disturb anything up here." He looked up, sweeping the large area with his soft brown eyes. "Oh, hey, at least there are cameras here."

Scott had chastised me gently for our lack of cameras in the back when Troy was killed. Now I had to admit the awful truth. "There are cameras, but they ... they aren't hooked up."

"Then why—"

"Troy bought some cameras when that antique mall in Fountain

Inn closed a couple of years ago, but he never got them hooked up." He had also tried to buy out some of the dealers in the mall, with no luck, thank God. "He put up signs that there are cameras"—I pointed to one—"and people can see them. They just can't tell that they don't work."

Scott sighed heavily and shook his head.

"I know, it's dumb. Rebecca and I kept telling him to get them hooked up. He said he needed to get the recorder working first. The owner of the mall in Fountain Inn told him it didn't work when he bought the stuff. That's why he got it cheap. Troy thought maybe he could fix it, but he decided just having the cameras and the signs where people could see them would be a deterrent—and cheaper."

"Please get them hooked up."

"Could your nephew do it?"

"He probably could, but, you know, child labor laws. It wouldn't look good, me being a cop—"

"Scott, I'm just kidding." I put a hand on his arm. He can be a little too serious and too literal. "I'll call somebody today. I promise you." One more item on that already long to-do list.

"And a locksmith?"

I nodded. Make that two more items. "We do have sprinklers and smoke alarms, you know," I pointed out in my defense.

"Only because you have to, to be up to code and allowed to open."

"This place isn't exactly a gold mine. It was more of a hobby— okay, an obsession. Troy cut every corner he could."

"I don't mean to give you a hard time, Maureen, especially right now. I just want you to be safe." He scratched Pepper's head. "I have to go. I'm glad you've got the dog with you. When the techs are done, be sure you lock up back there. Are you going to open the store to-day?"

"I wasn't planning to. I need to think about what I'm going to do with the place. I don't want to deal with customers yet."

With a quick kiss and a promise to call later, Scott left and I settled into the office, which is halfway between the front and back doors. The original office and restrooms for the department store were on the second floor overlooking the main floor, so Troy's father had walled in a portion of the first floor to create an office and handi-cap-accessible restrooms and an elevator.

I could understand why Troy had loved this place so much. The floor in the back storage area where he died was concrete, but the rest of the building still had the original wood floors. They creaked, and the air had just the right nip of mustiness in it. The crowded furniture absorbed and muffled sound. The pictures and knick-knacks made it as comfortable as your favorite sweater and jeans, a kind of three-story man cave. I turned off the lights except in the office and felt something like an embrace, as though the building was welcoming me. Or maybe it was some vestige of Troy. When he was in Afghanistan, Rebecca said she sometimes felt his presence.

I shook off that odd sensation and sank into the desk chair. Pepper lay down on the rug next to it, his regular spot. I wasn't even sure why I was here. I had passed the first test—standing in the very place where Troy had died and looking at the piece of furniture that had fallen on him. What more did I hope to prove?

I turned on the computer and logged in. Since I had worked in the store as recently as three years ago, I was familiar with Troy's bookkeeping methods, but I was going to have to ask Rebecca about some of the refinements she had apparently introduced. What I wanted to do today was get a sense of the inventory and any money owed to the store. Troy sells—no, sold—furniture to poor people at ridiculously low prices and on installments, with no interest. And he didn't press hard for payment. Whether I sold the store or let Rebecca run it, I needed to have some idea how much income it could generate. Right now it was hard to see how it could match the offer the developer had made.

Half an hour later one of the techs came to the office to tell me they had finished and were "releasing the scene."

"We do need one more thing, Ms. Cooper," the young woman said diffidently, "if you don't mind."

"Why would I mind?"

"We'd like to get your fingerprints and swab your cheek for a DNA sample, just so we can compare it to samples we took back there." She jerked her head toward the rear of the store. "Since somebody was killed here recently, we think it's a good idea. It helps us eliminate people. It'll just take a minute."

"Sure, that's no problem."

She closed the office door, like this was some intimate process, and took the swab. She was taller than me, with dishwater blonde hair done up in an efficient bun and more freckles than would be considered cute. As she took my fingerprints on her tablet I noticed that her name tag said Hightower, the name of a prolific local family.

When the techs left, I locked the back door, with Pepper by my side, and looked over the last batch of furniture Troy had bought. He hadn't had time to enter it into the inventory, so I would have to figure that out. As I ran my hand over the dresser I suddenly knew why it seemed familiar. This was from my paternal grandparents' house, an historic home known as the Lemand house, after the man who built it and made the furniture. Even though several families had lived there since World War II, it was still the Lemand house.

I hadn't been in the house in almost twenty-five years, and the furniture looked different, not being in the context where I had always seen it. My grandfather, the chief of police, had been killed leading a raid. Not long after that, my grandmother had sold the house and moved into an apartment. She said the place was too big for her by herself and had too many memories that she couldn't bear.

I don't like the Arts and Crafts style, but I knew this was high-end stuff—late nineteenth-century and in very good condition—the kind of furniture Troy would put on the first floor, near the front, and probably would sell to support the rest of his "habit." Even when we were dating and I had taken him to meet my grandparents, he had been in awe of the furniture. He must not have been able to afford more than a few pieces. The house, as I remembered it, was chock-full of this kind of thing.

I wasn't sure I could stand to have the armoire out where I would have to see it every day until it sold. It was about eight feet tall with short legs. Troy should never have tried to move it by himself. The evidence techs had put the drawers back in the dresser and chest that made up the rest of the set .Whoever had rummaged through them had scratched them in a couple of places.

As I stepped around broken glass, the smashed display case puzzled me. It contained coins and old paper money. Some of the pieces had been taken, but not all and probably not the most valuable ones. I wasn't surprised that someone had broken in. The store was obviously not being watched. What I didn't understand was why only certain things had been disturbed or stolen. Thieves could have had the whole place to themselves for hours. Maybe they saw the cameras and did get scared off.

I was surprised to hear the bell over the front door jingle. I thought it was locked. Scott, amid all his grumbling, had checked it from outside as he left. The last thing I wanted now was to have to deal with a customer. I stepped into the shadows behind the armoire. When I heard footsteps approaching the office, I put my hand on my phone, ready to dial 9-1-1.

"Hello? Is anyone here?" a woman's voice said. But not just any woman's voice. It was Anna Maxwell, the woman Troy had had an affair with, the affair that ruined our marriage! Pepper trotted toward the front of the building, giving what I've already learned was his bark of recognition and welcome.

"Well, hello, Pepper. I didn't expect to see you here. Who's with you? I know you're a smart dog, but unlocking doors is a bit beyond you."

Maybe not, with our crummy locks, I thought. Peeping around the corner of the armoire, I saw Anna kneel to pet the dog and I realized that Pepper knew her better than he did me. I stepped out into the dim light filtering into the store from the windows on the upper levels, stopping beside a display case filled with knives and military memorabilia—stuff that sells pretty well in a small town in South Carolina.

"What are you doing here?" I asked. "How did you get in?" I struggled to keep my voice level. My mother had raised me by a strict code of Southern gentility, and I had tried to remain on good terms with Troy and pay as little attention as possible to Anna, but right now I wanted to scratch her eyes out—for a start.

Anna stood up, her hand over her heart. "Oh, Maureen. I'm sorry to intrude."

In my store? Or in my marriage?

"I didn't see any lights on. I ... I have a set of keys. I thought I should return them, and I hoped I could do it when nobody was around. Then I could just leave by the front door and it would lock behind me."

Which she couldn't do if we had deadbolts. "A set of keys'? To what?"

"To this place, to Troy's apartment, and to his truck."

Although their relationship was no secret, Troy and Anna never moved in together. I had never asked why. Because of her kids, I assumed, or maybe because I owned the house where Troy had an apartment. Anna has an accounting business on the north side of the square and sells insurance. She and her husband were divorced eight years ago. She has two daughters, eleven and nine. I dislike confrontation—have ever since I was a child—so I have avoided her as much as I could in this small a town. I do my own taxes. And I would certainly not buy any insurance from her. Perhaps Troy had, but that wasn't a question I wanted to ask during our first encounter since his death.

Anna wasn't a native of Lawrenceville. You're not considered a native until three generations of your family have been born here. She had moved into town with her teacher husband and then stayed—just because she liked the place, she said—after they divorced and he left. I had met her a few times before she and Troy began their affair.

Like any woman whose husband has betrayed her, I suppose, I looked at the other woman and asked myself what he found in her that he couldn't find in me. Anna was certainly attractive—about thirty-five, taller than average, blonde, with an angular face and enough curves to satisfy a man—but no bombshell. She was wearing a gray business suit with an off-white blouse and a red necklace. Was there something about her personality that Troy found more appealing than mine? I knew she was a fitness buff, like Troy. They had met while running a half-marathon, something I would never do. I walk every morning—or use the treadmill in bad weather—but Troy had always pushed me to get as serious about working out as he was, without success.

I should hate Anna, and I guess I do, but I knew she had struggled after her own divorce. I had heard that child support payments were few and far between. She had not flaunted herself in front of me in the time she and Troy were together. That sort of decorum is something I appreciate.

"I'll take those," I said, holding out my hand.

Anna gave me the keys. Neither of us moved.

"Look, I'm not sure how to put this," I said, "but thank you for not coming to the funeral. That would have been … well, awkward."

"Even more than you know."

"What do you mean? The woman scorned and the cheating girl-friend at the same funeral—how could it get any more awkward?"

Anna flinched. "I guess I deserve that. Your son came to my office the day before the funeral and told me that, if I showed my face, he and his partner would remove me."

I put a hand on the display case to steady myself, or maybe my subconscious was reaching for one of the knives. "That was his do-ing. I swear to you, I knew nothing about it."

She shook her head, looking at the floor. "I didn't think you did. You've never seemed vindictive, and I thank you for that. I wouldn't have been there anyway. I couldn't risk giving potential customers a reason to snub me. I've had a hard enough time gaining acceptance in this town."

I couldn't resist the opening. "Why don't you leave? I'm sure an accountant could find work pretty much anywhere." My mother would just have to forgive me for the snarkiness.

"You'd like that, wouldn't you?" She squared her shoulders. "But my girls love it here, so I'm going to stick it out until they finish school."

"Well, I assume this will be our last conversation."

She nodded.

"Is there anything of yours in Troy's apartment that you want to retrieve?"

"No. While everyone was at the funeral I had a chance to go to the apartment and clean out anything of mine. I never went past the kitchen and the powder room. I made him keep his hoard out of there so I could stand to be in the place."

That explained why the kitchen looked so neat when I glanced through the back door as I was getting supplies off the porch for Pepper.

Her tears began to well up. "I didn't take him away from you, you know."

"What?"

"I don't mean to be cruel, Maureen, but I guess you have a right to know this, and I'm the only one who can tell you. Troy said that he had decided to leave you before he deployed to Afghanistan the first time."

I had to take a couple of breaths before I could say anything. "Why should I believe you? You need to leave. Right now!"

She still didn't make a move toward the door. "My mother used to say, 'If he'll do it with you, he'll do it to you.'" Her tears started to flow in earnest; I was still fighting mine back. "I'm pretty sure he was getting ready to dump me, if that makes you feel any better."

I couldn't fully appreciate the *schadenfreude*, but I took some satisfaction from her tears. "What makes you say that?"

"The last month or so ... he was acting different ... strange."

"It's called PTSD."

She took a handkerchief from her purse and dabbed at her eyes. "No, more than that. He would be gone for most of a day and wouldn't tell me where he was or what he was doing. And he seemed to be afraid of something. Or somebody. I'd never seen him like that before."

CHAPTER 3

I tried to focus on getting more acquainted with the office than I had been in the last few years, but Anna's parting comment and the fact that somebody had broken in made it difficult for me to concentrate on trivialities like where Troy kept the staples and the paper clips. I called the only locksmith in town and then called a couple of security firms in the area to get estimates about cameras and alarms. Then I decided to call Rebecca and ask her if she had noticed anything unusual about Troy's behavior recently.

This wasn't a call I looked forward to making. My relationship with my daughter has been rocky for the last seven or eight years, since she was a junior in high school. In spite of my best maternal advice, she became sexually active at that time. I never condemned her and tried to keep communication open—everything the advice columnists say you should do—but she seemed determined to shut me out. During those years she grew much closer to Troy, who couldn't accept that his son was gay.

Even with our history, I was surprised by how cool Rebecca sounded when she answered the phone. "How are you doing, hon?" I asked.

"My dad died. How do you think I'm doing?"

"It's hard, isn't it, a real shock? Especially when it's so unexpected. I had time to prepare—if you ever really can prepare—when my parents died."

"What do you want, Mother?" she asked abruptly.

It took me a second to decide to put her rudeness down to grief and move on. "Well, I was talking to somebody a little while ago who said your dad had been acting differently lately. You worked closely with him. Did you notice any change in his behavior?"

Rebecca sighed, as though she did not want to have this conversation any more than I did. "He kept more to himself for the past month. He would be gone, sometimes for most of the day, and I wouldn't know where he was. He wouldn't have his phone on."

"Did he say or do anything to indicate he was afraid of somebody?"

There was a long enough pause that I thought we had lost the connection, but she finally said, "Yeah ... you."

"What ... what on earth are you talking about?"

"He was afraid of you. That's why he never would put my name on the deed to the store."

"Wait a minute. I told him any number of times that he ought to put your name on it and take mine off."

"He didn't believe you. You lorded it over him because you made most of the family's income." The intensity in her voice was ramping up. "You wouldn't even take his name when you got married, Mom."

I tried to stay calm. "We talked about that. Lots of women keep their own names. He said he was fine with it." My family name is one of the oldest in Lawrenceville. Since I am the only child—and a daughter—of an only child, I thought I would be the last to carry it. The only way I could pass it on was to give it to my children as a middle name. But then, when Robert and Derrick got married, they chose Cooper as their last name.

"What else could he say? You're a ball-buster, Mom. That's why Dad took up with Anna. Hell, it's probably why Robert is gay."

I slapped my hand on the desk, startling Pepper. "You know that is utter nonsense. Robert is who he is. Nobody *made* him that way. Where is this coming from?"

"From years of watching you emasculate Dad."

I gasped like I had been hit hard in the gut. "Okay, look, I know we're both upset. We've lost somebody ... dear to us, but why are you talking to me like this?"

"Because Dad wouldn't let me say anything. I told him he needed to confront you, to tell you to get off his case, but he was afraid to."

"Afraid? Why would he be afraid of me?"

"Why *wouldn't* he be? I mean, you let yourself get pregnant so he would have to marry you."

"Hey, stop right there, young lady. We thought we were both being careful, but the only way you can be sure not to get pregnant—"

"Is not to have sex. I know. You told me that all the way through high school."

"Well, it was the voice of experience. I'm sorry you didn't listen. And I did *not* force your father to marry me. We were already engaged. We had an accident, so we just moved things up a little. Did he ever say I forced him to marry me?"

"He didn't use that word, I guess, but you could tell it was what he meant."

"Did he actually say he was afraid of me?"

"No, but he was afraid of somebody. Who else would it be? Everybody in town loved him."

I felt like I was listening to a stranger talk about people I didn't know. "Rebecca, I worked hard to support Troy, even when he was having so much trouble. I never made him feel inferior, and I know damn well I never gave him any reason to be afraid of me."

"Mom, you own the house where his apartment was, and he couldn't afford to buy your interest in the store. His truck was the only thing that was his. Maybe that was why he spent so much time in it."

I was too stunned to say anything for a moment. What I thought of as generosity—extreme generosity to a cheating spouse—Rebecca obviously saw quite differently. In exchange for Troy giving up any claim to my house, I let him have an apartment in another house two blocks away that my parents left me, one that had been converted to a three-family rental before the town's historic district was established. In return for free rent, he acted as the super in the building. He was always good about minor repairs, painting, that sort of stuff. Everyone thought we were quite civilized about the arrangement. I was just glad not to get calls about leaky pipes or furnaces that didn't work. Troy was quite handy with plumbing, wiring, just about any kind of small job. And he had enough sense to call somebody for the big jobs. I still got the bills, but those I could manage without having to deal in person with tenants or plumbers or electricians.

"Well," I finally said, "I've just learned that Shakespeare was right."

"What are you talking about?"

That's what you get—or don't get—with a business major, I guess. "'How sharper than a serpent's tooth' and so on. It's from *King Lear.*

Google it. And when you calm down, maybe we can talk about why you hate me so much and why you picked now to unload this on me. Don't you have any idea what I'm going through right now?"

"Mother, I don't hate you. I couldn't hate you." She took a deep breath. "I'm just sorry you couldn't see how much Daddy was hurting. You always had your nose in some book that you were writing—"

"Which is how I paid for your college education, and your brother's, if you'll recall. And law school for him as well." I was proud of the fact that both of my children got their education without the burden of student loans.

"I appreciate that. You know we both do, but please don't start on me like you did on Dad."

Dear God! Could she be right?

"What are you going to do about the store?" Rebecca asked with an edge still in her voice, but a softer one with a hint of an apology in it.

"I'm still thinking about that. I'm in the office now. Somebody broke in sometime during the last couple of days." I stroked Pepper's back, just to reassure myself.

"Oh, no! Did they take anything?"

"Not that I can tell. They smashed one display case, the one with the money in it. But you would probably know what's missing better than I do. They don't seem to have gotten any farther than that."

"Have the police been there?"

"Yes, come and gone."

"You still get special service, don't you, just like your parents did."

"I don't ask for anything," I said. "They didn't either." My paternal grandfather had been the much-revered chief of police here for fifteen years. I guess Rebecca was right. We never had to worry about lack of patrols on our street or slow response time if we did need to call.

"You know, my friend Laura's apartment was broken into," Rebecca continued in the same petulant tone. "The cops wouldn't even come out. They told her to give them a list of anything that was stolen."

"She wasn't hurt, was she?"

"No, but that's not the point. All you have to do is call Scott Kelly. It must be nice to have your own personal cop on speed dial."

Rebecca never has liked Scott. At least she has never been rude to his face. I don't know how she deals with Anna and frankly don't care. "For your information, I called 9-1-1, just like anybody would. He heard it on his scanner and stopped by. We go out some, but—"

"Okay, Mother. Whatever. I don't care if you're his booty call. But we really do need better locks and a security system. I don't know how many times I told Dad."

"I've called a couple of people to get estimates."

"Good." She was quiet for a minute. "Mom, I am sorry I went off on you. I've got a lot on my mind right now, and I just can't believe what's happened."

I could hear her voice choking. "I know, hon. I still expect him to walk in the door."

She blew her nose loudly. "When do you think you'll reopen the store?"

"When will you be ready to go back to work?"

"Any time." I could tell she was putting on her brave face, like she did when she had to get braces. "It's your store now, so it's your call."

"Rebecca, it's *our* store. I don't care what the documents say. It always has been our family's store."

"Whatever."

Both my children know how much I hate 'whatever.' The dismissive tone with which the word is spoken only emphasizes how much it means 'I don't give a rip about what you're saying.' It seemed like it was becoming Rebecca's mantra. "Okay, today's Wednesday. Why don't we open again on Friday? That FoodFest thing is this weekend. There'll be vendors set up on the courthouse lawn and all around the square, so there should be pretty good crowds."

"Do you want me to come in today?"

"No." We both needed time to cool off. "I want to sort through some things. Why don't you come in tomorrow afternoon and we'll talk over the situation, see where we go from here. You can see what was taken from the display case. Call Joseph and tell him to be here Friday morning."

"That sounds like the manager's job. Should I think of myself as the manager now?"

"Yes, you should."

Her voice perked up. "Maybe we could talk about a raise then. I've got a lot of good ideas. We need a web site, and a Facebook page. We need to be able to sell things online. Dad never wanted to get into that."

"I'm not sure he really wanted to sell anything."

"Yeah, but I do, and you can't run a business today without—"

"Rebecca, we'll talk about all of that, I promise. See you tomorrow."

I let Pepper do his business in the alley behind the store, cleaned up after him, then made sure both doors were locked because I planned to walk around the store, on all three floors, while I considered my options. I didn't want to be actively involved in running the place. I did it to help Rebecca when Troy was in Afghanistan, but my introvert nature and my tense relationship with my daughter made it a real chore.

I was the only child of a teacher and a lawyer, born when my parents were in their late thirties. Both of my parents were only children, so I grew up a loner, with no cousins or extended family. I read a lot and by the time I was in junior high had developed my desire to write. If I sold the store, I could get back to writing and—if the developer's offer was legitimate—give both of my children a decent sum to help them get established.

But Rebecca loves the store, always has. She hung around here as a child and started working here when she was in junior high. She isn't a hoarder—at least not yet—so she doesn't mind selling things. She understands that the purpose of a business is to make money, not fill up a building with stuff. But could she do the buying that her father and grandfather did? If Troy had lived longer, Rebecca could have learned more about the antique business.

Using social media and selling things online might actually improve our profit margin. It would mean an investment of time and money, though. I knew from Rebecca's excitement at the end of our conversation that she would be crushed if I sold the store, but I wouldn't let her force me into a decision.

It would be a huge disappointment to Troy's father, too, if I sold the store. Troy's grandfather bought the building, but it was his father, Wyatt, who really started the business. With his eye for antiques he can spot the one valuable piece in a room full of junk. At the same time, he's always been the real hoarder, although Troy was strongly inclined in that direction.

I repeated my new mantra: I do not want to be involved in running this store, especially now that I know how deeply Rebecca resents me. Wyatt is still alive, a healthy, active man of 70. I wondered if he could come back in and help Rebecca for a few years. Troy's mom died from multiple myeloma ten years ago. His dad still lives in Lawrenceville but spends some time in Florida in January and February, during what passes for winter around here. Troy's sister lives near Tallahassee. Wyatt drives a big van, like Troy's, and he always comes back with a full load of items for the store. I had spoken with him only once since the funeral. He was involved with his daughter and grandchildren, who came up for the service. He had said he would do anything to help us out. Maybe it was time to take him up on that offer.

Pepper followed me back to the office. I was reaching for the office phone to call Wyatt when my cell phone rang and I saw Dave Siegler's number. I knew he would keep calling until I somehow managed to convince him that I did not want to get involved in another book project right now, when I hadn't even quite finished the current job. His persistence is an admirable quality when he's working on my behalf. At other times it just makes him a nag.

I answered, ready to cut him off, but a soft woman's voice said, almost apologetically, "Ms. Cooper, hi. This is Artemisia."

CHAPTER 4

"Excuse me? Who?"

"Artemisia. Artemisia Johnson. I'm the singer. Mr. Siegler said he talked to you about writing a book with me."

"Oh, yes. Sure. How are you?" It was all I could think of to say.

"I'm fine, thanks. I know this is a surprise. Mr. Siegler let me use his phone. I'm in his office right now, in the conference room. He said you don't answer calls if you don't recognize the number."

"Yes, that's true."

"Well, I hope you don't mind my calling you."

"No, it's all right." With that sweet young Southern accent, how could I object?

"When Mr. Siegler told me about what happened to your husband, I felt like I had to tell you how sorry I was to hear about it and about the trouble he had after he got back from Afghanistan."

"Thank you, hon. I understand your dad was injured pretty badly over there."

"Yes, ma'am, but he's getting along better than you might expect. At least he seems to be. Sometimes I wonder."

"I'm glad to hear that." I had to remind myself that I was talking to someone younger than my daughter. She was polite and sounded so mature.

"Ms. Cooper, I can understand you not wanting to work on the book with me. This must be a difficult time for you."

"It is. I'm sure Dave will hook you up with somebody who can do the job. He has several clients with this kind of experience."

"He wants me to work with a woman named Cassondra Willis. I just came out of a meeting with her." After a long pause and a heavy sigh, she asked, "Can I be really honest with you?"

"Sure."

"I can't *stand* her, Ms. Cooper," she said, as though I was another sixteen-year-old with whom she was sharing her deepest secret about which member of the latest boy-band she had a crush on. "I told Mr. Siegler I could never work with her."

I bit my tongue so hard I was surprised it didn't bleed. Putting my phone on speaker, I made a quick Google search that brought me to Artemisia's website. She looked like the wholesome, fair-haired daughter many parents would love to have, with just enough of something provocative in her smile to appeal to a wider audience, mostly teenaged boys. Her music seemed to be a blend of country and soft rock.

It helped to see a face as the girl went on enthusiastically. "I've looked over a couple of the books you wrote with people—Mr. Siegler has copies here—and I just *hope* you might reconsider about doing this project with me. I know I'm young and people don't think I've done enough to write the story of my life, but I want this to be a good book. I think it would be, if you helped me write it."

"Let me think about it, hon." Why did I keep wanting to call her 'hon' when I didn't even know her? Was I turning into a Southern matron? "I have to get my husband's store reopened and there's a big food festival here this weekend. I ... . I can give you a decision on Monday." I couldn't believe I wasn't saying a flatout no.

"You know what, Ms. Cooper," Artemisia said as though the most amazing idea had just bubbled into her head, "I don't have anything scheduled this weekend. I'm doing a concert in Charlotte on Thursday. It's not a long drive from there to Lawrenceville. My mom and I could rent a car. What if I came down and hung around your store on Saturday? Maybe I could sing a couple of songs, meet people. It might help draw some customers into your store, and it would give us a chance to get acquainted."

I was struck dumb. Having one of the most popular singers in the country in my store *might* draw in some customers? "Well, hon, that's ... . I don't know what to say. I'm afraid I couldn't afford your performance fee, though."

Artemisia laughed. "Oh, Ms. Cooper, I wouldn't charge you anything. It would be fun. I don't get to do much of anything for fun these days." I couldn't miss the sadness in her voice—a childhood already lost. "There's just one favor I would ask, though."

A-a-a-and here it comes. "What's that?"

"Mr. Siegler said you took him to a great barbecue place when he was down there. He showed me their web site. It's cool. Could you take me?"

By the time our conversation was over I had several more items on my to-do list. Artemisia and her mother, who travels with her on her concert tours, would arrive Friday evening. They would bring a stack of publicity photos she could autograph and give out and CDs to sell. She said I could make a poster or two, although she seemed amused by the very concept of a "poster." She asked that they not be put up until Saturday morning and that I not tell anyone about her visit before then. She didn't want the local media to have advance warning of her appearance. She would notify her fans on social media that morning. By her estimate, she had several thousand followers in the Upstate.

A place for her and her mother to stay was the major issue. Lawrenceville isn't flush with hotel rooms to begin with. The places I called were booked solid because of the festival. That left me with no real options. I would have to put them up in my house, where I certainly had room—six bedrooms and four bathrooms, in fact. But that would make *me* very uncomfortable. Troy had, at one time, suggested we open a B&B, but having to be sociable with strangers over breakfast, maybe even for a whole weekend? No way could I do it.

I was prioritizing my list when Pepper got up and trotted out of the office. I didn't think much of it—I'm just not accustomed to having an animal around—until he reappeared with Joseph walking beside him.

"Oh, hi. I didn't hear you come in."

"Sorry, Ms. Cooper. I didn't mean to startle you."

"I guess I was absorbed in some planning for this weekend."

Pepper returned to his rug and Joseph stopped in the doorway, filling it with his muscular six-foot frame. "Rebecca called me." His soft, cultured voice surprises people who know him primarily as a running back knocking over would-be tacklers. "She said you're going to reopen on Friday. Do you want me to be here?"

"Definitely. With the festival and ... and all, I think we might have a good couple of days. There certainly should be a lot of people around."

"I'm ready to get back to work. I do appreciate you paying me while we've been closed. You didn't have to do that."

"It's only fair. Our being closed wasn't your fault, and you've been somebody we could depend on these last few years."

"Rebecca said you were thinking about setting up a web page and doing sales online."

"Oh, well, that possibility ... has been raised." I had the sense that I had already lost control of this situation. "We would have to find somebody to set it up. All that would take time."

"It's not hard to do, Ms. Cooper. I've taken a couple of courses. I set up the web site for my uncle's restaurant. And his Facebook page."

"*You* did that web site?" Joseph's uncle runs the barbecue place I had promised to take Artemisia to. It's just a hole-in-the-wall, with four tables. Until Artemisia mentioned it, I hadn't thought about it having a web site, but a Facebook page as well? Who can exist without one these days, I suppose?

"Yes, ma'am. We've had about five thousand people like us."

"That's not surprising. You've got the greatest barbecue in the Upstate."

"Thanks. You should put that on our Facebook page."

I wondered what it would do for their business if Artemisia "liked" them. "Well, I have a lot of thinking to do the next few days. I'll talk things over with Rebecca and you before I make any final decisions." I stood up, indicating our chat was over. "Oh, and thank you for coming to the funeral. Thank your grandmother for me."

Joseph nodded and joined me as we walked toward the back of the store, with Pepper between us. "We wouldn't have missed it. And my grandma made a contribution to Wounded Warriors. I'm sorry it couldn't be more."

"Thank you. Everything helps." I wasn't surprised that they had donated something, probably more than they could afford. That's the kind of people they are, even though the family has struggled along at or below the poverty line for several generations. Joseph's grandmother was a single mom with two children. Then her daughter, Dolores, got pregnant. When Joseph was two months old, Dolores left him with her mother and nobody saw her for several years. She has reappeared a couple of times, but the last I'd heard was that she was in jail in Atlanta.

"I still can't believe it happened," Joseph said, looking over the scene as we stopped by the back door.

"It doesn't seem real, does it? Oh, by the way, the police may ask you for a DNA sample and fingerprints," I said as casually as I could. "They got them from me. They want to compare us to the samples they took back here."

Joseph lowered his head. "Well, mine are already in the system, unfortunately."

"Oh, right." I needed to change the subject. "Listen, do you know anything about this last load of furniture Troy bought?"

"Yes, ma'am." Joseph stepped over to the armoire. The mirror over the dresser caught his reflection. He's a handsome young man, there's no denying that. "He got it at a sale in a big old house on West Main Street. He said your grandparents used to live there. A Mrs. Boyd owns it now. She's really old and not doing too well."

I had seen the sale advertised and thought I might go by there, just to walk through my grandparents' house one last time. As often happens in small towns, the historic homes come to be known by one family's name—sometimes the original owner's, as in this case, even though the Boyds had lived there for a quarter century. They were long-time Lawrenceville stalwarts themselves, but they could never eclipse the Lemands' reputation.

West Main Street was the other arm of Lawrenceville's L-shaped historic district, and the Lemand house was one of the largest and most beautiful there, one of only three in Lawrenceville done in the Arts and Crafts style. It couldn't get any more ironic than this—my husband crushed by a piece of furniture from my grandparents' house.

I shook my head to stop that train of thought. "I haven't found any paperwork on that furniture," I told Joseph.

"The receipt's probably in that accordion file he keeps in the truck. We were there just a couple of hours before ... ." He looked at the armoire like it was a guillotine or an electric chair.

"Why was he trying to move a heavy piece like that armoire by himself then?"

Joseph shook his head slowly. "He dropped me at my grandma's house on the way back from the sale. She called me and said she needed me to do a couple of things for her. I asked her if it could wait a little while, but she said no, she needed me right away. I told Mr. McKenzie I would come in later and help him unload. I don't know why he didn't wait for me."

Joseph began to choke up. Twenty-one years old, he has had a checkered history. He was an outstanding football and baseball player in high school and a capable student, but trouble with the law— serious enough for him to spend six months in jail—kept him from getting a college scholarship. Troy ran interference for Joseph with the police—even bailing him out a couple of times—and gave him what guidance he could.

"Mr. McKenzie meant a lot to me," Joseph said, running his hand over his eyes. "He helped me so much. I just feel like, if I'd been here, he wouldn't have been killed."

I put a hand on his shoulder. "Don't beat yourself up, Joseph. Nobody can know what might have happened. You know how stubborn Troy could be. If he decided to do something, he was going to do it." It hurt to hear myself talking about him in the past tense, but I had to get used to doing that. "We may need you to work more hours now. Are you taking classes this summer?"

Joseph has straightened himself out over the past couple of years and is going to the University of South Carolina's campus in Spartanburg, better known as USC Upstate. He is an avid reader and, Rebecca says, does well in school now. They had a class together two years ago, right before she graduated from USC. History does repeat itself, I guess. Troy and Dolores were in the same year in school, two years ahead of me, and had classes together. Now his daughter and her son had done the same.

"I'm not taking anything this summer," Joseph said. "Just working at my uncle's place a little bit and playing in the Wooden Bat League. I'll be taking two classes in the fall. I'll be glad to have all the hours I can get here. Not many people are willing to take a chance on me like Mr. McKenzie was."

"Okay. I'll talk with Rebecca." I walked back over to the desk and shuffled a few papers. "She's going to be managing the store now."

"Are you going to keep it open then?" His voice lifted in hope. "I know somebody made Mr. McKenzie an offer to buy the place."

My head jerked up. "Did he say anything to you about whether he might accept the offer?"

The question obviously made Joseph uncomfortable. I wondered if Troy had reached some kind of agreement that I didn't know about.

"What's the matter?" I asked.

"Well, Ms. Cooper, I don't quite know how to say this." He paused and looked down.

"What?"

"He said he wouldn't sell because, if he did ... well, you'd get half of it since your name is still on the property."

As soon as Joseph's car was out of sight I turned off the lights and locked up the store. I had to get out of there. Waving to Pam as I passed her shop, I started walking up West Main Street. The historic district covers seven blocks, then transitions into more modest homes before giving way to businesses. If I kept going, I would arrive in Anderson and, eventually, cross the state line into Georgia. At the moment that possibility appealed to me. Pepper seemed to have enough energy to keep up with me.

I've heard of women who, after their husbands' sudden deaths, find an unsuspected cache of porn or evidence of gambling debts or cross-dressing or affairs. I guess these days they find things like that on computers or phones instead of in desk drawers. Those discoveries might be easier to deal with than being told—by three different people within a couple of hours—how much my husband hated me. And *feared* me.

My God! Did I even know the man I had slept beside for over twenty years? I wish I could have convinced myself that I didn't care about Troy after our divorce, but we still had connections—our children, the store, the house where he lived, which I own. And it pained me deeply to see him suffering from the PTSD. Yes, he had betrayed me, but I could see how he wasn't really himself the last few years. He wasn't the Troy I had fallen in love with and, maybe, never completely stopped loving.

If only one of those people I'd talked to this morning, especially Anna, had said something, I probably could have dismissed it, but three independent sources? When I'm working on a book project, I consider three sources sufficient to corroborate anything a client wants to say.

Money was always a delicate subject in our marriage, because I made a lot more of it than Troy. He and his father had been partners in the store until Troy's mother was diagnosed with multiple myeloma twelve years ago. Wyatt had turned the business over to Troy so he could concentrate on caring for his wife, who went through a long and difficult cycle of treatment, remission, recurrence, and finally her death.

Wyatt was supposed to receive an annual payout as a consultant. It wasn't much—five thousand dollars a year—but he insisted on it. When his wife died, he sold his house, bought a small condo on the edge of town, and spent time traveling between here and Florida, where his daughter lives. On his trips he bought furniture and other antiques, for which Troy would pay him, but sometimes his hoarding instinct put a strain on Troy's resources.

Within a couple of years Troy was having trouble keeping the business afloat and paying his father. Eight years ago I put up the money to keep it going. I would have gladly just given it to him, but Troy's damnable pride wouldn't let him accept that. He insisted that I become part owner, since he knew he couldn't pay me back any time soon. We didn't tell his father about the loan because that would reveal that the business was struggling. It was vital to Troy to keep up the payments to Wyatt and not to appear a failure in his father's eyes.

Wyatt McKenzie has never been one of my favorite people. I admire the way he took care of his wife when she was sick, but I always felt that he expected people to admire him. Troy said he was never abusive to his children, just brusque and distant. He was attentive to Robert and Rebecca when they were younger, but never what you'd call a doting grandfather. And yet, as unappealing as I found him, I might need to invite him back into the business to help Rebecca and me figure out what we were doing.

"Maureen, good morning," a man's voice said off to my right.

I slowed and Pepper's head went up. Completely absorbed in my thoughts, I hadn't noticed how far I had walked. I was at the boundary of the historic district and into the area of more modest homes on the west side of town.

Roger Martin, one of my children's teachers in high school, stepped out from behind a hedge, clippers in hand. "I didn't know if I should speak to you," he said. "You looked like you were deep in thought."

"Drowning might be more like it." I ran a hand through my hair. "I'm glad you threw me a line."

"Well, I haven't had a chance to tell you in person how sorry I am about Troy."

"Thank you, Roger."

"I won't ask how you're doing. I'm sure it's a difficult time for you, even though you and Troy weren't together any longer."

"It has been, but the support I'm getting from everyone means a lot."

Roger laid his clippers in his wheelbarrow. "Everybody in town knew Troy. His death certainly brought back memories for me."

"How so?"

Pepper sat down as though he sensed a long conversation about to start.

"Not only did I teach his children—and yours, of course—but Troy was in a couple of my classes the first few years I taught here."

"I'll bet he was a handful." I managed a smile.

"Let's just say he ... had his moments. Him and the Hughes girl. But, of course, that was before he met you," he added quickly.

"The Hughes girl?" I said it, even though I was sure who he meant.

"Yes. Dolores. You know, her brother runs that barbecue place on the northeast side."

On the northeast side is local code for "the blackest part of town."

"So Troy and Dolores were an item?" I was aware that they knew one another. Dolores worked for Troy's dad for a couple of years after high school, but I didn't know any more than that. Troy's family and mine did not move in the same circles. Lawrenceville has two middle schools—East and West—which funnel into one large high school that serves the whole county. Troy and I were in the same school for only two years. He was one of the cool kids, two years older than me, and I was a loner, the mousy girl with the glasses and her nose in a book.

We did not get acquainted until we were in college at the University of South Carolina in Columbia. Our mothers were teachers together in an elementary school. His parents offered for him to drive me to Columbia and bring me home on breaks, to his obvious annoyance. I returned the favor by tutoring him in several classes. He wasn't stupid, just undisciplined. In his senior year, when we were engaged, I wrote a paper for him, the first step along the path toward my career of writing things with other people's names on them. I finished college in three years, while it took Troy five, so we graduated together and were married a month after that. Our first child was born seven months later.

"I guess you could call them an item," Roger said. "They were in my Biology 2 class. Lab partners, in fact. Do you know whatever became of her?"

I just shook my head. I wasn't going to provide grist for the rumor mill.

"I understand her son works for you folks." He was still trying to glean a grain or two.

"Part time, yes." I petted Pepper. "He's a very nice young man."

"I'm glad to hear that," Roger said. "When he was in my class, he was the typical athlete, more concerned with that week's game than with his schoolwork. As a biology teacher, though, I was always interested in his genetic make-up."

"I'm sorry. What?"

"Don't misunderstand me. I'm certainly no racist—"

Yes, I know. Some of my best friends—

"I'm a scientist, but it was obvious that Dolores had a white father. Then her son's father must also have been white. It's funny that many Southerners get so exercised about mixing the races, but we've been doing it for centuries. Strom Thurmond, as staunch a segregationist as there ever was, had a child by his family's black maid. He never acknowledged her, but he supported her all his life."

I looked at my watch and tried to think of a gracious exit line.

"And there was Thomas Jefferson and Sally Hemings," Roger continued. "We've often found the children of those relationships to be quite beautiful, from the days of Dorothy Dandridge and Lena Horne to Halle Berry and Dolores and Joseph. If we were to sample the DNA of everyone in this town, we would probably get some real surprises. And what does race mean? If you have twenty-three chromosomes from a white parent and twenty-three from a black parent—as President Obama did—why does that make you black or white?"

South Carolina no longer flies the Confederate flag atop the state capitol building. A lot of its people still salute that symbol in their hearts, though. This was not a conversation I wanted to continue. "Well, I need to get home, Roger. There's a lot of stuff to take care of right now. It's been nice talking to you." Another lie for the sake of Southern gentility.

On the return trip I walked more slowly, taking some deep breaths and admiring the gorgeous houses. The 1880s and 1890s were a boom time for Lawrenceville. Prosperous bankers and lawyers showed off their wealth here, on the "white" side of town. I stopped when I came to the house next door to the Boyd house.

It's known as the Nichols house, from the family who built it, although no one by that name has lived there for two generations. It is a glorious, flamboyant Queen Anne—if that's not a redundancy—as lavishly tarted up as any of the famous Painted Ladies in San Francisco. The front door is set on the north side of the house, with a porch that runs across the front of the house and along one side and a *porte-cochère* on the other. The body of the house is a gray-green color, with brick red and darker gray trim and accent colors. It has three gables of different sizes on the third floor.

The house is so large and so eye-catching that it overshadows my grandparents' neighboring house, which is a Craftsman style bungalow, if that word can be applied to a two-story house. I was so absorbed in my contemplation of the Nichols home that I didn't realize someone was sitting on the Boyds' porch until she spoke.

"It's quite the sight, isn't it?"

"Oh, good morning." I took a step up the sidewalk and saw Mrs. Boyd sitting near the front door, with a blanket over her lap. Her walker was on one side of her and a small table on the other, with a pitcher on a tray. I hadn't seen her in several years and was surprised at how much older and more feeble she looked. Her white hair was done up in the tight curls favored by women of that age, or at least by whoever did her hair.

"Yes, it is impressive."

"I suppose you could call it that, if you like things gaudy and overdone. Would you like a glass of tea?" she asked, beckoning me to join her and ringing a small bell.

"That would be lovely." I told Pepper to stay and climbed the steps to take a seat beside Mrs. Boyd. A woman in nurse's scrubs came out of the house with another glass, which she filled with tea. She fussed with Mrs. Boyd's blanket.

"Do you need anything else?" the nurse asked.

"I think we're fine," Mrs. Boyd said. She turned to me. "Would you like anything, dear?"

I picked up the glass of tea. "This will do nicely. Thank you."

"It's such a lovely day, isn't it?" Mrs. Boyd said as the nurse went back into the house. "Much too nice to spend in the house, even if all I can do is sit here and look at it. And I won't be able to do that for much longer."

I sipped and savored the sweetness of old-fashioned Southern iced tea, even sweeter than mine. My grandmother made it this sweet. Most people these days are too health-conscious. I guess at her age Mrs. Boyd doesn't have to worry.

"The yard is lovely," I said. "When my grandparents lived here, they never paid much attention to it."

"My daughter-in-law loved working in it when they lived here with me. I haven't been able to keep it up the way she did."

We sat in companionable silence until she said, "When are you folks going to come get the rest of the things your husband bought at the sale?"

I didn't point out that he was my *ex*-husband and I was not his widow. "I'm sorry. The rest of the things?"

"Yes. They're out in the garage."

"But we have the things he bought. They're in the store."

"That must be the first load, what he bought when that young man was with him. He came back a short time later, by himself, bought some more and said he would come get it when he had some help."

CHAPTER 5

Getting Mrs. Boyd down the steps with her walker was awkward, but she insisted on coming with me to the garage. After trying perfunctorily to keep her on the porch, the nurse, whose name was Joanne, pitched in and helped. I had the sense that she knew she could do only so much with her elderly charge, so it was better to go along with her and be sure she didn't get hurt.

"Several people left things back here to be picked up later," Joanne said. "I think everybody else has gotten their pieces."

That's because the other people didn't die, I wanted to say, *without telling anybody what they'd done.* "I'll get someone out here later today. Tomorrow at the latest."

"I expect it will take a couple of trips."

She was right. There were several rooms of furniture in the garage, all in the Arts and Crafts style and each piece carrying a SOLD tag with the price and Troy's name on it. Each tag had an original price, marked through, with a much lower price below it. Even at the lower prices, I had no idea he could lay out that much money at one time. Rebecca and Joseph would have a busy afternoon. Well, she wanted to be the manager.

"Does this bring back memories?" Mrs. Boyd asked.

I ran my hand over the buffet from the dining room. "Yes, it certainly does. I remember getting out the good dishes for Thanksgiving and Christmas. My mother got that set, and now I've got it. It seems to belong here, though."

"He bought some of our nicest pieces," Mrs. Boyd said, "although I guess you would think of them as your pieces, since your grandparents lived here before I did."

"It's hard to say who 'owns' old pieces like this."

"I was surprised they didn't sell earlier in the day." She pushed a drawer back in. "Drawers shouldn't be left partly open like that. They'll warp."

I noticed that the drawers on several other chests and dressers were also hanging out. The piece that caught my attention, though, was a large armoire from my grandparents' bedroom, its doors open. "It looks like somebody has been going through this stuff."

"We did leave the garage unlocked," Joanne said, "so people could get their items."

"Who else had things out here?" I asked.

Joanne shrugged. Mrs. Boyd said, "I think you'd have to ask the woman who ran the sale. She would have a list."

"Who is that?"

"Her name was Maxwell. Anna Maxwell."

I blinked in disbelief. "The accountant?"

Mrs. Boyd nodded. "She's done my taxes for several years. When I mentioned that we were going to hold a sale, she asked if she could run it. She said she wants to branch out."

"She did a good job," Joanne volunteered.

"How would she know what anything was worth? She's an accountant."

"She had a young woman working with her," Mrs. Boyd said. "She seemed quite knowledgeable. What was her name?"

"Rebecca," Joanne said. "I never did hear her last name."

"We just tried to stay out of their way," Mrs. Boyd said. "That's not easy to do when you're using a walker."

I leaned against a massive mahogany sideboard, my hand to my mouth, as I tried to comprehend that my daughter had worked with The Other Woman and hadn't bothered to mention it to me.

"Are you all right, dear?" Mrs. Boyd asked. "You look a little shaken."

"Yes, I'm fine. This is ... a lot to take in. Rather unexpected." I waved a hand over the furniture as though I was talking about it. "Thank you for letting me see it. I need to go make a couple of phone calls. We'll get these things out of your way just as soon as we can."

"There's no rush," Mrs. Boyd said. "My children don't want them. They're old and too much trouble to take care of. Like my house." She turned her walker toward the door. "Like me."

Pepper rejoined me and we started back into town. I made myself walk a couple of blocks to vent some anger before I called Rebecca. She must have been working with Anna Maxwell while I was in Asheville, going over the final draft of Mudcat's book with him. I stopped at a small park two blocks west of the square and sat on a bench to make the call. Pepper sat down as close to me as he could get. I stroked his head, realizing for the first time that he was becoming *my* companion dog.

Rebecca picked up on the second ring. "I just had a glass of tea with Beatrice Boyd," I said, my throat so tight I could feel my voice choking.

"Oh, how is she doing?"

"Damn it, Rebecca! Don't play games with me. When were you going to tell me about the rest of the furniture Troy bought? And when were you going to tell me you worked with Anna Maxwell to set up that estate sale?" I didn't know which question to ask first because I didn't know which bothered me more.

"In all honesty, Mother, not until I absolutely had to, because I knew you would react just like this."

"Well, how do you *expect* me to react?"

"You don't have any reason to react at all. It's none of your business."

I clenched my fist. "But you were working with that woman—"

"And I will again. I'm an adult. I don't have to hate the people you hate. Anna and I are going to handle a sale in Clinton in a couple of weeks. We made a nice bit of money at Mrs. Boyd's house."

I took a couple of deep breaths. "Speaking of money, how did your father afford all that furniture that's in the garage and that you and Joseph will have to pick up, by the way?"

Rebecca paused before she finally said, "I paid for a lot of it."

"You? Where did you—"

"I used the money Anna paid me and some of what Gramma left me."

Then a realization hit me. "And you set the prices on those pieces particularly low, didn't you, for yourself and your father?"

"Not at first." She paused, then said, "Okay, look, before the sale opened Dad picked out pieces he wanted. I priced those really high and marked them FIRM, so nobody else would buy them, and we put them in places where people would hardly notice them. Then

Dad came back at the end of the day and we lowered the prices, just to clear things out."

"So you and Anna and your father ripped off an old lady. An old lady in a walker, for cryin' out loud."

"Don't let that old biddy fool you, Mom. She's hard as nails. People usually get thirty percent for handling a big sale like that one. She wouldn't budge over twenty percent. She knew it was Anna's first sale, so the old bat had her in a corner."

"Anna could have walked away from it."

"She really wanted to do it, to establish herself. So Dad said to take the offer and we could find other ways to make money off it."

"Are you saying it was your dad's idea to rob her?"

"We didn't *steal* the stuff. Maybe she didn't get as much as she could have, but some of those pieces probably wouldn't have sold at all. They're big, and Arts and Crafts isn't everybody's favorite style. And she should have paid us more than she did."

I got up and walked along the gravel path in the park, glad that no one was in earshot. "Do you hear yourself rationalizing? This is like insider trading in the stock market. You can't take advantage—"

"Get off your high horse, Mother. People do stuff like this all the time in the antique business."

"How did you know what prices to set?"

"I know more about antiques than you think. And if I wasn't sure about a piece or couldn't find something comparable on the internet, I sent pictures to Dad and he told me."

"This is why you've been so bitchy with me the last few days, isn't it? You know you did something dishonest."

"No, I don't know that, but I knew you'd look at it in the worst possible light."

I stopped beside the fountain in the center of the park. "You and your dad were supposed to pick the stuff up, weren't you? Once you got rid of the price tags, nobody would be any the wiser."

"Mother, nobody got hurt. Mrs. Boyd made $30,000 from the sale, *after* she paid us. We didn't cheat her. We *bought* the damn furniture. She wouldn't pay us what we should have gotten. We just made it another way."

"That's not the point, Rebecca. You did something dishonest. If anybody hears about it, you'll never get to handle another sale."

"How is anybody going to hear about it? You're the only one who knows, and you can't prove anything. It was our first sale. Maybe we just weren't as accurate as we could have been in the pricing." She began to mock. "Oops, my bad. I'll do better next time."

"You know, I'm not sure I want somebody who can think like that working in my store."

"Oh, now it's *your* store? What happened to 'it's *our* store. It always has been *our* store.'"

"I'm the owner. My name is on the title. If you're cheating people and you're connected to the store, that affects my reputation."

"So, are you firing me?"

"I didn't say that." I felt like a boxer must feel when his opponent comes off the ropes with a sudden flurry of blows.

"Are you going to run the place by yourself?"

"You know I can't do that."

"Yes, I know."

The phone went dead.

I hesitated to ask a favor of Scott. I enjoy going out with him. I know he wants more of a relationship, but I'm just not sure what I want. He's often said he would help me with anything I needed. Fortunately I'm not a person whose life runs afoul of the law with any regularity. I could have just called him now, but I felt like this request might sound better if I made it face-to-face, so I drove out to the Judicial Center, without even knowing if he would be there or free to talk to me.

"This is a pleasant surprise," he said, when he came out to meet me in the visitors' area. "Has something else happened?"

I explained to him about the furniture in the Boyds' garage and my concern that someone had been looking through it. "I just wonder if you could have your techs dust that furniture for prints."

He wasn't as eager as I expected him to be. "Why?"

"If we could compare prints found there to prints found on the furniture in the store, we might know who we're looking for."

"That's an awful long shot, Maureen. Anybody who came to that sale could have touched the furniture in both places, and, from what you say, there's a lot of stuff in the garage. You see, the thing about fingerprints is that you have to have a group of people to compare them against. We would have to have the prints of everyone who went to the sale and everyone who ever lived in or visited that house. That would include you and your entire family, wouldn't it?"

When he put it that way, it did sound pointless. I wasn't ready to give up, though. "But, Scott, somebody went through those things, just like they went through the pieces in the store. That can't be a coincidence."

"Actually, it could be, but it's probably not. Look, if the techs don't have anything else to do tomorrow, I'll send them out there. They can use the practice, I guess. Right now I think the best thing for you to do is to go home and try to take your mind off this business. I'll have a patrol car go by the store once in a while tonight."

At least he was taking me that seriously.

On my way home I stopped to pick up a barbecue sandwich and some slaw, leaving Pepper in the car. It was a few minutes after the noon rush, but I was afraid there might still be a line. I hate standing in lines. Only two of the five tables were occupied, though. The linoleum tile floor, a red and white checkerboard pattern, had a path worn from the screen front door to the counter, with its ORDER HERE sign. Blues music played softly from a device that I couldn't see behind the counter, mingling with the rich aroma of the barbecue over a sinful undertone of grease. Artemisia and her mother would love the place, I was sure.

"Mornin', Miz Cooper," Joseph's uncle said from behind the counter. "How are you doin'?"

"I'm all right, Zeke. Thank you. And thank you and your family for coming to the funeral." I didn't know if he was aware that his mother had made a contribution to Wounded Warriors, so I didn't mention it.

Zeke wiped his hands on his apron. "Troy was a good guy. He really helped Joseph get himself turned around. We'll always appreciate that."

I wondered if Joseph knew about the scam that Troy, Rebecca, and Anna had run on Mrs. Boyd. Rebecca hadn't mentioned him, so I hoped they hadn't dragged him into it.

"Do you want the pulled pork sandwich?" Zeke asked. "That's your usual, isn't it?"

"Yes. Creature of habit, guilty as charged. With some slaw, please."

While he was fixing my order, I watched his daughter Estelle, standing beside a computer at the other end of the counter, away from the food preparation area. She studied the screen, printed something off and began making a sandwich. The bell over the door jingled as a customer came in behind me.

"Here you go, Miz Maxwell," Zeke said, picking up an order packaged in a paper bag from a shelf beside the register and handing it to her.

Geez. Of all the gin joints—

"Rebecca called me," Anna said, barely looking at me.

"I'll bet she did."

"This isn't the time or the place, but we'll need to talk."

"Definitely."

She turned and left, and I realized I hadn't seen her pay. Zeke eyed me as he put the finishing touches on my order. I wanted to break the tension, but he beat me to it.

"You know, Miz Cooper, you ought to order ahead," he said, "like she did. It would save you standin' around waitin.'"

And avoid run-ins with people you obviously don't want to see. I could see him thinking it.

"Do a lot of people phone in orders?" I assumed that was what Anna had done.

Zeke shook his head and smiled. "Not as many as used to. Most people order online now. And they pay that way, too, like Miz Maxwell did." Zeke jerked his head toward Estelle and the computer. She packed up an order, stapled the computer printout to it, and set it on the shelf close to the register.

"I know bigger places let you order you online," I said. "I've done that. It just hadn't occurred to me that you would."

"Big business or little, it's what people want."

"So you find the web site helps you?"

"Oh, definitely. About 60% of our business now comes from orders through the web site. People can get to it from their offices or from their phones. Including people who don't want to spend too much time in this part of town. Joseph made it pretty simple. All we ask is a fifteen-minute lead time. You got your phone? I'll show you."

I dug my phone out of my purse and followed his instructions to place the order for my sandwich and slaw and pay for it. Estelle printed it and handed Zeke my receipt.

"That is easy," I said.

"These days people expect to do everything online, you know. A business can't survive if they don't adapt. We even keep track of what people like and let 'em know when we run a special."

Big brother in small-town America. I shuddered. Maybe Mudcat Jones was right about not wanting to be on "that interweb thang."

Zeke looked over my shoulder. "You got Pepper in the car?"

"Yes, I guess he's mine now. I'm getting used to him."

"He's a sweet dog." Zeke dropped bones and scraps of meat into a take-out bucket. "Health Department wouldn't be happy to see me doin' this, but I always sent Troy home with somethin' for Pepper. He never did mind bendin' a rule or two for his dog."

Or for his girlfriend and his daughter.

A pulled pork sandwich with slaw and a bottomless glass of iced tea—Troy used to say my tea was so sweet it made his teeth hurt—are a vital part of my process when I'm finishing a project and getting it ready to send to Dave. I was glad to have the final edit of Mudcat's book to occupy me for the rest of the day. I needed to finish it before reopening the store and playing host to Artemisia, and I didn't want to think about people breaking into my store, or about my husband and daughter ripping off an old lady.

The wizened old mountain man—a legend to many people, even though he had performed in front of only a few hundred in his entire life—was the perfect antidote.

As I slowly chewed the last bite of the sandwich I had a moment of ironic realization. If I accepted the new assignment, I could go from writing a book about a sixty-six-year-old man who would be more at home in the nineteenth century to writing about a sixteen-year-old girl who epitomized the twenty-first century entertainment business—gaining fame by winning a contest on television and drawing legions of fans who "followed" her without ever seeing her in person.

And I didn't particularly care for either one's music.

About eight o'clock I clicked "send" and was done with Mudcat, at least until Dave sent me his suggested revisions. I took a shower and slipped into my preferred sleepwear—panties and one of Troy's

National Guard T-shirts. If anybody knew I slept in it, they would think I still had a problem letting go. And I guess I do. Or *did*. In one sense, it wasn't a problem anymore. Troy was dead. But my feelings for him weren't.

After everything I had heard and learned about Troy today, I was surprised that I still wanted to sleep in his T-shirt. I had found it in the laundry hamper after he moved out. It's big and comfortable, I told myself, that's all, olive green with the National Guard logo on the front and his name on the back. And it reminds me of having his arms around me, a little voice said. The T-shirt is the only visible reminder of Troy still in my house. My wedding ring, which was my grandmother's, is in a drawer, in case Rebecca wants to use it. When Troy moved out I kept up a brave front. I was the one who got cheated on, after all, and I had every right to be angry. People were impressed with how I was able to take the high road.

When I found the shirt two days later, I sat down on the floor and cried for ten minutes.

Why did I still love Troy? In the years since we'd been divorced, I had asked myself, and my therapist, that question numerous times and had come up with dozens of answers. He was the first—and only—man I'd ever slept with. I knew Scott would gladly change that statistic, but I wasn't ready for that. I knew that I eventually could be, just not yet. Troy had brought me out of my shell. He was funny, audacious, but not truly a "bad boy." When I was with him I felt like Mackenzie Phillips' character in "American Graffiti," an awestruck little girl riding around with the coolest guy in town.

Then he came back from his second tour in Afghanistan, lost and vulnerable, and that made me love him even more. I still believe that whatever happened to him over there—not his lack of love for me or his interest in another woman—had been what led to our divorce.

I checked the news to see what the terrorists had blown up else-where while my own life was imploding in safe little Lawrenceville. Pepper settled down in his spot in the mud room at the back of the house. I knew he had slept on Troy's bed, and he seemed disappoint-ed and puzzled to find himself relegated to the boondocks, but I just couldn't adjust yet to the idea of having a large animal roaming in-side my house during the night. Besides, Pepper snores.

I was coming out of the bathroom—probably not for the last time, considering how much tea I'd consumed—when the phone rang. It was one of my tenants in the house where Troy lived. *Damn,* I thought. *What's busted now?*

"Hey, Connie," I said.

"Hi, Ms. Cooper. I'm sorry to bother you this late, but I think there's somebody in Troy's apartment. I just wanted to be sure it wasn't you or somebody else in the family before I called the police."

"It could be Rebecca. Let me take care of it. Thanks for the call."

I slipped on a pair of jeans, dropped my phone into my pocket, and stepped into my shoes. When I went out the back door Pepper jumped up and followed me. By cutting through the yard behind mine, which belongs to a rental house, I shortened the distance to my own rental. It's just one block over and two blocks down.

One part of my brain said to call the police right now. Somebody broke into the store; now somebody's in Troy's apartment. But, I argued with myself, it could be Rebecca. She has no business in Troy's apartment. Maybe she's trying to get rid of evidence of her scam. I wanted to confront her.

And whoever broke into the store was interested in the furniture from the Boyd house, not in Troy. They didn't even go into the office. That's why they looked through the other furniture in the Boyds' garage. Whatever was going on, it was about that furniture, not about Troy.

When my rental house came into view Pepper trotted ahead of me, probably eager to go home. I didn't see any lights in Troy's apartment, on the first floor, though, so I stopped him. I knew Troy kept his curtains drawn. Would I be able to see anything? Then I saw a light moving into the kitchen. Someone was using a flashlight. "Stay, Pepper. This doesn't look right."

I called 9-1-1 and gave the operator the information.

"Are you in the house, ma'am?"

"No. I'm across the street."

"All right. Stay there. I'm sending a patrol car."

"Okay .... Oh, wait, somebody's coming out." I was directly across the street from the house, behind some bushes, with the phone to my ear. What had been the rear entrance to the first floor had been converted into the entrance to the stairs for the upper floors. The "rear" entrance to Troy's apartment opened from the side of the house onto the driveway. Somebody was coming down those steps now. "It's just one person," I told the operator.

"Ma'am, stay where you are. The officers will be there in a couple of minutes."

"But he's getting away."

"Ms. Cooper, he could be dangerous. Please stay where you are."

The intruder seemed about average height. That was all I could tell in the little bit of illumination coming from nearby houses and the light over the garage at the end of the driveway. I thought about taking a picture with my phone, but realized it would be useless. Then the intruder turned and I saw the figure in profile—wearing a shirt that fit snugly over breasts.

"It's a woman," I told the operator.

"She could still be dangerous. Please wait for the officers."

I wanted to take her advice, but Pepper lunged across the street and barked. The woman saw him coming and turned toward the back of the house.

I stepped out from behind the bushes. "Stop! The police are on their way. I've got them on the phone." I held the device up to prove my point.

Okay, not the smartest thing to say to somebody who's broken into your house.

Lights were coming on in neighboring houses. The woman disappeared around the back of my rental house with Pepper in pursuit. I felt I had no choice but to go after them. Then I heard a dog's sharp yelp of pain.

CHAPTER 6

I didn't hear any sirens yet or see any lights, so I tore across the street and up the driveway. When I turned the corner of the house I saw Pepper lying at the bottom of the chain link fence that runs across the back yard. The woman had jumped the fence and was heading into the patch of woods on the other side, rapidly putting distance between us. I would never catch her, and I had to see about Pepper.

The woman had grabbed a shovel that somebody left propped against the garage and hit Pepper with it. There wasn't much blood, but his left front leg was bent at a funny angle.

I looked up to curse the woman and saw that she had tripped over a tree root and was still on the ground. Maybe I *could* catch her. In the distance I heard an approaching siren.

"Help's on the way, Pepper," I said, petting his head.

Then I hoisted myself over the fence, which is four feet high. But, as I came down on the other side, Troy's big, comfortable T-shirt got caught on the top of the chain links. I was struggling to unhitch myself when the woman got up and disappeared into the woods, limping noticeably.

"Hold it right there!" a male voice shouted behind me.

I turned to see two police officers running across the yard, flashlights out and hands on their guns. Suddenly I realized how exposed I was. Since I'd been ready for bed, I wasn't wearing anything under the T-shirt which was now bunched up on the fence.

"Hurry up," I said. "She's getting away." I pointed into the woods.

"Just hang on," the first policeman said. "It doesn't look like anybody's getting away."

"You don't understand. I'm the one who called you. And my dog is hurt."

The officer shined his flashlight away from my bare back into the woods, which sloped down to a stream. "I don't see anybody."

"Because she got away." I gave one more tug on Troy's T-shirt and heard it rip. "Oh, God. No." I couldn't stop the tears.

"You stay right where you are," the policeman said, "until we get this sorted out."

"It's all right, Eric," Scott said from behind the officers. "She's the owner of this house."

One of the officers jumped the fence and helped me back over. Scott caught me when I landed and held me against his chest longer than he needed to. When I straightened up, he got a good look at what I was wearing.

"Well, that T-shirt reveals a lot."

Another patrol car arrived. Scott sent them to check the other side of the woods, where the intruder would most likely have come out. The officers already on the scene did a quick search of Troy's apartment to be sure nobody else was in there. A window in the back of the house had been broken. They covered that with a piece of plywood from the garage and sealed everything with yellow tape. Scott assured me that a patrol car would come by several times during the night in case the intruder came back.

"I'll send the techs over tomorrow morning," Scott said in a flat tone.

"Don't you want to do it tonight, while the evidence is fresh?"

"Nobody was hurt. There's no blood or other evidence of that sort that we have to get to right now. Fingerprints and footprints will still be there in the morning, along with the incredible mess in that place. Your husband really was a hoarder, wasn't he?"

I nodded. I had not let Troy accumulate any mess in our house while we were married. He seemed content to have the store. As soon as he moved into his own place, though, he began surrounding himself with stuff.

"It will be difficult to do any forensics work in there," Scott said. "It would be impossible tonight. They can do this in the morning instead of wasting time on the furniture in Mrs. Boyd's garage." His voice, underlined by the way he leaned away from me, made it clear that he had read a lot more than just the National Guard logo from my T-shirt. "They work better in daylight, especially if they're look-ing for footprints in those woods."

"Yeah, that makes sense. Okay, thanks." I folded my arms over my chest, covering the logo on the shirt and the fact that I wasn't wear-ing a bra. "Scott, I'm sorry."

"You've got nothing to be sorry about, Maureen. Do you have a key to this place that I could give to the techs? They'll be here first thing."

I removed the key from my ring. Scott took it without saying any-thing and turned to one of the other officers, who was kneeling be-side Pepper. "Help Ms. Cooper get her dog to a vet." It had been a long time since he called me Ms. Cooper.

My phone rang at eight the next morning. Since I hadn't gotten back from the vet's until almost one, I hadn't set my alarm. It had been a relief to learn that Pepper's injury wasn't serious, just a frac-tured leg. He would be in a cast for a few weeks but should be fine after that. They wanted to keep him for a couple of days for observa-tion and to catch up on his shots and other routine things Troy had fallen behind on. When the officer dropped me at home, I gave in to exhaustion and decided to let myself sleep as long as I needed to. It hadn't been long enough.

"Ms. Cooper?" a man's voice said when I answered the phone.

"Yeah. I mean, yes."

"This is Greg Compton, with the Crime Scene Unit. Sorry to bother you this early. We're done over here at your rental place. If you'd like to come over, we can release the apartment to you and return your key."

"I'll be there in five minutes."

I ran a comb through my hair, put on a clean T-shirt and jeans, and drove over, because I was just too tired to walk. I parked on the street in front of the house. The techs' van was parked in the driveway; they were packing up their equipment when I arrived. The yellow tape was down. My other tenants and several neighbors provided the crowd that one always sees in the background on TV shows and in movies when the police are examining a place. Compton greeted me in the driveway. To judge from his unlined face, he was a few years younger than me but had already lost a lot of his dark hair and was losing the battle to keep his waistline trim. He handed me the key.

"I'm pleased to meet you, Ms. Cooper. My dad started on the force shortly after your grandfather became chief. He always spoke so highly of the Chief." He pronounced it, as most people did when they talked about my paternal grandfather, so that you could hear the capital C. I guess Rebecca was right. I was getting special treatment from the police because of who my family was. Right now I would take it.

"Thank you. My family is certainly proud of him." I pointed at the techs. "I didn't expect you to be finished so soon."

"Well, there were only two rooms where we could actually check for any prints—the kitchen and the office. There's so much stuff piled up in there. But it's not garbage, like you find with most hoarders. It's just stacks of newspapers, magazines, and apparently everything he or his kids ever wrote in school. The room that he used as a study or an office wasn't as bad. It looked like somebody had gone through the file cabinet in there, so that's what we focused on."

"Did you find anything?" I asked as I hooked the key back on my ring.

"It's too early to tell. We took some prints. We'll have to run them, though, before we know anything. And we'll need to take prints from you and anyone else who might have been here to compare them. Could you come by the station today?"

"I was fingerprinted yesterday, after the break-in at my store."

"Okay, that's helpful. Your husband's prints will be on file because of his military service. You have a son and a daughter, don't you?"

"Yes. Rebecca lives here, but Robert is in Greenville. He did go in a few days ago to pick out clothes for the funeral." I had let Robert handle that chore because he has such good taste and because I didn't want to go into the apartment. I suspected I would find what Compton was describing, or that I would find evidence of Anna Maxwell's presence.

Compton jotted something in the notebook he was holding—names, I presumed. "We'll need their prints. Is there anyone else who might have been in the apartment?"

"Joseph Hughes works for us. He might have been there recently."

"Oh, yes, Mr. Hughes. His prints will be in the system. Anyone else?"

"Troy was seeing a woman. Anna Maxwell."

"The accountant here in town?"

"Yes."

"It should be easy enough to get her prints."

I couldn't suppress a smile as I imagined Anna talking with a client when the police arrived to fingerprint her.

"I'm not sure any of this will do any good," Compton said, glancing over a couple of pages in his notebook. "We also found some smudged prints, which suggest the intruder was wearing gloves."

"Could you tell if anything was missing?"

Compton sighed. "Ms. Cooper, we don't know what was there to begin with, so it's hard to say if anything might have been taken. And in this case, the place is packed."

"Like you said, my ex-husband was something of a hoarder."

Compton gave me a sympathetic nod. "I have an aunt in Spartanburg who's like that. I don't know what we'll do when she dies." He pointed to Troy's place. "Most of what's in there is pretty well organized, unlike at my aunt's, and there is some room to walk. I'll give him that. The kitchen and the powder room off of it are as clean as in a normal person's house."

So Anna Maxwell really had insisted, like she said, on that much of the apartment being neat enough that she could stand to be in it. I wondered if they'd had sex on the kitchen table. I would donate it to Goodwill, just in case, and maybe have the kitchen counters replaced.

"In the office," Compton continued, "stuff has been pulled out of a file cabinet, as I mentioned, but you'd probably know what's missing better than we would."

I shook my head. "This is my ex-husband's place. I've only been in there twice in the last five years." As the owner of the house, I had the legal right to go in any time I wanted, but Troy and I had an agreement that I would not go into his apartment unless he asked me to, and, except for two occasions to approve repairs, he had not.

"Well, it's not like you see on TV. We can't look at a bookshelf and see that one book is out of place and therefore the killer must be—"

He must watch as many police procedural shows as I do. "I don't expect that. I just thought there might be something obvious."

"Not in a mess like that." He closed his notebook. "You saw the intruder leaving, right?"

"Yes. It was a woman."

From his expression I gathered he hadn't been told that bit of information. "Was she carrying anything?"

"Not that I could tell, and certainly not when she jumped the fence. She could have had something tucked under her shirt, I suppose. Or in a pocket."

"So, something flat or small. Money or jewelry, most likely."

"I don't think Troy had much of either." Not if Rebecca had put up money to buy some of the furniture.

"Well, we're done here. We're going to see if we can pick up any footprints in the woods, but you can do as you like with the apartment. I don't mean to be unkind, but I would suggest having somebody drop a dumpster in the driveway, to start with. That's what needs to happen at my aunt's house."

"It will probably come to that. I've given my kids a month to get anything of their dad's that they want. Then I'll empty the place, paint, and get it ready to rent."

"You'd better have it checked for mold."

I groaned. "Did you see any?"

"No, but behind and under all that stuff, it's almost inevitable. And the dog smell was pretty bad."

"Okay, duly noted." As he stepped toward his van I asked, "Do you want me to show you where the woman jumped over the fence?"

Compton turned back to me, picked up a roll of yellow tape, and motioned for one of his men to come with us. "That would be very helpful."

"Are you going to bring in a dog to track her?" I asked as we walked into the back yard. I knew the local police had a K-9 "officer." My grandfather had hired the first one.

"We don't have anything from the intruder to give the dog a scent to work from. He might go off after anybody who's been in the woods in the last few days—couple of kids smoking pot, it could be anybody." Compton's indifference, on top of Scott's reaction to my T-shirt last night, gave me the feeling that my free pass from the police department was in danger of expiring.

Compton was well past his fence-leaping days, so the other officer went over the fence and took a few steps. "I don't see any prints," he said.

"It's too bad it hasn't rained recently," Compton said.

I pointed to the spot where the intruder had tripped and fallen.

"That's a place where a dog might pick up a trail. You could be pretty sure whose scent it was."

Compton nodded. "I'll see what the boss says about that. Hey, Fisher, put some tape around that spot and don't tromp all over it yourself." He tossed the roll of yellow tape to the young officer. "He's new," he confided to me, then raised his voice again. "We'll meet you over on Church Street."

Compton and the other tech got in their van to drive around to where the woods ended at the next street over. As I watched them back out of the driveway, I felt a wave of uneasiness sweep over me, a mixture of anxiety and vulnerability. Aside from the trouble in my marriage, I have lived a rather quiet life since my grandfather's death. Chatting with police officers has never been a part of my daily routine.

I turned toward the house but couldn't make myself go in just yet. As long as I didn't go in, I didn't have to confront the mess I had long suspected I would find in there—Troy's personal hoard. Robert had been evasive about the condition of the place after he got the clothes for his father's funeral. "It's going to take some work to clean it up," was all he would say. "When you're ready, Derrick and I will help you."

Standing on the steps, I also felt that sense of violation that people often have when their property has been invaded by a person or persons unknown and the gnawing fear that they might come back. If I knew what somebody was looking for—if I had even a hint—all of this might make some sense. The fact that someone had searched the furniture in the store and the pieces in Mrs. Boyd's garage led me to believe that the furniture, or something supposedly in it, was the issue. Troy might have stumbled into the middle of something when all he was trying to do was rip off an old lady.

But then why break into his apartment? Did someone believe he had found what they were looking for and brought it here? But he hadn't had time, had he? He was killed when he was unloading the furniture from his truck. Anything he might have found there must still be in the store. What was somebody looking for here?

The door from the driveway opened into the kitchen. I closed and locked the door behind me and took a minute to orient myself. My parents had bought this place fifteen years ago, fixed it up, and rented it. I had no personal connections with it, other than helping them paint and wallpaper. For the kitchen my mother had chosen a pleasant sage green on the walls, with off-white cabinets, and a brownish tile floor. That color scheme continued into the powder room. The kitchen appliances were white, the countertops an inexpensive laminate. They had fixed the house up nicely, but it was, in the end, a rental.

Giving grudging credit to Anna Maxwell for a clean entry into the apartment, I stuck my head through the kitchen door into what should have been the dining room. Instead it was just as Compton had described—a wall-to-wall pile of stuff with a couple of paths allowing passage to the living room. The darkness from the closed drapes, which I couldn't even reach, heightened the gloom. Edging my way through that mess and trying not to touch any of it, I came to the first of the three bedrooms in the apartment, the one that Troy used for his office.

Once again Compton's description was accurate. The room wasn't so much of a mess that a person couldn't work here, although the musty smell would make it impossible for me to be in here for more than a few minutes. A desk and chair sat against the wall under the window, with a metal file cabinet on each side and a rug for Pepper in the corner. Since I could reach the curtains, I opened them, raising a cloud of dust.

One file and the desk were locked. The woman who broke in here had pulled stuff out of the unlocked cabinet and strewed it over the desk. Had she found what she was looking for and left, or had she given up in frustration?

I figured the keys to the desk and the locked file were on Troy's ring, but I didn't have that with me now, and I wouldn't be able to stay in here until I had dealt with the smell and at least some of the mess.

On top of one pile of magazines and newspapers was a cardboard box half-full of more magazines. I dumped them and filled the box with as much material from the open file cabinet as I could carry, starting with what was spread over the desk. I would sort through it when I got back to my place.

I was back in the kitchen when my phone rang. I put the box of Troy's stuff on the counter, took my phone out of my pocket and was surprised to see that Scott was calling. I hadn't expected to hear from him again.

"Good morning, Maureen," he said, all business. At least he didn't call me Ms. Cooper.

"Hi, Scott. How are you?" I tried to sound like I was talking to a friend.

"I'm fine. Listen, Greg Compton called me. It looks like your intruder went through the stream at the bottom of that incline behind your house. There were some footprints leading up to the parking lot of that little picnic area on the other side. They figure she had a car parked there. That's where the trail stops."

"Don't you think a dog could help you track her?"

"Not unless he can sniff out a license plate number. Maureen, I'm sorry I can't give you any more help on this. As a department we have to do a kind of triage. I'm sure you heard some of this from your grandfather. Violent crimes, with personal injuries, are our top priority. There's a whole range of felonies below that. Way down at the bottom of our list is a B&E where nobody got hurt and we're not even sure anything was stolen."

"Somebody smashed a display case in my store."

"Can you tell me what was taken?"

"Well, no ... . Some old money." I ran a hand through my hair.

"Give me a list, with serial numbers or some way to identify it."

"I can't do that."

"Then there's really nothing I can do for you. Somebody took advantage of the store being closed and of your old locks. I guess they also figured Troy's apartment would be empty. Thieves read the obituaries, Maureen. I'm sorry we can't do anything about this. We're already understaffed and, with this FoodFest thing this weekend, we'll have every available officer working overtime. That's always a madhouse. And this year they're adding a beer tent."

I wondered if I should give him a heads-up that Artemisia was going to be in my store on Saturday and might draw x-number of her fans on top of everything else. But she asked me not to tell anyone in advance.

"Thanks anyway, Scott. I'll be talking to you."

"Yeah, I'll see you around. Be sure you get those new locks installed."

"I will. And somebody's coming to give me an estimate on installing real security cameras."

"Glad to hear it."

CHAPTER 7

On my way home I stopped by the vet's to check on Pepper, who was doing fine. I petted him and sat with him for a few minutes.

"He perked up as soon as he heard your voice," the vet's pretty young assistant said. Why is it that everybody seems pretty and young these days?

I perked up as soon as I saw him, in spite of the lump in my throat.

My next stop was the police station, where I asked Compton if they had any results from the prints they'd taken in the store later in the day or at the apartment.

"Nothing from the apartment," he said. "And there weren't many prints on the furniture in the store. It looks like Troy was wiping it down when the accident happened. I'll give you a call as soon as we know something."

When I got home I called Joseph and told him to bring Troy's truck out to Mrs. Boyd's house to get the rest of the furniture. His surprise at hearing there was more to be picked up seemed genuine. Rebecca and Troy must not have included him in their scheme. We agreed to meet right after he got off work at his uncle's barbecue place, after the noon rush.

I carried the box of stuff from Troy's apartment up to the third floor of my house. My parents had finished the attic space into a large family room, which I always found ironic, since we were such a small family. I decided I would bring Troy's stuff there, to avoid messing up the rest of my house and to keep the musty smell at bay, especially with Artemisia and her mother coming in for the weekend.

I picked up some more boxes and Troy's key ring and drove back over to his place to empty the other file drawers and his desk. I wasn't going to clean out the place today, but I wanted to get anything that

Albert A. Bell, Jr

an intruder might be interested in.

Standing in Troy's study, I felt a wave of dismay sweep over me. How was I ever going to deal with this mess? I called Robert. His secretary extended her condolences and put me through to Robert's office.

"Hi, Mom. How are you?"

"Don't ask unless you really want an answer."

"Well, of course I do."

"Here goes then." I told him about the extra furniture, the break-in at Troy's apartment, and Pepper's injury.

"Good Lord! What's going on?"

"That's what I'm asking myself. The police think it's just a B&E, somebody taking advantage of the store being closed and the apartment being empty. But somebody also went through the furniture that your dad hadn't picked up yet in Mrs. Boyd's garage. I think they're looking for something. I just can't imagine what it would be."

"Well, be careful. Lock doors. They might come back. Where are you now?"

"I'm in your dad's study. I did lock the door when I came in."

"Maybe you should just go ahead and start cleaning the place out."

"Do you have any advice about what I should do with this stuff? What I see is mostly old *Sports Illustrated, Sporting News, Baseball Digest*, that sort of thing."

"I don't want it," Robert said.

"Could any of it be worth anything? That's what bugs me. I don't want to throw out some collector's item."

"You won't be. They print so many copies of those magazines that the supply pretty well keeps up with the demand. Hold on, let me check something."

I figured he was searching online.

"Well, some of the swimsuit issues are for sale online for eight to twelve bucks, depending on condition and who's on the cover. You might put those in a separate stack and sell them in the store."

"I'm not sure I want to become a purveyor of soft-core porn."

Robert chuckled. "I know what you mean, but in general those sports magazines aren't worth keeping. Let me check something else." He came back on a moment later. "The first few of issues of *Sports Illustrated* can be worth a couple of hundred dollars, depending on the condition, but that's from 1954."

I skimmed the issues in one stack, wiping my hands on my jeans afterwards. "I don't see anything here before about 1985."

"Let me check ... . Those aren't worth more than a couple of dollars. Be careful, though. Dad might have gotten something autographed, especially programs from Greenville Braves' games or Atlanta Braves' games. We went to a lot of games and got some autographs. Chipper Jones, Tom Glavine—there's no telling who might be in there."

"Robert, you saw this mess. The stacks are waist-high. You mean I'm going to have to look through every piece individually?"

"It's up to you, Mom. There could be a couple of gems in all that dreck. I wouldn't know how to spot them. Like I said, Derrick and I will help you. We could come down this weekend."

"No, this weekend is FoodFest. You don't want to deal with all that hassle. How about next weekend? I did promise you kids you could have a month to get whatever you wanted."

"Mom, sadly, I did not see anything in the apartment that I wanted when I got Dad's uniform for the funeral. We could come down next weekend. You can wait for us, if you want to. If you decide to get started before then, just look things over a bit before you chuck them."

I heard Derrick's voice in the background.

"Derrick just reminded me," Robert said, "that he knows a guy in Columbia who specializes in sports memorabilia. We could hook you up with him."

"That sounds good. I want to concentrate on getting the store re-opened tomorrow and then Artemisia will be—" I stopped myself, but it was too late.

"Artemisia? The singer?" Robert said. "She'll be what?"

"Oh, I wasn't supposed to say anything. My agent wants me to work on a book with her. She and her mother will be in town this weekend and will be in the store on Saturday, and it looks like they'll be staying with me. I don't have any other place to put them."

Robert repeated what I had said to Derrick. "Okay, you've just about made Derrick pee himself. He is Artemisia's biggest fan. He voted for her, like, fifty times on three different phones."

"Hey, Mom," Derrick's voice cut in as I assumed he had grabbed the phone from Robert. His parents disowned him when they learned he was gay. He has called me 'Mom' for as long as he and Robert have been together. "Are you serious? Artemisia is going to be in your store this weekend and staying with you?"

"Yes, but you can't tell anybody. Please. She's going to tweet her followers Saturday morning, but she didn't want any advance notice."

"Why would I tell anybody?" Derrick said. "I'd love to be the only one there. Oh, my God! I can't believe this."

Derrick is two years older than Robert. They've been together since they met in law school. Most people, I think, don't recognize that Robert is gay when they first meet him. Derrick, on the other hand ...

Robert took the phone back. "I apologize for my partner's rudeness. Let me ask you more politely. Would it be all right if we came to see you this weekend? I know you're going to be busy."

"I'll be happy to see you, dear, and I can use the help. May I ask, what is Derrick's attraction to Artemisia?"

It's funny how you can hear someone roll his eyes. "Well, it's kind of like Cher or Bette Midler. Once in a while a female singer strikes a chord with some gay men. I don't think she's aware of it. She doesn't play it up."

"You don't sound like you share his enthusiasm."

"Oh, I agree that she's talented, but I'm not drawn to her the way Derrick and some of our friends are."

"Well, remind him that she's under eighteen."

"Every time he mentions her, I ask him, 'Now, once again, how old is this child? And aren't you twenty-seven?' I promise you, other than drooling a lot and worshipping the ground she walks on, he'll behave himself. I'll see to that. We'll be in tomorrow evening, if that's okay."

"That will be fine. I look forward to seeing you. Oh, by the way, you'll need to go by the police station and let them take your fingerprints. They need to eliminate people who might have been in the store and the apartment."

"That's no problem. You have to be fingerprinted before you're admitted to the bar."

"Oh, yeah, I'd forgotten that."

"You know, it just occurred to me that we are going to have a problem about this week-end." He must have said something to Derrick.

I could barely hear an exchange. First Robert, "We said we would do it this weekend. Maggie's coming on Monday." Then Derrick, "But it's *Artemisia*. I'll never get another chance like this." Finally Robert, "All right, but we won't go to bed Sunday night until it's done."

"Robert," I said, "is there a problem?"

"No. We had planned to paint our spare room this weekend."

"Is it urgent? Who's Maggie, if I'm not prying?"

"Oh, you heard that?"

"Yes, I did."

"I didn't want to say anything yet, but Derrick and I are going to have a baby. We're turning our spare room into a nursery—"

"Wait! You're doing what?"

"We're going to have a baby. Maggie is our surrogate."

"Oh, Robert! That's wonderful. When?" I was bouncing like a teenager. Thankfully, no one could see me.

"She's six months along. We want her to see how we're fixing things up."

"But how ... . I mean—"

"You mean, who supplied the sperm?"

"Well, yeah, that cuts right to the chase." And it wasn't a conversation a mother expects to have with her son.

"We both did, and they inseminated her with a mixture from both of us. So we won't know who the biological father is. We could find out, if there was some medical reason, for instance, but otherwise he or she will just be our child."

"This is amazing. Wonderful." I was still bouncing.

"Are you okay with it? I know you're really big on family and you won't actually know if this is your biological grandchild—"

"Oh, Robert! What the hell difference would that make? If it's your child, it's my grandchild. But why didn't you say anything?"

Robert paused, then said sadly, "I knew how Dad would react, and I just didn't want to face that until we had a child."

I decided to leave the sports magazine stuff for Derrick's friend from Columbia to look through. Emptying Troy's desk and the other file cabinet, I packed the boxes in the car and headed home. Joseph had said he would be at Mrs. Boyd's by two. I called Rebecca and left a message for her to get herself fingerprinted and meet us at Mrs.

Boyd's. We would need all the bodies we could muster to load that furniture into the truck.

With the boxes of Troy's stuff deposited in the family room on the top floor, I had a couple of hours to get some lunch. Pulling the makings of a salad from the refrigerator, I decided to eat at the kitchen table rather than on the porch. Right now I didn't want to tempt any of my neighbors to drop in. I had a lot to sort through.

I've never been any good at writing fiction. In a class I took in college we were told that conflict is what makes stories. Your main character must have a problem. "Get that character up a tree and then start throwing rocks at him or her" is how the professor put it. I made a C in the class—the only grade below a B that I ever got in high school or college—because, the professor told me, I seemed unable to create a conflict for my characters that felt believable or that readers would care about. Ten years ago I wrote a few chapters of a novel and showed them to Dave. He was kind, but he advised, even urged, me to stick to non-fiction.

In the last week I felt like I had been run up a tree and the rocks that had been thrown at me had hit their target. My ex-husband was dead. I'd been told that he didn't love me, even feared me. Someone had broken into my store. Someone—the same person?—had broken into a house I own and injured my dog. My *ex*-husband and my daughter had colluded with my ex-husband's girlfriend to scam an elderly woman.

Robert's announcement that he and Derrick were going to have a baby was the one ray of hope I'd seen this week. And it came from the least expected source. For the past ten years I'd thought Rebecca was my only chance of having a grandchild, and I was afraid she'd do it without benefit of a husband or partner.

I understood why Robert hadn't said anything about the surrogate. He told us he was gay when he was fifteen. I had had my suspicions before that, mostly because of his disinterest in dating. Robert always was a good-looking guy, one that girls openly flirted with, but he never returned the attention. Books and sports were his passion—especially baseball and track.

I knew Troy was homophobic, but I was surprised by how extremely upset Robert's admission made him. "Where did he get the queer gene?" he asked me that night as he finished his third beer.

That was the closest I ever came to slapping my husband. "Don't you *ever* talk about our son like that. He's gay. It's part of him, just like having blue eyes or being left-handed."

"He got both of those from me." Troy pulled another beer out of the fridge. "Are you saying I'm the one who made him gay? Is there some queer gene lurking down inside of me?"

"Troy, nobody *makes* somebody gay. He was born that way and he'll be a lot happier if he—and we—can accept it."

After that realization Troy withdrew from Robert. He seemed to pay more attention to Joseph, who was already hanging around the store and helping out. He was actually relieved when Rebecca started having sex with her boyfriend at age sixteen. "At least she's not a dyke," was his only comment, while I was trying to offer advice about safe sex and STD's.

When Robert introduced Derrick to us at their graduation from law school, Troy refused to shake Derrick's hand. He just walked away, muttering to himself. Robert wouldn't let me go after him. "That's a milder response than I expected," he said. They rarely spoke after that.

I finished my salad and put the dishes in the sink. I would wash them by hand after supper. When you live alone, it takes too long to fill a dishwasher. Mine comes to life now only when the kids come over or if I have a few friends in for dinner.

Troy's truck was backed up to Mrs. Boyd's garage when I pulled up in front of the house. Rebecca was wearing shorts and a tank top, *not exactly professional,* I thought, *but probably suitable for the weather.* Joseph had on a polo shirt with the name and logo of his uncle's BBQ place. I wondered if he had designed that, too. They were talking to Mrs. Boyd and her nurse. Standing next to the truck, Mrs. Boyd looked even smaller than she really was.

"Well, a deal is a deal," Rebecca was saying as I walked up to them.

"I know, dear," Mrs. Boyd said. "But Joanne showed me some pieces like these on the internet and the prices were much higher than what you paid. I saw a dresser just like that one going for $1200. You paid $400."

Rebecca shot me a guilty glance. "Those are retail prices, ma'am. When we sell these in our store, we'll ask a higher price. But if we paid $1200 for that piece, we couldn't make any money on it. There's a saying in this business: 'There has to be some meat on the bone for us.' We wouldn't buy it at that price. You'd be stuck with it."

"Maybe I could sell it for $1200." Mrs. Boyd shifted her walker to take me into the conversation. "What do you think, Maureen?"

I thought I ought to tell her that she had been conned and offer to make up some of what she'd lost, but I said, "Maybe you could sell it, Beatrice, but you'd have to advertise and ship it to someone. And it would be sitting here until you found a buyer."

"These pieces didn't sell," Rebecca said in relief, "so my dad did you a favor by taking them off your hands at the end of the day. We're not trying to cheat anyone, Mrs. Boyd. We're just trying to operate a business. Remember, you made over $30,000 after you paid us."

"Well, I suppose that's true," the old woman said, and I thought *suppose?* It's a fact, lady: you made over $30,000, even after my family skimmed some off the top.

"We need to start loading," I said. "This will probably take a couple of trips."

"Yes, we'll get out of your way. Joanne, why don't you bring these folks some tea? It's turning into a warm afternoon."

When Mrs. Boyd had hobbled her way out of earshot, Rebecca sighed and said, "Thanks for backing me up. I wasn't sure what you were going to say."

"We can talk about it later. Just remember, you owe me big time."

It did take two trips and several glasses of iced tea to get all the furniture moved. Most of it came from bedrooms—dressers and another armoire, several night stands—but there was also a massive mahogany sideboard. For me the physical activity was just what I needed after finishing the Mudcat book and before plunging into another project.

When Joanne was refilling my tea glass, I took the opportunity to ask her why Mrs. Boyd was selling the furniture. "It was designed to go in this house," I said. "It's as much a part of the house as the windows and doors."

Joanne glanced over her shoulder, as though Mrs. Boyd could have sneaked up on her. "I know. We talked about that. She's in really bad shape financially, though. Her kids have drained her the last couple of years. Mrs. Maxwell has put a stop to that, but Beatrice didn't have good advice about her investments for a number of years. I know she regrets having to strip the house, but she has no choice."

"It will probably lower the value of the house."

Joanne nodded. "It was a real dilemma for her, but Mrs. Maxwell said this was the best choice. The house will have only a limited local market, but people all over the country may want the furniture."

And so my family not only took advantage of an elderly woman, but an elderly woman who needed to get as much money as she could out of what she was selling.

Joseph and Rebecca worked adroitly, leaving me feeling like I would do better just to get out of their way. This was the first time I'd seen them together for more than a few minutes. They seemed to share a kind of chemistry—a glance, a touch—something more intimate than just two people moving furniture.

When we had the last piece unloaded in the back of the store, I began pulling out drawers and opening doors. I was determined to understand why somebody was so interested in this stuff. It had to be the furniture itself, since all the contents had been emptied. I turned things upside down and knocked on the backs and sides. Perhaps there was some hidden compartment.

"Hey, take it easy," Rebecca said. "Don't scratch anything. I've got a potential buyer."

"Already?" I was amazed. "Nobody's even been in the store to see it."

"The store doesn't have to be open. I sent pictures to a guy in Spartanburg, somebody Grandpa Wyatt knows. That's how you do business now."

I had to confirm a suspicion. "How much are you asking for that piece?" I pointed to the $1200 dresser.

Rebecca's hesitation was all I needed, but she said, "$1400."

"And somebody's offering to pay that, without actually having seen the piece?"

"It's called the twenty-first century business model, Mother. If we had a web site, I could sell half the furniture in this store by the end of the summer."

"But you can't sell this stuff yet," I protested. "Not until we know why somebody was messing with it."

Rebecca heaved a mother-weary sigh. "Somebody broke in. Okay,

I get that. They also smashed a display case and took stuff out of it."

"Probably to make us think they weren't just interested in the furniture."

"Or maybe they moved the furniture around to draw attention away from the display case. You don't know what they were interested in." Her voice rose in exasperation.

I stood in front of the armoire that had ... fallen on Troy. I still couldn't grasp that a piece of furniture that I had grown up with— that I had hidden in as a small child—had killed him. "But this stuff is the only evidence we've got."

"Evidence of what, Mother? Dad's death was an accident. This isn't a crime scene. The police have finished with it."

"But somebody broke in. Somebody broke into Troy's apartment last night. Isn't that a crime?" I looked to Joseph, but he had stepped back out of the line of fire.

"One that will never be solved. You saw the woman running away. She wasn't carrying anything. You ought to just leave the door open and hope people will come in and take stuff. It's the only way you'll ever get Dad's apartment cleaned out. Right now, we've got to get these pieces ready to sell."

"Before Mrs. Boyd realizes how badly you ripped her off?"

Before Rebecca could say anything else, Greg Compton appeared in the door. "Am I interrupting something?"

"No," I said, sure that he could read guilt on my face and in my awkward body language. Suddenly I couldn't stop primping my hair. It was the only thing I could think of to do with my hands. I wondered how much Compton had heard. "Come on in. Do you have a lead about the break-ins?"

"In fact, I do." He opened his notebook. "And it's not at all what we expected. Like I told you earlier, there weren't many prints on those first few pieces that we dusted back here. Troy was cleaning them off."

"We always clean things before we put them out on the floor," Rebecca said defensively.

Compton nodded. "There were a few prints we couldn't identify. I'm sure they're from Mrs. Boyd or members of her family. But the freshest set of prints belonged to Dolores Hughes."

❖❖❖

CHAPTER 8

"What? Dolores was here?" I looked at Joseph, who seemed to be trying to slip even farther into the shadows. "I thought she was in jail."

"She was released a month ago," Compton said. "She got early parole because of over-crowding. The authorities in Georgia said her crimes were non-violent and her behavior had been good." He turned to Joseph. "Have you heard from her?"

Joseph hunched his shoulders. "She called Grandma right after she got out. She said she'd be coming through here, but she wasn't going to stay."

"Have you seen her?" Compton asked.

Joseph shook his head. "I don't *want* to see her. Why would I? My grandma's the only mother I've ever had."

Rebecca stepped closer to him, taking his hand. He looked at her gratefully. Once again I had a fleeting vision of history repeating itself. Her mother and his father had had some sort of relationship in high school. Was there more between them than just friendship?

"So, her fingerprints were on this furniture?" I said. "Where?"

Compton found a page on his tablet and then stepped up to the armoire. Slipping on a pair of latex gloves, he raised his hand to a back corner of the piece but didn't touch it. "The clearest set of prints—most of her hand—was right here. It's fortunate that this is a really fine piece, finished on the back as well as the front and sides. I'd like to dust everything again."

"Including what was in the Boyds' garage?" I asked hopefully.

Compton nodded. "Everything."

"But I've already got a buyer," Rebecca whined.

"We're not going to sell anything," I said sharply, "until we figure out what's going on here. You can take a deposit and assure the guy that we won't sell to anyone else, but not one piece of this furniture is going out of here until I say so."

"We'll also need your fingerprints," Compton told Rebecca. "We've got your mother's, your father's and Joseph's. I can take yours right here. And I'd like to get DNA samples, if you're willing. I've got my techs waiting outside."

"I thought this was just a break-in," Rebecca said, "and you don't care about break-ins."

"We have the fingerprints of a convicted felon on this scene now," Compton said, glancing apologetically at Joseph. "That makes everything seem more serious."

"Don't you want to take Pepper's paw prints?" Rebecca asked. "He's been in here, too. He was here when Daddy died."

"Actually, the dog was closed up in the office when we got here," Compton said, revealing a detail I hadn't heard before. "We have some samples of his hair. If we need anything else, we know where to find him."

"Wait. Pepper was in the office? Why would he be there? He was always right beside Troy."

"We figured Troy put him in there so he wouldn't get out while that garage door was open and he was bringing furniture in."

"That doesn't make any sense. Pepper is a very obedient dog. "

"Ma'am, all I know is he was in the office when we got here. Now, can we get the samples?"

"Let's do this," I said.

Compton brought in his team. Officer Hightower smiled when her eyes met mine. I didn't know the other officer. They took Rebecca's fingerprints electronically and swabbed her cheek and Joseph's. With that done, the two of them were about to leave.

"If you hear from your mother again," Compton said to Joseph, "please let us know. We want to talk to her."

"Is she a suspect in something?" Joseph asked.

"No. We would just like to know if she can help us understand what happened to Mr. McKenzie. There's no denying that she was here."

Joseph nodded. "I'll remind my grandma."

As they got to the door I said, "We'll be opening tomorrow morning at nine. Please be here then, both of you."

"Whatever," Rebecca said over her shoulder.

Joseph stopped and turned to face me. "Would you like for me to show you some possibilities for a web site?"

"Let's plan on that." Even if I ultimately decided to sell the building to a developer, a web site could help us reduce inventory so we wouldn't be stuck with finding another place for all this stuff.

Once I heard them drive off, I took Compton aside. "Do you really just want to talk to Dolores Hughes? Do you think she might be involved in what happened to Troy?"

"I didn't want to say anything in front of Joseph, but, if somebody was going to push that armoire over, that's where her fingerprints would be."

I gasped. "Do you think she might have killed Troy?" Even though I didn't know Dolores, I didn't want to believe the worst right away. "Couldn't her fingerprints have gotten on it when it was at Mrs. Boyd's?"

"Only if she attended the sale. Joseph was there. He said he hasn't seen her. And why would she go there?"

"Why would she come here? Why would she kill Troy?"

"Answering the 'why' questions isn't my job, Ms. Cooper. All I know is that her fingerprints are on the piece of furniture that killed your husband. We'll dust all the pieces that came from Mrs. Boyd's house. If her prints are on that second batch of furniture that you just brought in today, then it would indicate that she had been out there. If her prints are only on these pieces that your husband brought here in the first load, then it looks like Dolores was here. Why she was here and what she might have done, I can't say."

I had to put aside questions about Dolores and spend the rest of the afternoon designing a poster announcing Artemisia's appearance in the store. Downloading one of the pictures from her web site, I came up with what I thought was an effective bit of publicity, given that I'm a writer, not an artist.

One of the items Troy had picked up somewhere was a printer big enough to do blue-prints and posters. He had tinkered with it to get it running again and sometimes did posters for businesses around the square. When he bought it, I had rolled my eyes, but I was glad to have it now because it meant I didn't have to email my design to an office supply store on the edge of town and blab the secret of Artemisia's arrival.

On my way home I stopped by the vet's to see Pepper. As I petted him, they assured me that he was doing fine and I could take him home right then. "He'll need the cast for a couple of weeks," the vet explained, "but it shouldn't limit his mobility too much. He won't be chasing any Frisbees for a while, though."

Suddenly it dawned on me that I didn't know how Artemisia and her mother felt about dogs. What if they had allergies?

"Could I leave him one more night? I have company coming and I don't know if they have issues with pets. If they're okay with it, I'll pick him up tomorrow morning."

"That'll be fine," the vet assured me.

When I got home I vacuumed the two bedrooms where Artemisia and her mother would be staying and cleaned the bathroom between them. I use a cleaning service, but they weren't scheduled to come in for another week. I called Dave to get Artemisia's phone number. She assured me that she and mother would have no objections to a dog in the house. They had two of their own.

By eight-thirty it was getting dark. I was in the kitchen fixing myself a late supper when a car pulled into the driveway and the back doorbell rang. I flipped on the outside light and opened the door to find myself facing a light-skinned black woman about my age and height, although with a fuller figure. She wore jeans and a loose-fitting top with half-sleeves. I recognized the car as Joseph's, but I was still surprised when the woman said, "Ms. Cooper? I'm Dolores Hughes. May I talk with you for a few minutes?"

If I hadn't seen Joseph sitting behind the wheel of the car, I would have slammed the door and called the police. Instead I stepped back. "Come in."

With a bandage on one ankle and walking with a cane, Dolores hobbled painfully into the kitchen. I was relieved to hear Joseph turn off the car's engine. "Should we ask Joseph to come in?" I said.

"No. we need to do this one-on-one," Dolores said. "He's going to wait out there, to take me to the ER when we're done. As you can see, I can't walk it."

I couldn't muster up much sympathy for her injury. It was obvious she was the one who broke into my house and injured Pepper.

"Why don't you sit down?" I gestured to the kitchen table. "Would you like some tea?"

"No, thank you. I'm sorry to disturb your supper." Dolores lowered herself into a chair and glanced around the room. "This is a beautiful place."

"Thank you."

She sighed and laid the cane across her lap. "Okay, I guess that covers the polite chit-chat. My mama and Joseph said I had to come talk to you or they would turn me in to the police themselves. And that would mean I'd go back to jail."

I sat down across from her, leaving my supper plate on the counter. She truly was an attractive woman. Allowing for what time and her hard life had done to her, she must have been quite beautiful when she was younger. "What do you want to talk about?"

"I want to apologize for breaking into Troy's place and for hurting your dog." Her voice was soft, bordering on sultry. "If you don't press charges, we'll pay for the window and the vet's bill."

I shook my head. I knew they couldn't afford the window, let alone the vet's bill. "There's no need for that. In fact, I'll make an offer of my own. I won't press charges if you'll answer some questions."

She looked at me suspiciously, as though prison might be a better option than talking. "What kind of questions?"

"Let's start with what you were doing in Troy's store a few days ago."

Her grip on the cane tightened. "What makes you think I was there?"

"The fingerprints you left on one of the pieces of furniture." I've watched enough police shows to know that you keep a few things back when you're questioning someone, to see if they reveal something that only the perp could know.

"Oh, yeah, when I helped him move that armoire."

That was at least an admission that she was there, if not a confession that she murdered him.

"You mean the armoire that fell on him and killed him?"

"My God! Is that what happened? I just heard he'd had some kind of accident."

"Your family didn't tell you the details?"

"Tonight's the first time I've seen them. I talked to Mama on the phone, but I've tried to stay away from them since I got out of jail, so I wouldn't get them mixed up in my problems. I was staying with some people I know, but I had to have some help with my ankle. I think it might be broken."

Home is where, when you have to go there, they have to take you in.

"What did they tell you?"

"You mean after reminding me what a huge disappointment I am?"

The crestfallen look on her face reminded me of a celebrity for whom I had ghost-written an autobiography. He told me much of the turmoil in his life had been caused by his parents who, at separate times during his childhood, told him they wished he'd never been born.

Dolores pulled herself together. "They just said Troy had an accident in the store."

"He was crushed by the armoire. The one that has *your* fingerprints on it."

She glanced toward the door, as though considering an escape. "That's because I helped him scoot it into the store so he could get some other pieces out of his truck. I told him he ought to wait 'til Joseph came back to help him."

"It was convenient that your mother called Joseph to come help her with something. That left Troy by himself in the store."

"Yeah, I asked her to call Joseph so I could talk with Troy alone."

"So we're back to my original question. What were you doing in the store?"

"I came to ask Troy for some help."

"What kind of help?" I guess her experience with the police over the years had taught her not to volunteer one bit of information more than she was asked for.

"I needed money. And somebody to drive me to Philadelphia."

"What's in Philadelphia?"

"A gal I met in prison said her brother could give me a job there when I got out, an actual legit job to help me start over. I knew if I stayed in Atlanta, I'd be back in jail in six months, probably sooner. I had to get away from there, from those people."

"What did Troy say?"

"He said he would, if I could wait a few days."

I refilled my tea and poured Dolores a glass. "How could he help you? He didn't have any money." Not if Rebecca had put up the cash for their furniture scam.

She shrugged. "He just said he would help me. That's all I know."

It was time to ratchet up the tension. Joseph's presence in the driveway and her bum ankle gave me the courage. "Then why did you kill him? Was it an accident?"

Dolores sat bolt upright. "What? My God! I didn't kill him."

"The police said your fingerprints were on the armoire at the very place they would be if you had pushed it over."

"But I didn't! I told you, I just helped him move it a few feet across the floor. Like this." She held up her hands as though she was pushing the armoire. "Then, after we talked, I left. He was still alive, I swear to you."

I've learned from interviewing people when I'm writing a book that a sudden shift in a line of questioning can elicit sometimes unexpected answers. "Why did you break into his apartment?"

Dolores sat back, still alert but less tense, and took a sip of her tea.

"Yeah," she said, "about that. In the last couple of months before I was released, I wrote Troy to see if he would help me. Real, old-fashioned letters, 'cause we didn't have email in jail. When I heard he was dead, I knew I needed to get those letters back. I was sure everybody would think I killed him if they knew I'd even been in touch with him."

"Why would they think that, just from some letters?"

"I guess I used some kind of ... strong language."

"You mean you threatened him."

"No," she snapped. "I just reminded him that he owed me something."

"Why?"

"Well, because of what we had ... back when."

"And you figured he would still have the letters?"

She laughed. "Did that man ever throw anything away? I'm sure he still had stuff I wrote back in high school. I didn't think he'd keep it in his office. But everything in the apartment was locked up. I just had time to pop open that one file cabinet before I started hearing noises. People upstairs coming in, I guess. I was afraid somebody would see the window I broke, so I got out. I never was very good at

Albert A. Bell, Jr

that B and E stuff. That's why I was in jail. Well, partly why."

My supper was getting cold, but it seemed rude to eat without offering Dolores something—in spite of what she'd done; damn Southern gentility anyway—and I didn't really have anything else. I was planning a trip to the store tomorrow, to get ready for Artemisia and her mother. "What kind of relationship *did* you and Troy have in high school?"

"We were ... good friends. We had a lot of fun together."

"That's not exactly how your biology teacher put it."

"Old man Martin?" She hooted. "He was just jealous 'cause he wanted to get in my pants. He had a thing for light-skinned girls like me. You know, the Halle Berry type. I think he had this fantasy of being a slave owner on a plantation." She twirled an imaginary mustache.

She was probably not far off in her assessment of the man, or in comparing herself to a woman as lovely as Halle Berry. "You worked in the store after you graduated. Did you and Troy continue to have fun together? Maybe after Troy and I were married?"

She tented her fingers in front of her face. "Ms. Cooper, that was a long time ago. Stuff in the past, you know, it's better just to leave it there."

I looked her straight in the eye. "Was Troy Joseph's father?"

She answered without hesitation "No, ma'am. I swear to you by all that's holy, Troy was *not* Joseph's father."

"Then who was?"

"Okay, you've got a right to ask if it was Troy." She shook a finger at me. "Beyond that, if you'll forgive my saying so, it's none of your business."

"If I press charges and you go back to jail, how long do you think you'll get?" I hated myself for threatening her, but how else could I learn anything?

She smiled at first, then looked at me more closely. "Wait, you're serious, aren't you? You'll press charges against me."

"You hurt my dog, and I think you know more about what happened to Troy than you're admitting. So, yes, I'm serious. Who was Joseph's father?" If my daughter was interested in a man, I wanted to know as much as I could about him and his family.

She leaned back and looked up at the ceiling before she brought her eyes down to meet mine. In a soft voice she said, "Ms. Cooper, I was raped."

I took in a quick breath and put my hand to my mouth. "Oh, no. Who did it?"

"That's something else that's none of your business."

"Did you go to the police?"

"In this town, what good would that do?"

"So I'm assuming it was a white man."

Dolores nodded quickly.

"And you had Joseph—"

Her voice started to break and the painful words gushed out. "My mama couldn't pay for me to get an abortion. And she wouldn't have, even if she could. The baby didn't ask for it to happen, she said. We shouldn't punish him. She said the same thing happened to her, and Zeke was the result. I would have to deal with it, just like she did. Make the best of it, like she did. She said she never regretted having Zeke, or me. I guess mothers have to say stuff like that. It's sure not how I feel."

"Has she ever told you who your father is?"

Dolores shook her head and rubbed her eyes. I got a box of tissues off the counter and placed it in front of her. She pulled out a couple and blew her nose.

"When I was growing up, I used to try to get her to tell me, but she never would. She said I was better off not knowing. Our whole family was better off." Another outburst of tears and another wad of tissues. "I tried to be a mother to Joseph. Honest to God, I did, Ms. Cooper. But whenever I held him and tried to take care of him, all I could feel was that man's hands all over me. I would start to have panic attacks. Mama told me just to leave the baby with her and come back when I could get over it. I'm not sure I'm over it yet."

She put her elbows on the table, held her head in her hands, and began to sob so hard she couldn't speak anymore. I scooted my chair closer to hers and put my arm around her heaving shoulders. She leaned into me. Beyond her I noticed the back door was barely open and in the porch light I could make out the side of Joseph's head.

How much had he heard?

❖❖❖

CHAPTER 9

By the time Dolores had settled down enough to leave, the back door was closed again. When I opened it, I was not entirely surprised to see that Joseph's car was gone. Obviously he had heard quite a bit.

"Oh, damn!" Dolores said when she saw the empty driveway. "What's got into that boy? He was supposed to take me to the hospital."

"I'll take you. Let me get my keys."

Dolores put a hand on my arm. "No, Ms. Cooper. You haven't had your supper. I can't impose on you. Just call Zeke. He'll come get me."

For some reason I wanted to help this woman. Maybe, as weird as it sounded, because we both had a connection to Troy. Maybe because of the tragic story she had told me. "Zeke doesn't close until nine, and then he has to clean up. I'll take you."

Dolores was quiet on the short drive to the hospital. I had the sense that she was thinking about things—awful things—that had happened to her twenty years ago. I regretted stirring up those memories, so I did not intrude.

I let her out at the ER entrance and went to park. By the time I got inside, she was filling out the usual forms. At one point she put the pen down and said, "I know they have to treat me, but I don't have any insurance, and I can't pay for this myself. They're just going to slap an Ace bandage on my ankle and send me home."

I took the clipboard from her and went up to the desk where a chunky middle-aged woman was sitting behind a computer. Her ID had her first name, Christine, in large letters and her last name in smaller letters and her picture beside it. She looked vaguely familiar.

"I'm Maureen Cooper," I said. I don't like to throw my name around, but it does sometimes get people's attention, and that was what I needed right now.

"Yes, I know," Christine said. "We were in high school together. I'm Christine Marshall. I was Chrissie Armstrong back then."

"Oh, yes. You were head cheerleader."

She looked down at herself. "Hard to believe now, isn't it? Four kids, you know. Well, what can I do for you?"

"I was wondering what I need to sign to take responsibility for this bill."

From the arching of her eyebrows, I gathered that this was not a question she heard every day. She craned her neck to look around me at where Dolores was sitting. "Is that who I think it is, Ms. Cooper?"

"Why does that matter? I just want to sign whatever form you have so I can cover this bill."

"Whatever you say." Christine clicked a few times on the computer and printed out a form. "Fill this out, please, and sign by the X. I'll need to see your driver's license."

"Do I need to pay anything in advance?"

"No, we'll send you the bill."

"All right. Let me get my wallet."

As I picked up my purse from the chair beside her Dolores asked, "What are you doing?"

"Just settling an account."

I had barely gotten the form filled out when Dolores' name was called. "Do you want me to come with you?" I asked as she stood up.

Tears rose in her eyes. "I wasn't going to ask, but yes. Thank you."

We were led to a ward with four beds in it, each surrounded by a curtain. A nightstand and a chair completed the furnishings in each bay. A nurse attached an ID bracelet to Dolores' left wrist. The doctor was a young Pakistani, whose accent had a pleasant lilt to it. He unwrapped the bandage on Dolores' ankle, probed and turned it, then ordered x-rays. While she was gone I called Zeke and told him where she was.

"I'll take her home when we're done."

"You know, Ms. Cooper, it would be better if you brought her to the restaurant. She and Mama aren't getting along so well right now. I'll take her home after I close."

"All right. I can do that."

The technician who brought Dolores back to the bay said we

would have the results of the x-rays in less than half an hour. Dolores stretched out on the bed.

"Are you comfortable?" I asked. "I know hospital beds aren't the greatest."

"I've slept on prison beds. This is like lying on a cloud."

I took a deep breath and decided to plunge in. "Could I ask you a couple of more questions?"

"About what?"

"About the day Troy died."

Dolores sat up on the bed. "Is that why you're being so nice to me, so you can interrogate me? I told you, he was alive when I left the store. That's all I know."

I ignored her jibe. "You said you left the store about one. Where did you go?"

"Back to my friend's house, where I was staying. I didn't leave there again until the next morning. There were people there who can vouch for me, although they're not the kind of people who like to talk to the police."

"Okay. Troy was found about six-thirty. The coroner said he died between three and three-thirty. That's our timeline."

"'Timeline'? You sound like some kind of damn detective. Do you think Troy's death wasn't an accident?"

"In all honesty, when I heard about your fingerprints on the armoire, I thought maybe you killed him. Maybe it was an accident," I added quickly. "You could have been helping him move the thing, like you said, and it tipped over. You were scared, didn't think the police would believe you because of your record, so you ran."

Dolores chuckled. "Is this where I'm supposed to break down and confess?"

"Only if that's what happened."

"Ms. Cooper, the armoire was wobbly, on those skinny legs, and there's a couple of rough spots in the concrete floor. Troy must have been trying to move it by himself after I left." She made a pleading gesture, her hands out and palms up. "Why couldn't it just have been an accident?"

"Because somebody was looking for something *in* that furniture. They broke in sometime after Troy died. They might have been there earlier and Troy caught them. I just don't think it was an accident.

Troy was a strong guy and he'd been moving furniture around since he was in high school."

The curtain around the bay parted and Dolores' doctor stepped to the end of the bed, looking at images on a tablet. He asked to see Dolores' ID. When he was satisfied on that point, he said, "Well, Ms. Hughes, the good news is that your ankle isn't broken, just badly sprained. We're going to put a boot on you, which you'll need to wear for a week, and give you something for the pain. Then we'll have you check in with an orthopedist for any further treatment that might be necessary."

Dolores shook her head. "Doc, I can't afford any of that. An old tennis shoe, maybe, but not some kind of fancy boot and nothing more than a couple of aspirin."

The doctor flicked to another screen. "It says here that all the costs are being covered."

Dolores turned her attention to me. "Is that the account you were settling? Ms. Cooper—"

"Don't worry about it," I said. "I'll be in the waiting room while they fix you up."

"That's a good idea," the doctor said. "It will get a bit crowded in here."

When I got back to the lobby I saw Zeke talking with Christine. She pointed in my direction and Zeke walked over to me.

"Is it true?" he asked. "Are you paying Dolores' bill?"

"Yes, I am."

"Why?"

"Because she couldn't and she needed the treatment."

"We'll pay you back, Ms. Cooper, even if it's just a few dollars a week."

"No. Don't worry about it."

He looked down and then back up at me. "Well, from now on your money's no good at my restaurant."

"Zeke, you don't have to—"

"I mean it, Ms. Cooper. I will not take any money from you from now on."

My mother used to tell me that, when people want to return a kindness—even though you did it without expecting repayment—you just have to thank them graciously and let them retain their dignity.

"Thank you, Zeke. I really appreciate that." But now could I bring Artemisia and her mother there? Surely I could insist on paying for a group.

"By the way," Zeke said, "do you know where Joseph is? He was supposed to take Dolores to see you and then bring her here."

Zeke took Dolores home with him. I got back to my place about ten. When I called Joseph's cell it went straight to voice mail, so I left a short message. I heated my supper in the microwave, locked all the doors, and climbed the stairs to the family room on the third floor, now a. k. a. the repository of Troy's papers. Dolores was right. Troy would not have thrown away anything she wrote him—not now, not twenty-five years ago. What I had brought home so far couldn't be all of his correspondence over the years, but it was what I had to start on.

With all that was happening this weekend, I wouldn't be able to get through even a fraction of what was here. Each jam-packed four-drawer file cabinet—and there were three in his study, for want of a better term—had produced eight boxes of musty-smelling stuff. His desk accounted for four more boxes. My kids often wonder why I insist on driving a mini-van. I tell them because it's comfortable and because, when I do need room, I've got it. With the seats down, I had been able to transport all of the boxes in one trip. It was lugging them up here that had nearly done me in.

The third floor has a separate heating and cooling system. I knocked the a/c down a couple of degrees and prepared to commit myself to a few hours of what I do best—prowling through other people's lives.

Unlike most hoarders, Troy had some sense of organization. I decided to build on that and do a sort of triage of the boxes, just to get an overview of what was in each one and some idea of where I might start looking for anything pertaining to Dolores.

I had cleverly dubbed the three file cabinets Right, Center, and Left. The drawers I numbered with a marker, starting with #1 on the top and going down. The two boxes taken from each drawer were "a" and "b." That allowed me to preserve the exact order, in case that became important. I had set the twenty-eight boxes on the floor of the family room in the same arrangement as the file cabinets and the desk they came from. Now I hoisted box R1a onto the game table in the center of the room, being careful not to knock over my glass of tea.

It didn't take me long to realize that this box contained papers from Troy's college days. My first impulse was to get a recycling bag and just dump everything into it. But, until I better understood his relationship with Dolores and whether that had anything to do with what had happened to him, I hated to think I might destroy something that would give me a clue. There might even be something about me in all this mess.

"Is this how hoarders get started?" I muttered. The nagging sensation that I *might* need this, someday? I swore I would throw stuff out. I had to, just not quite yet. The three file cabinets in Troy's study were only a fraction of what I had seen in his apartment. In his business he must have bought out a lot of offices and amassed enough file cabinets to supply a small bureaucracy—or a really serious hoarder. Just keeping everything on a computer couldn't have given him the sense of satisfaction, or security, that paper in file drawers did.

I understood him better than I wanted to admit. I not only back up all of my documents; I print paper copies. I still have the final "manuscript" copy of every book and article I've ever written, plus my research notes. I've always thought that's just what writers do.

I was thinking about quitting for the night when I got into box R3b. It contained a collection of newspaper articles about the death of my grandfather, Russell Cooper, whom Troy had admired greatly. He was chief of police in Lawrenceville for fifteen years, a local hero, virtually a saint—killed in a gun battle with a gang of drug dealers. There's a big memorial plaque for him in the foyer of the town's Justice Center. The Lawrenceville paper put out a special edition about him. Troy had that. But he also had articles from the Greenville, Spartanburg, Greenwood and Columbia newspapers. We used to be able to get upstate newspapers at the drug store on the corner of the square opposite our store, before everything went online.

Glancing over the material brought back memories of my grandparents. "Papa" was a large, affable man with reddish-brown hair. His smile was the feature I remembered best. All of the articles and stories spoke about him in the most glowing terms.

One piece puzzled me, though. It was an op-ed from the Greenwood paper, a column called "I'm Just Sayin,'" dated two weeks after my grandfather's death. Troy had underlined a few phrases. I had to read the article twice to make sure I understood what it was insinuating:

> Yes, Russell Cooper was a hero who died protecting the people of his town from infiltration by a gang of drug dealers. There can be no debate about that. For some years Lawrenceville has been notable for its low rate of problems with drugs and related criminal activity. That could be due to the high moral character of the town's citizenry, or to exceptional police work—which was most likely the case here.
>
> But, as has been shown recently in Mason, Alabama—a town quite similar to Lawrenceville in many ways—drug trafficking tends to be less noticeable when police officers are involved in it. In the Alabama case it was several mid-level officers. No one has suggested that the chief there was complicit. Nor is anyone here suggesting that Chief Cooper was involved in any malfeasance. But police chiefs, <u>like generals in an army, rarely put themselves at risk in the front line of battle, as Chief Cooper did, without some compelling reason.</u>
>
> In the two weeks since Russell Cooper's death, there have been several shootings and robberies that appear to be drug-related. Lawrenceville obviously misses the strong hand of its beloved chief of police. Maybe there are questions that need to be asked. There <u>might be people who are willing to talk now,</u> perhaps people who have insight into how things work in Lawrenceville.
>
> I'm just sayin'.

I slapped the piece of paper back down. "That son of a bitch. He's accusing my grandfather—"

One of my older computers sits in a corner of the family room. I looked up the Greenwood paper online and was surprised to see that the guy who wrote that piece was now the associate editor. I emailed him and left a message with my name and number but no mention of why I wanted to talk to him. I suspected the words "Cooper" and "Lawrenceville" would get his attention.

Shortly before midnight I had to make myself quit, after going through ten boxes. I kept pushing myself to work in a cursory fashion, but I kept getting bogged down. As someone once said, "No person who can read is ever successful at cleaning out an attic." Troy's apartment was just a big first-floor attic.

The next morning I picked up Pepper from the vet's. They assured me he was doing fine. "It's easier for a dog to have a broken front leg than the back," the vet said.

I noticed Pepper licking his cast. "He won't need one of those cone things?"

"He would with stitches but not with a cast." He reached up on a shelf and handed me a small spray bottle. "It won't hurt him to lick the cast, but if he seems to be obsessing about it, just spray a little of this on it. It's a bitter apple spray. It tastes vile. Be careful. It will burn the dog's eyes—or yours—pretty badly."

I settled the bill and we headed for the store. The square was blocked off so FoodFest vendors could set up, but we have enough private parking behind the store—room for Troy's truck and a couple of cars—that I didn't have any problem getting into a space. Rebecca's car was already there. I was disappointed not to see Joseph's car, but it was still early.

Pepper managed pretty well with his cast. Rebecca petted him and baby-talked to him and he settled on his rug in the office. I noticed that the door to the men's restroom was closed and assumed that Joseph was in there. Someone in his family must have brought him in. I was surprised when the door opened and Troy's father emerged.

"Oh, good morning, Wyatt."

"Good morning, Maureen." He put a hand on my arm. I hate for people to touch me right after they come out of the bathroom. "How are you doing?"

"I'm ... managing. How are you?" Though I don't particularly like the man, I had to sympathize with him. He'd lost his wife, now his son. He rubbed my shoulder and I wished I could take two steps back.

"You know, a friend once told me, after her daughter's funeral, that she had done the hardest thing she would ever have to do. I thought I'd hit bottom when my wife died, but the loss of a child is like a punch in the gut that you never saw coming."

He hugged me and we stepped away from one another, to my great relief. "Rebecca called me," Wyatt said, "and asked if I could give you folks a little help. I need to earn my consulting fee."

Oh, yes, his "consulting fee," which Troy had insisted on paying, no matter how much money the store lost and which I would now be paying. "Thank you for coming in. I think we're going to have a busy weekend."

He nodded. "There are certainly going to be a lot of people around."

"Some of them might even want to buy something. Will you be okay with that?"

Twisting his mouth and surveying the store, he said, "In the words of Ecclesiastes, 'For everything there is a season ... . a time to keep, and a time to cast away.' This is my time to cast away. None of this stuff has any meaning for me anymore. I love my daughter and all my grandkids—you know I do—but I've lost my son." He waved a hand over the furniture around us. "You could open the doors and give all of this away, for all I care."

I hugged him. "Wyatt, I'm so sorry. I think about my own kids, and I can't imagine what you're going through."

"Mother, what is this?" Rebecca came out of the office holding the poster I'd made for Artemisia's visit.

As I explained that Artemisia would be in the store on Saturday and staying with me over the weekend, Rebecca's mouth dropped open.

"Are ... you ... kidding ... me?"

She had pushed one of my buttons. "Why do people always say that? Somebody on 'Antiques Roadshow' is told that their four-dollar, garage-sale painting is worth $50,000 and they say 'Are you kidding me?' I keep hoping the appraiser will say, 'Yeah, I'm just messing with you.'" I took the poster. "No, I'm not kidding. Artemisia and her mother will arrive tonight and she'll spend the day in the store tomorrow."

"Oh, my God!" Rebecca gasped. "We've got to tell everybody."

"No! That's exactly what we *cannot* do." I shook my finger at her. "She doesn't want anybody to know about it in advance. She'll announce it on social media in the morning and we'll put this poster up. Until then we cannot say a word."

"If it got onto the news tonight," Wyatt said, "we would be swamped tomorrow. The whole town would be overrun. It'll be bad enough, I'm sure, even with the little bit of publicity on social media."

I cocked my head at him. "Do you know who she is?"

He actually blushed. "She's had four #1 hits in the last year and a half. Her first album went platinum in less than a month. She's a sensation, and a damn good singer. Don't you watch 'America's Icon'?"

"Well, no one has held a gun to my head lately, so, no, I don't."

The back door opened and closed and Joseph walked into the front of the store, his head down. "Sorry I'm late," he said quietly. "Hello, Mr. McKenzie. Nice to see you."

Wyatt nodded.

"Zeke was wondering where you were last night," I said. "You were supposed to take your mom to the hospital."

"I needed some time to think ... about things, and somebody to talk to." He glanced at Rebecca, who suddenly seemed very interested in arranging some items on the shelf beside her.

I took his arm and led him into the office, closing the door behind us. He remained standing by the door while I leaned against the desk.

"Joseph, I know you heard your mother saying some things that weren't exactly kind last night, and I'm so sorry."

"'Not exactly kind'? Ms. Cooper, she might as well have cut my heart out." His lower lip was quivering, his voice about to break. "All my life, I've thought she left because of something she couldn't control or somebody that she was afraid of. But she left because she couldn't stand to be around me."

I stepped over to him and hugged him. His back stiffened. "You have to hear the whole story, Joseph. Everything has a context. Your mother is trying to turn her life in a different direction. She needs as much support as she can get from her family. You abandoned her last night."

"Well, now she knows how I've felt all my life."

CHAPTER 10

Closing the door behind me, I left Joseph in the office to give him a few minutes to collect himself. The top item on my agenda this morning was to examine the furniture Troy and Rebecca had bought—stolen was more like it—from Mrs. Boyd before Rebecca sold it out from under me. I feared that she would, even though I had explicitly told her not to.

"Wyatt, could I ask you for some help?" I said as Troy's father stood over the broken display case with the old money in it, sipping his coffee. I had to remind myself that he was seventy. When my father was that age, he looked even older. People who didn't know us mistook him for my grandfather, with his thin, wispy hair, his jowls, and his rotund waistline. Wyatt was trim and still had thick hair, even though it was white.

"Sure. What can I do for you?"

"You can help me look over this load of furniture from the Lemand house. Somebody thinks there's something about it that makes it worthwhile to break in here and sneak into the Boyds' garage. I grew up with this furniture in my grandparents' house, but I don't know much about it. You know a lot more than I do. Maybe you can see what I can't."

"All right. Let's have a look."

The furniture had been set up in the back of the building, what had been the stock room when this was a department store. The pieces were arranged, as I had asked, so there was room to walk around and between them, to examine them from all angles. Rebecca must have come in early enough to remove the price tags.

Neither of us said anything at first as we stood in front of the armoire that had crushed Troy. Though it was heavy and solid, like much Arts and Crafts furniture, it looked like it should have stood securely on its short legs.

"It must be difficult for you," Wyatt said, "seeing furniture from your grandparents' house stripped from its familiar surroundings."

I nodded, fighting back tears. "I used to hide in this armoire when my mother and I played 'hide-and-seek.' It's so solid—I would imagine I was in a cave. I can't understand how it could tip over." The armoire had only two drawers, side-by-side, on the bottom. It was designed for hanging clothes.

"The floor back here is uneven," Wyatt said.

"Yeah, I guess that's it." I couldn't bring myself to reach out and touch the piece.

"What did Troy pay for these?" Wyatt finally asked.

"You'd have to ask Rebecca. I wasn't involved in the deal." I couldn't bring myself to admit that my daughter and her father had pulled such a con on old Mrs. Boyd—and with the collusion of Troy's girlfriend.

He nodded and pursed his lips. "Well, the first thing I can tell you is that they're very high quality. They should sell quickly and at a good price."

"Rebecca already has an offer on a couple of the pieces from someone you put her in touch with."

"Oh, yes. Michael, over in Spartanburg. I told her to send him some pictures."

"She did. I'm not going to let anything go out of here, though, until I understand why somebody broke in and went through this stuff. I think it may have something to do with Troy's death."

"I can't say anything about that." Wyatt began to walk around the furniture. "I'll tell you what I can about what you've got here." He squinted and bent down behind the largest dresser. "The light never has been good back here, has it? I'm sure it's not that my eyes aren't as good as they used to be."

"Let me get the shop light," I said. I stepped over to the work bench and picked up the light, the sort of thing on a long cord that mechanics hang from the hood of a car when they're working on the engine, and handed it to Wyatt.

"That's much better," he said, clicking it on and running it over the back of the dresser. "Okay, here's what I was hoping to see—the maker's mark. Take a look."

I squatted next to him so I could see a 150 in a square.

"This is a piece by Christopher Lemand," Wyatt said. "I'm sure we'll find they're all his work."

"How do you know that?"

"In Roman numerals CL is 150. That's how he signed his pieces. He was a little quirky. His son was Christopher the second, so he signed himself 152."

"I'm assuming Christopher Lemand is the eponym of the Lemand house."

"Yes. He built it. He was a master craftsman." Wyatt stepped over to the next piece, a chest of drawers, while he talked. "He moved here from Philadelphia about 1880, just after the end of Reconstruction. He thought the South, because it wasn't so industrialized, would be a better place for the burgeoning Arts and Crafts Movement."

"That's mostly handmade furniture, isn't it?" I had absorbed enough about furniture from Troy to recognize the style, even though I don't particularly like it.

"Yes. It was a reaction against the ornate Victorian style."

"You mean places like my house."

"Well, yes. But Arts and Crafts was a philosophy of life as well—simplicity, naturalness, some of the same ideals that people espouse today about getting off the grid, back to nature. Lemand and his family made exquisite furniture, adapting to new styles, of course, until after World War II, but the Arts and Crafts stuff from the 1890s to the beginning of World War I is their best."

"And that's what this is?"

"Oh, definitely."

"What happened to them? Did they move away? Outsource jobs?"

"No. Their factory—really more on the order of a large workshop—was on the west end of town. It burned in 1950 and they never rebuilt."

"Do they have anything to do with Lemand Park then?" I'd heard the name all my life, but never really known much about them.

"That's where the factory was. The family donated the land to the city after the fire. Unfortunately, it wasn't a good location for a park and it's been neglected for some time."

Lemand Park has always been surrounded by small businesses

and warehouses. For years it has been a hang-out for junkies and drug dealers, its attractions consisting of a few dilapidated swing sets with rusty chains and a couple of rotting seesaws. It wasn't a place I had ever taken my children or would take my grandbabies.

"Are there still any Lemands in this area?" I asked. I couldn't recall hearing the name.

"Not with the family name. Christopher Lemand II took over just before World War I. The Arts and Crafts movement was passé by then."

"Art Deco was the next fad, right? In the 1920s and '30s?"

Wyatt smiled. "We'll make an antiques junkie out of you yet. By 1940 Art Deco was out and a grandson was running the business. He had two daughters, no sons. I've heard that he just didn't have the passion for woodworking—or the skill—that his grandfather and father had. The rumor was that he set the fire to collect the insurance. Forensics weren't as sophisticated in that day, so he might have."

"But he had a big building full of wood and stains and so on—"

"Sure, the place was probably a tinderbox. No sprinkling system. People smoked wherever and whenever in those days. It could well have been accidental."

I bent over to take a closer look at a nightstand, the one from my grandparents' guest bedroom, if memory served. Its legs tapered, growing more slender from the bottom to the top. The brass drawer pull matched the hardware on the dresser that must have come from the same room. "So this isn't something you would have bought at Ikea."

Wyatt chuckled. "No, my dear. Every piece was custom designed and handmade. The house was built about 1890, wasn't it?"

"1892." Those of us who live in the historic district know the pecking order. My house is five years older. "Boyds' place is Arts and Crafts style all the way through."

"That was when the movement was at its height. This furniture was built for that house and for the specific places where it sat in the house. Each piece is unique." He ran a hand over the chest of drawers, caressing the drawers as lovingly as he might touch a woman's body. "Arts and Crafts furniture makers disdained machines. That was a key part of the philosophy of the movement. 1892 would have been when Lemand senior was at his prime. It's a crime that these pieces have been removed from the house."

I explained Mrs. Boyd's financial problems.

"Well, she may have profited in the short term, but she'll get much less for the house now."

I wondered if Anna and Troy had planned to scoop up the stripped house at a bargain price and then replace the furniture. "How much are these pieces worth?"

"That nightstand that you're fondling so affectionately would probably go for $1200, give or take."

I gasped and drew my hand back.

"And the larger pieces, like the two armoires, would probably go for close to three thousand."

"Apiece?"

Wyatt nodded and pointed to the sideboard. "A few years ago I saw a sideboard similar to that one sell for $3500 at an auction. I stopped at $3000."

And Troy and Rebecca paid only a few hundred for each piece! I rubbed a hand over my face. Wyatt turned off the shop light and laid it back on the workbench.

"Is something bothering you, Maureen? I suspected Troy wasn't making any money in the store. I didn't think he could pay me back for that sideboard or make any money on it at that price. That's why I stopped bidding. How could he afford these Lemand pieces?"

I leaned against the workbench and folded my arms over my chest. "If you bought a painting for four dollars at a garage sale and later found out it was worth, say, $50,000, wouldn't you have an obligation—a moral obligation—to go back to the person you bought it from and, I don't know, share the money?"

Wyatt waggled a finger at me. "In this business, it's not only 'buyer beware.' It's also 'seller beware.' If you don't know what you've got, you shouldn't be selling it, especially to people who *do* know."

"But if the buyer has a better sense of what it's worth than the seller does, isn't he taking advantage of the seller?"

"That's called good business. Buy low, sell high. It's the oldest axiom in the market-place." Wyatt turned toward the front of the store. "Now, I'm going to do some research on Lemand's furniture and see just how much my friend Michael is going to have to part with."

"Rebecca said he'd offered $1,400 for one of the dressers."

Wyatt shook his head. "He's not *that* good a friend."

"But if the pieces are so valuable," I called after him, "why has somebody been going through them, pulling out drawers?"

Wyatt stopped by the armoire that had fallen on Troy. "That I can't tell you. I do know that Lemand senior is known for sometimes putting little secret pockets in some of his furniture. Unless you know how to find them and open them, they're undetectable." He ran his hand over the side of the dresser. "I could be touching one right now."

"Then how do people know they're there?"

"A couple of them have been found when damaged pieces were being repaired."

"Didn't he leave drawings?"

"All of his papers seem to have perished in the fire. That's all I know."

Wyatt vanished through the swinging doors that separate the loading dock from the front of the store and I was left alone with my thoughts and the furniture. I had so many memories of this furniture in my grandparents' house, as well as the beams, the woodwork, the built-ins. Even though I didn't understand its significance when I was a child, I had the sense that it was special. When I brought Troy to meet my grandparents, he had been overawed, his mouth practically hanging open. And now Lemand's work had been ripped out and would be sold, piece by piece, scattered to the four winds, all to make some money for my family. Quite a bit of money, it looked like. I felt like we were tearing the "Ode to Joy" out of Beethoven's Ninth Symphony to make a car commercial.

I made sure the rear door was locked and returned to the front of the store. While Wyatt and I were talking I had heard the bell over the front door jingle several times. Rebecca and Joseph were talking with customers. I stepped into the office, picked up my bag and climbed the stairs to a mezzanine area on the second floor. When Wyatt had remodeled the store, he converted the original office into an employee lounge, with a refrigerator and small stove. Troy had added a microwave. Through the large window that Wyatt had installed, one could keep watch on the store while taking a break.

As I crossed the mezzanine I stopped and looked out over the first floor. The thought occurred to me that a performer might use this as a stage. With its railing it could be a way to protect Artemisia from an overly enthusiastic crowd and still let them get a lot closer to her than they ever would at a concert. Robert and Derrick and Joseph could block the stairs and the passenger elevator. We could shut down the freight elevator.

I wondered what our liability might be if something happened to her or to some fan. For that matter, what if a customer tripped over the old, uneven floors in this place? There were so many reasons I did not want to be involved in running this store.

But right now I wanted to know more about Christopher Lemand and his family. Somebody might have known about the secret compartments in the furniture. Maybe it was a family legend. Maybe some of his papers hadn't been destroyed in the fire. Someone who knew the secret couldn't barge into Mrs. Boyd's house and start poking around in the furniture, but once it was removed, they could get access to it. And they would have to check it out before it was sold and scattered all over the country.

I sat down at the table in the employee lounge, looking out over the store toward the front door, and got out my laptop. A Google search quickly verified everything Wyatt had told me and provided a couple of pictures of the Lemand men, with their mustaches and high starched collars, and their factory. There was no mention of the fire being suspicious. Christopher the third had indeed had two daughters, Hannah and Grace. That struck me as curious, since "hannah" in Hebrew means "grace." What I couldn't discover immediately was what happened to those two daughters. If anyone was likely to know about Christopher senior's quirks, it would be a family member, and that meant those daughters or their children.

Because of the work I do, I subscribe to an online service that lets me search for people's addresses, phone numbers, and criminal records. I can write off the cost as a business expense, and it has let me contact people who, years earlier, knew someone I was writing about. It is much cheaper than hiring a private detective.

With an unusual surname like Lemand, it wasn't hard to find marriage records for the two women and, sadly, their obituaries. The older daughter had died in 1995, leaving no children. The younger daughter, Grace, had died only a year ago. She had married a man named Proctor and had apparently spent her life in Greenwood, only forty miles from here. She was survived by a son, two daughters and several grandchildren. The son was named Christopher Lemand Proctor. No doubt I had the right people.

"Ms. Cooper." I looked up to find Joseph standing at the door of the lounge, carrying his own laptop. "I hope I'm not disturbing you."

"No, that's all right. What can I do for you?"

"I was wondering if you'd like to look at what I've got so far for a web site for the store."

"Definitely." I pulled out the chair next to mine and Joseph sat down. For the next half hour we looked at options for the site. He uploaded a few pictures he had taken around the store.

"If you like," he said, "we could sign up with this web host, buy a domain name, and have the site up and running this weekend. We can put a statement on here that we'll be adding items every day and encourage people to check in regularly."

My stomach knots up when people start pushing me to do things in a hurry. When I was taking Latin in high school I ran across an axiom dear to the emperor Augustus: "Make haste slowly." That sentiment appealed to me, and not just because I like oxymorons.

"I'd like more time to think about it, Joseph. We're not set up to ship anything bigger than a shoe box right now. I don't want people ordering pieces of furniture and then getting frustrated with us because we can't deliver. We need to figure out how to factor in shipping costs, insurance, and so on."

"I've got some preliminary figures." Joseph clicked on another page.

I didn't even look. "Joseph, there's just too much going on right now. You've done a really fine job on this, but I can't make the commitment with everything else I'm dealing with this weekend. You and Rebecca and I will sit down Monday and talk about it. That's all I can promise."

"Sure, I understand. I didn't mean to pressure you."

I put a hand on his arm. "I know Rebecca's pushing you to do this, but we're going to have to do it at my pace. By all means, keep working on it over the weekend. Right now, though, I want us to rearrange some things on the first floor, to improve traffic flow."

Joseph closed his laptop, then stood up as though surprised by

something. I followed his gaze to the front door of the store and saw
his grandmother bustling in.

Joseph's grandmother, Maribelle Hughes, has always been Mrs.—
pronounced Miz—Hughes, although I'd never known or heard of a
Mr. Hughes. Some Southern women are given that honorific, like
housekeepers on a PBS drama. We Southerners began using "Miz"
long before the women's movement created "Ms." More commonly,
though, she was Miz Maribelle. She was a heavyset woman of about
sixty, but she still showed traces of what must have been real beauty
and a dignified carriage. At that moment, though, her face was contorted in anger. She spotted Joseph and motioned for him to come
downstairs. She started across the store to meet him.

"Oh, crap," Joseph muttered.

"You'd better see what she wants," I said. "Take her into the office.
I'd rather not have a scene and frighten away customers."

"Yes, ma'am."

Joseph trotted down the stairs and met his grandmother by the
office door. By the time I got down the stairs they were inside. I didn't
have to put my ear to the door to eavesdrop, since it was partial-
ly open. Even if the door had been closed all the way, I could have
heard Miz Maribelle.

"Where were you last night?"

Joseph was standing behind the door and his voice was indistinct,
but he must have said that he had stayed with a friend.

"A friend? What friend?"

Joseph spoke louder as he defended himself. "Mama, I'm twenty-one years old. I don't have to tell you where I am every minute or
who I'm with."

"Let's see," Miz Maribelle said, her voice dripping with sarcasm.
"Where have I heard that before? Oh, yeah, from your mother. And
you see where she ended up."

"Mama, I'm not like her. You don't have to worry about me."

Miz Maribelle's voice broke. "My precious baby boy, you've already been in jail. How can I *not* worry about you?"

"That's all in the past, Mama. I haven't been in any trouble like
that in a long time."

"Joseph, like you said, you're barely twenty-one years old. You haven't *had* a long time in your life yet."

Rebecca, who was behind the counter at the front of the store, motioned for me to come up there, so I had to miss the rest of this moving encounter.

"You really shouldn't be eavesdropping," she said as I stopped beside her.

"The door was open. Miz Maribelle's voice carries."

"And you're just accustomed to snooping in people's lives."

"At least I don't cheat them, my dear. Wyatt says that furniture from my grandparents' house is worth many times what you paid for it, but I suspect you knew that."

"Arts and Crafts pieces can bring a good price." Rebecca shrugged. "Everybody knows that. It's business, and I'm not going to argue with you about it anymore. What's done is done."

"Well, it's not going to be done again, not as long as I have any connection with this store."

I smiled as the bell jingled and an older couple—which means anybody older than me—came into the store. Right away I could sense that they would walk around looking at things and saying, "Oh, my mother had one of those. Look at what it's worth." Then they would use the restroom, instead of the port-a-potties provided for people attending FoodFest. They stopped first at a rack containing Depression glass.

"Are you the friend that Joseph stayed with last night?" I asked Rebecca.

She didn't hesitate. "Yes. We talked until two this morning. He was really upset about what he heard his mother say."

The door to the office opened and Miz Maribelle and a chastised Joseph emerged. He went back up to the lounge while his grandmother approached us.

"I'm sorry for the intrusion, Ms. Cooper," she said. "I was very worried about my boy."

"It's quite all right," I said. "I think you can trust him, though."

"Lord, I hope so." She sighed. "Thank you so much for what you've done for Dolores."

"How is she doing?"

"The pain pills have her sleeping a lot. She's at Zeke's house. I promise you she won't bother you anymore."

"Oh, she hasn't bothered me. I'll try to get by to see her today. In an odd way, I've enjoyed—if that's the right word—getting acquainted with her. I never really knew her in high school. You know, I even had the crazy idea that she would be an interesting person to write about. She's had some ups and downs in her life. Readers could learn something from those kinds of experiences, even if she's not a celebrity."

Miz Maribelle's face clouded. "Ms. Cooper, you don't want to go looking under that rock. You might see some things you'd never be able to unsee."

CHAPTER 11

The morning passed pleasantly enough. Although FoodFest officially opened at noon, we had traffic in and out of the store for a couple of hours before that. Our restrooms were a big attraction. The city had set up port-a-potties on a couple of the streets leading off the square, but people are always looking for alternatives to those things. Many of the businesses around the square were offices, like Anna Maxwell's accounting/insurance business, with no public restrooms. Pam's coffee shop had a RESTROOMS FOR CUSTOMERS ONLY sign on the door. That meant you had to cough up three or four bucks for some tarted-up cup of coffee just to use the facility.

I've always been sympathetic to folks who were looking for a place to stop—or maybe I should say, to go. My father, in his later years, had made locating a bathroom his first objective on any trip we took. My only restriction now was **NO MERCHANDISE ALLOWED IN RESTROOMS.**

The food vendors were set up on the courthouse lawn, in the street that runs around the square, and down the four side streets, all of which had been blocked off. A Greek restaurant from Simpsonville had a booth right in front of Palmetto Antiques. Across the street, on the courthouse lawn, sat a booth from a Thai restaurant on the outskirts of Lawrenceville. I could also see, to our left in the middle of the street, a truck selling elephant ears and other confections. Those folks obviously made a living traveling from one festival or county fair to another.

A "command center" had been set up on the landing of the courthouse steps. Music blared from speakers there, interrupted by occasional announcements. Several police officers strolled by. When Scott Kelly came around the corner, he paused at our door. I motioned for him to come in, not sure whether he would or not.

"Good morning," he said as he opened the door. He was wearing khakis and a dark green polo shirt—kelly green, I guess you'd call it—that made me aware of his Irish eyes. "It's good to see you folks up and running again."

"Thanks. Troy's dad is helping us. Listen, I'm curious about something. Maybe you can help me out."

"Be glad to, if I can." He leaned against the door frame, as if to say that was as far in as he would go.

"Would the police department have any information on file about the fire that destroyed the Lemand furniture factory in 1950?"

"I imagine so. What's your interest in that?"

"The furniture we bought from Mrs. Boyd was made by Christopher Lemand. I'd just like to know more about it."

"Was there anything suspicious about the fire?"

"Not that I know of. I was wondering, too, if there would be any record of anything that survived the fire."

"I'll take a look, but today and tomorrow crowd control is the top priority. Last year we had over 10,000 people at this thing in the rain. With the great weather, I'm sure we'll top that." He pushed away from the door frame. "I'd better get back out there."

I resolved to call him tonight to let him know that Artemisia would be here tomorrow, so he could call in extra officers, or whatever he had to do. It wouldn't be fair to sucker-punch him and maybe create a dangerous situation for everybody. And it would put more stress on our relationship—whatever it was—after the T-shirt incident.

Joseph and I spent an hour rearranging some of the tchotkes near the front of the store. At least that's what I would call things like the little ceramic burro pulling a cart with pink wheels or the myriad of glass and ceramic vases that Troy seemed to have been enamored of. Judging from the prices he put on them, I didn't think he really wanted to let go of them.

"Get that sheet of red stickers from the office, please," I asked Joseph as an inspiration hit. "And bring me a marker, some tape, and a few pieces of paper." If Wyatt was willing to start selling stuff, I wanted to prime the pump.

It took Joseph only a moment to find the items. "Here you go."

"Thanks." I took the markers, paper, and tape. "Now, put those stickers on three or four items on each shelf."

"Which ones?"

"Any ones you want." On the paper I wrote "**20% OFF ITEMS WITH RED STICKERS**" and taped the signs at strategic spots around the store.

Rebecca emerged from the restroom as I was putting up the last sign on the front door. "Mother, what are you doing?"

"We're having a sale."

"But we haven't talked about that." She looked around like a teacher noticing a measles outbreak in her classroom. "How are you determining which items to mark down?"

"It doesn't matter. They're all over-priced." At the moment there were no customers in the store, so I could speak truth to power, as they say.

During the rest of the morning we did sell some small red-tagged items, just things that people could carry while they walked around the square. I didn't expect to sell any furniture over the weekend, but it was gratifying to see merchandise actually going out the door, and that stupid burro was one of the first to go.

About 12:30 the front door swung open and, from my post at the register, I was surprised to see Dolores come in, limping noticeably and pulling a child's wagon with a cardboard box in it. She wore a blue plaid shirt and a pair of white shorts. I figured she couldn't get jeans on over the boot on her ankle, or maybe she just wanted to show everybody how good she looked in a pair of white shorts, and she's older than I am. If I looked half that good in anything, I'd wear it all the time. The aroma of Zeke's barbecue wafted around her like the little birds fluttering around Snow White in the Disney movie. Or maybe it was Cinderella.

"Lunch time!" she called out.

"Here, let me help you with that," I said, taking the handle of the wagon and pulling it toward the back of the store. "Sit down. We've got enough chairs."

"Thank you," Dolores said. She groaned as she took the weight off her foot. "I've been trying to help Zeke over at his booth, but I think I'm just in the way. He's really busy."

"You shouldn't be on that foot. Remember what the doctor said:

RICE—Rest, Ice, Compression, and Elevation." I pushed a footstool toward her. "Here, rest, elevate."

Dolores put her foot up on the stool. "Thank you, Ms. Cooper—"

"My name is Maureen." I turned and called upstairs. "Hey, Joseph!"

Joseph looked over the second-floor railing. I know he saw his mother, but he said nothing to her.

"Your uncle needs some help. Why don't you run over there for a while?"

"Yes, ma'am. I'll be back after the rush." I heard the freight elevator and then the rear door opening and closing. Joseph was going to circle around the block rather than walk through the store and past his mother.

"He'd go around the world to avoid seeing me," Dolores said with a heavy sigh. "I can't say I blame him."

I put a hand on her shoulder. "Look, I know you're tired. Why don't we take some lunch up to the employee lounge? There's a sofa in there. You can stretch out, put your foot up."

"I don't know—"

She stopped in mid-sentence when Wyatt came out of the office. He flinched when he saw her.

"Well, hello, Dolores. It's been ... quite a while."

"Yes, sir, it has been."

Her voice and Wyatt's face gave me the impression it hadn't been long enough, for either of them. Considering that Dolores had worked in the store for a couple of years when Wyatt was running it, I found the dynamic strange.

"How are you?" Wyatt asked.

"A little gimpy right now, but I'm managing."

"What happened?" He pointed to the boot.

"I tripped over a tree root."

"I'm sorry to hear that. I hope it heals quickly. It seems to be going around." He scratched Pepper's head as the dog emerged from the office, his nose working overtime.

"It's getting better, sir. Are you doing all right?"

"Not too bad. I've been roped out in the pasture and put into harness again."

The awkwardness between them was making me nervous. "We're

going upstairs," I finally said. "You and Rebecca will have to look after things down here. Grab some lunch. Zeke sent some of everything on the menu, I think."

"There's a bag in there with your name on it," Dolores said.

I found the bag with my sandwich and slaw. "There's no bill."

"Zeke said I wasn't to let you pay anything."

"Well, I'll talk to him later about that."

"There's also this for Pepper." Dolores found a bucket of scraps. "Zeke said I was to give it to him personally and apologize." She set the food next to Pepper's water dish in the office. "I am sorry, buddy. As you can see, I got my payback pretty quick. Karma's a bitch. But maybe that's not an insult when you're talking to a dog."

Wyatt raised his eyebrows. I said, "Later."

Dolores and I took the elevator up to the second floor and set our lunches on the table in the lounge. I got some bottled water and some soft drinks from the fridge. Dolores popped open a Coke.

"So, Maureen, does anybody call you Mo?" she asked as she leaned back in her chair and put her foot up in another.

I winced. "Not more than once."

"Ooh, girl, that's the kind of answer you'd have to give to survive in jail."

"Sorry, I didn't mean to be rude. I just prefer Maureen."

"I hear you. Troy used to call me Dee, but I didn't much care for it. It's not a name. It's just an initial." She took a sip of her drink. "Might actually be better, though. I looked up my name once. It means 'sorrows.' My mama was really a prophet."

"Mine's almost as bad," I said. "It means 'dark' or 'bitter.'"

"That is a load to carry." Dolores reached into the pocket of her shorts. "Before I forget, let me give you this." She handed me a key. "That's the key to the store that I had when I worked here. I found it in my stuff at Mama's house last night. Mr. McKenzie gave them out to anybody who was working for him, even a few hours a week. He used to say that, since his father didn't change the locks when he bought the place, there were probably members of the family of the original owners who still had keys."

I slipped the key into my pocket. "Well, that's going to change. A locksmith is coming next week. We're going to get deadbolts and alarms—the whole nine yards." And I knew my decision to make that investment meant I wasn't going to sell the place. "Let me get us some more napkins."

While we ate we talked mostly about Joseph. As Dolores poured out her pain and frustration over her inability to love him as a mother should—as she wanted to—I found myself feeling compassion for her. Logically I had no reason to feel any connection with her. We were from totally different worlds, even though we grew up in the same town. She had done things I could never imagine doing and had gone to jail for some of them. She had suffered the trauma of being raped, something that had changed the whole course of her life. She had broken into my property and injured my dog. And yet I cared about what happened to her and wanted to help her.

I could blame my mother for that. She had held what I always thought was an impossibly romantic view of human relationships, namely, that sometimes a person will cross your path and you know at once that it's important for you to establish a connection with that person, whether it be as friend or lover. If you don't, you regret it for the rest of your life.

She never said it in so many words, but I suspect there was someone other than my father that she thought she should have been with. Her idea had sunk more deeply into my subconscious than I realized. I thought I had been lucky to find Troy, and maybe that was why I couldn't completely let go of him, but ... .

Dolores finally broke down and started to cry. Grabbing a box of tissues off the counter, I moved around the table and put my arm around her. She leaned into me and sobbed for a few minutes. "I gotta stop crying every time I'm around you." When the wave of tears had subsided, she sat up and dabbed at her eyes. "Why are you being so damn nice to me?"

"Do I have to have a reason?" I hoped I didn't, because the only reason I had sounded silly when I thought about how to put it in words: "I think we were meant to be friends."

"People always have reasons, Maureen."

"What's your reason for opening up to me like you just did?"

She shrugged. "I felt like I could talk to you. I've never had anybody to talk to, unless they wanted something from me. But I don't think you want anything."

"I don't."

"I've told you things I've never told anybody. Being back here has brought it all up again." She stood up suddenly and winced when she put her weight on her foot. "I've got to get out of here."

I patted her arm. "Hey, it's okay. Sit here as long as you like. Keep that foot elevated."

"No, you don't understand. I really need to get out of here."

Then it hit me. "Oh, God, Dolores, was this where it happened? Were you raped right here in the store?"

"Yeah," she said softly. "Not in this room, but in the store."

"Did Wyatt—"

"No, it wasn't Wyatt, and it wasn't Troy."

I couldn't help but feel relief along with sorrow and pity. "Did they know about it?"

"Maureen, I really don't want to talk about it anymore. I just want to get out of here."

When we got back downstairs Rebecca was with a customer and I didn't see Wyatt. We retrieved the wagon from the office and Dolores petted Pepper again. There was enough food left in the box that I would have to put it in the fridge. Robert and Derrick could have it for supper.

"Tell Zeke I'm not going to let him keep feeding us for free, but I do appreciate it and hope to return the favor, maybe as soon as tomorrow."

Dolores' brow furrowed. "Is something happening tomorrow?"

I put a finger to my lips. "Just tell Zeke to expect a crowd."

I found Wyatt in the back of the store, measuring and photographing the Lemand furniture. "Wyatt, could I talk with you in the office?"

"Sure. Just let me—"

"*Now*, please." In the twenty-six years I've known my father-in-law I had never spoken to him in that tone. I turned and walked to the office, not looking back to see if he was following me. Before I entered the office I saw Dolores standing just outside the front door, talking to Joseph. He took the handle of the wagon and they walked off toward Zeke's booth together, certainly not arm-in-arm but at least side-by-side.

Wyatt's uncertainty showed as he came into the office. He couldn't decide whether to sit down or to remain standing, as I was. "What ... what's up?"

"Close the door." I leaned against the desk.

"Am I going to be fired?" He tried to make it a joke, but I would have none of it.

"What do you know about Dolores Hughes being raped in this store?"

He responded so quickly that I suspected he had rehearsed his answer many times. "I know that neither Troy nor I had anything to do with it and that the statute of limitations expired a long time ago."

"But you knew it happened."

"Yes."

"What did you do about it?"

"Troy beat the hell out the guy."

"So you know who did it?" My voice rose in anger.

Wyatt nodded.

"Well, who was it?"

"Maureen, what's the point—"

"The woman was raped, Wyatt. That's the point. Who did it?"

Wyatt folded his arms and looked at the floor before looking back up at me. "Guy's name was Brian Dunmoore. He played football and baseball with Troy. Big guy, a lineman and a catcher."

I remembered Brian from high school. "Big" was putting it mildly. I remembered that he had torn up his knee during his freshman year in college and that he had to quit school because of that. He was a policeman here for a few years, then moved away. "How did it happen, Wyatt?"

"Troy and Dolores were working in the store, just the two of them, late one afternoon. Troy got a phone call and said he had to go see somebody. It wouldn't take him long. He would get them something to eat while he was out. He'd only been gone a few minutes, Dolores said, when Brian came in. Dolores knew him, and she knew he'd been accused of roughing up a couple of girls, but no charges were ever brought. He was a cop, so go figure. Brian said he was looking for Troy. She told him Troy wasn't there, and that's when he attacked her. Troy found her when he got back. She had a black eye and her blouse was ripped. She told us she'd been raped."

"Did he call the police?"

"Dolores told him not to."

I stood away from the desk. "What? Why not?"

"Who would ever believe her? A black girl accusing a white guy? A white cop? In this town, twenty years ago?"

"What did Troy do?"

"He called me. We took Dolores home, then Troy went and found Brian. Brian told him Dolores had come on to him. He knew Brian was lying, because one of the other football players had called Troy and asked him to meet him on the edge of town. He said his car had broken down."

"So Brian knew Dolores would be alone if he could get Troy out of the store. It was all a set-up."

"Yes."

"What did Troy do?"

"He pounded the guy." Wyatt's voice rose with pride. "Beat the absolute shit out of him."

I hadn't heard Dunmoore's name in years. "What became of Brian?"

"He left town a few days after that. I heard he was on the police force in Greenwood. Troy said he told him he'd kill him if he ever did come back here."

"And nobody ever reported this?"

Wyatt hung his head. "Sad to say, if every incident like this got reported, the police wouldn't have time for anything else. And what would be the point? He said, she said. No witnesses."

I shook my head in disbelief. "Wyatt, do you have any idea how traumatic this is for a woman? And then for her to get pregnant as a result of it? Can you even imagine what that's like?"

"I realize you're asking rhetorical questions, but I'll give you a nonrhetorical answer. I imagine it's about as traumatic as it is for a young man to go fight in some hell-hole of a country where the people won't fight for themselves and all that matters to them are the 'potato-potahto' differences in their religion." He took a breath and put his hand on the doorknob. "You know what that did to Troy. I really am sorry about Dolores—always have been—but bad things happen to people, Maureen. Every ... damn ... day."

❖❖❖

CHAPTER 12

When I'm working on a book, I sometimes find myself with such a mass of information that I have to make lists or charts—get myself organized in some visual way—or I completely lose track of what I'm doing. When Wyatt left the office I got out my laptop and opened a new document, one that I protected with a password. Starting with the date of my marriage, I listed Robert's birth (seven months later; yes, Mother, seven months, and he wasn't a preemie, like I tried to make you believe), then Rebecca's birth three years after that. I knew when Joseph was born, so I knew when Dolores was raped. I was about six months pregnant at that time. Rebecca was born three months later and Joseph six months after that.

During our conversation Dolores did say that she and Troy were not intimate after Troy and I got married. I didn't ask precisely when they stopped. If their last time was the night before the wedding, I didn't want to know. I never believed I was Troy's first, and I didn't want to know where I stood numerically or chronologically, or how I rated, in terms of performance, against the competition. After reading a magazine article on the subject, I did go to Greenville and have a test for STDs when Troy was doing his first tour in Afghanistan and another one when I found out about his relationship with Anna, so I had the assurance that he hadn't given me anything nasty.

But, even if they weren't physically intimate, Troy obviously still cared a lot about Dolores, even after we'd been married for several years. He cared so much that he "pounded" a guy who was a lot bigger and stronger than he was.

I remembered the night Troy came home from that pounding. He had a bloody nose and a cut over one eye, to go with a broken finger and some other bruises. He made that lame old joke about "you should've seen the other guy." But, from what Wyatt had said, maybe it wasn't a joke. What Troy told me was that he'd stopped for a drink at a bar on his way home from the store—which he often did, no matter how many times I asked him not to—and had tried to break up a fight. I wasn't to say anything about it to my grandfather because some of Troy's friends who were there couldn't afford to have the police asking them questions.

When I'd pressed him, Troy got testy. "Just let it go," he snapped. Wanting to be a dutiful young wife—at one time that had been my goal in life—I bandaged him up and didn't say any more about it.

I closed the document and set my laptop on the desk. So now I knew one more piece of the truth about my late ex-husband. I wondered how much more I would have to learn and if I would ever know it all. Did I even want to know it all?

One thing I did want to know was what happened to Brian Dunmoore. Logging onto the site I use to check on people, I found six men by that name but only one whose age would make him the guy I was looking for. He had an address in Greenwood and was a lieutenant in their police department.

His mug shot showed a man who had not aged gracefully, which is often the fate of big, burly football players. His receding hairline emphasized his puffy face. He had a scar on his left cheek. Had Troy given it to him that night? I hoped he had. I bookmarked the page.

Before I shut down my laptop, I sent the information about Dunmoore to Scott Kelly and asked him a few questions in the email. Could we know where Dunmoore had been the last couple of weeks? What if he had come back to Lawrenceville? Could he have gotten into an argument with Troy—maybe over Dolores, who had just gotten out of prison? He was certainly strong enough to push the armoire over on Troy.

I needed some physical activity. Doing more cleaning to get ready for Artemisia and her mother would suffice. I did need to make a trip to the grocery store. Reaching into my pocket for my car keys, I found Dolores' key to the store. It would be useless once I had deadbolts installed, but it was a symbol that I wanted to be rid of. I went to the work area in the back of store. Clamping Dolores' key in a vise on the work bench, I gripped it with a pair of pliers and bent it back and forth until it snapped in half—pointless, but it gave me some satisfaction.

As I tossed the pieces into the trash, I wondered how many other people did have keys to this place. If the locks were the originals from the 1920s, any number of former employees and their families could have been able to break in and mess with the Lemand furniture—if you're "breaking in" when you use a key. But I rejected that theory. The furniture came from the Lemand house. Someone's interest in it had to do with the furniture itself or the place or people it came from. I was sure of that. The fact that it was in our store was coincidental.

For the rest of the day business was brisk. Wyatt suggested locking the restrooms and making people ask for the key. That made most people who used our facilities instead of the port-a-potties feel guilty enough to buy at least a little something. The "sale" items proved so popular that I slapped on a few more red stickers. Starting at two o'clock, musical acts began performing on the landing halfway up the steps of the courthouse, blissfully unaware of the competition they would face tomorrow.

I convinced myself—and it wasn't hard to do—that my house was clean enough. I spent most of the early afternoon looking over the Lemand furniture, trying to find any sort of hidden pockets or mechanisms that would open some secret panel. It was probably a fool's errand, I kept telling myself. Just because Lemand was known to have put such things in a few pieces of furniture, there was no guarantee there were any in what he had made for his own house. But the job kept me away from the music and the people. Aristotle once said, "Whoever finds delight in solitude is either a wild beast or a god." He was wrong about a lot of other things, too.

Then, about four o'clock, my phone rang. "Hi, Ms. Cooper," Artemisia bubbled. "We're ten miles away. Should we come to the store or to your house?"

"Hi, hon. You can't get to the store right now. The streets are blocked off. I'll meet you at the house. Your GPS may have to recalculate for the last few blocks to get you around everything. We've got a huge crowd here." Scott's prediction of record attendance seemed sure to come true. "You can drive around to the back of my house for some privacy."

I could have left my car and walked home, but I had Pepper to worry about. I loaded him into the car and, with the help of one of the police officers, eased my way through the crowd on the street behind the store. I had to go several blocks east before I could turn south, then back west to South Arbor Street and my house.

Fifteen minutes later a car pulled into the driveway and two women emerged. The driver, I could assume, was Artemisia's mother, a tall, serious-looking brunette wearing navy slacks and a knit red and white top. But the other figure surprised me. Above her jeans with holes in the knees and a black T-shirt with some Goth design on it, Artemisia wore a black wig and sunglasses. I was amazed at how much the simple disguise changed her appearance from the sweet little blond I had seen online.

The older woman came around the car and extended her hand. "Ms. Cooper, I'm Fran Johnson. This is my daughter, Artemisia." Her handshake was as indifferent as her voice.

"Welcome," I said. "It's a pleasure to have you here."

"You're very gracious," Mrs. Johnson said, "to go along with Artie's little whim."

Artemisia had taken off her wig and sunglasses so I couldn't miss her eye-roll, but I wasn't sure if it was provoked by the nickname or the use of "whim."

"It was a very generous offer," I said. "We're looking forward to tomorrow."

By now Pepper had made his way laboriously down the back steps. Artemisia knelt in front of him and scratched his head and under his chin, looking for all the world like a typical pretty American teenager. I would have guessed she was closer to fourteen than sixteen. I hate clichés, but for this short, slender blond "cute as a button" popped into my head.

"Oh, sweetie," she cooed to the injured setter, "what happened to you?" Pepper closed his eyes, in the kind of blissful state I had yet to inspire in him.

"That's Pepper," I said. "He was my late husband's companion dog. He was injured by someone who broke into Troy's apartment." I wanted to forestall any further discussion of the incident. "Now, let's get you ladies inside and settled."

Without a smile and with no detectable enthusiasm, Mrs. Johnson popped the trunk and we were in the process of unloading four suitcases when another car pulled into the driveway.

I noticed the furrow that formed on Mrs. Johnson's brow. "That's just my son, Robert, and his partner, Derrick," I assured her. "They're coming up for FoodFest. In the interest of full disclosure, they are big fans of Artemisia, especially Derrick."

Robert and Derrick smiled as they got out of the car. Robert takes after me, shorter and more solid. Derrick is tall, blond, and lanky and has a penchant for taking pictures with his phone. He did a good job, though, of containing his enthusiasm as we made introductions. I could see Artemisia's mother sizing the guys up. I guess she has to be even more watchful than most parents about the people her daughter comes into contact with. She was polite and Derrick seemed to have his ecstasy in check, aside from a slight fluttering of his eyelids when his hand touched Artemisia's.

We had deposited the Johnsons' luggage in their rooms and were looking around the house when Rebecca came in the back door. In response to my introduction Mrs. Johnson said, "Oh my, the whole family's here. Or are there more?" I hoped Wyatt didn't decide to drop over.

"We haven't told anyone outside the family, I promise you. Right, guys?"

Derrick nodded vigorously. "I almost had to bite my tongue off, but I haven't said a word."

By the time we finished the house tour I said, "With FoodFest going on, there are all sorts of options for supper. Our treat, of course."

"No options for me," Artemisia said. "It's gotta be barbecue. I even skipped lunch today so I'd have plenty of room." She patted her flat stomach.

"This FoodFest is taking place right outside your store, isn't it?" Mrs. Johnson said.

"Yes, on the town square and some of the side streets."

"I'd like to see where Artie is going to be singing tomorrow. Could we do that when we get supper?"

"Of course. We'll need to walk over there, since everything's blocked off. It only takes about five minutes, though."

"Good," Mrs. Johnson said. "We'll get to see some more of your lovely little town."

She smiled when she said it, but I could read the subtext: You mean I have to walk through Hicksville?

"I don't know how you folks handle being out in public," I said, "but, Artemisia, if you don't mind putting on your disguise again, it'll be easier to get the barbecue tonight than it will be tomorrow, once people realize you're here."

"No problem," Artemisia said. "Mr. Siegler promised me that Zeke's ribs are the best I'll ever have." She opened the car door and retrieved her wig and sunglasses. As she put them on, she happened to be standing close to Derrick.

"May I, my lady?" he asked, tucking her shoulder-length hair up under the wig.

"Why, thank you, kind sir," Artemisia said. An image of Lolita flashed into my head.

As we started up the driveway Rebecca said, "I had barbecue for lunch, so I think I'll stay here. Mom, could you pick me up something from the Thai booth in front of the store? Something with seafood?"

"Of course."

"I think I'll stay here, too," Robert said. "I'd like to talk with Rebecca about a couple of things. Derrick, you know what I like."

"Oh, I certainly do," Derrick said, "but I'll get you some barbecued chicken." Robert's face turned red. Artemisia giggled, and her mother and I cringed.

On the walk over I learned a bit more about Artemisia's childhood, growing up in a suburb of Tulsa, and how much she idolized her father. Derrick knew it all and asked her several questions— about her older brother, about an automobile accident the family had been in when she was four—that showed just how much he did know. I could see he was making her mother uncomfortable, so I pointed out a couple of the more spectacular houses along our route. Mrs. Johnson evinced a keen interest and Derrick fell quiet.

We arrived in the square at the height of the supper hour. For a June evening in South Carolina, it wasn't particularly warm, but the humidity—increased by the presence of thousands of people—was reaching uncomfortable levels. The crowds were shoulder-to-shoulder.

As an introvert who spends most of her time alone, I intensely dislike such mob scenes. I've never had a panic attack, but if I ever did have one, it would be in a situation like this. I tried to look up, focusing on something over the crowd. A group of musicians with a young female singer were just about ready to cut loose on the landing on the courthouse steps. As we edged our way through the throng, the girl began a nasal rendition of a song that seemed somehow familiar.

"Hey," Artemisia said, "they're doing 'Misty Rainbow.'"

"Well, *trying* to do it," Derrick sneered.

I realized I had heard the song when I was getting acquainted with Artemisia through clips on YouTube. It was her first big hit after she won on 'America's Icon.' She had not only recorded the song; she had written it.

Mrs. Johnson took hold of her daughter's elbow. "Artie, don't you get any ideas," she said softly. "You'll have your chance to show them how it ought to be done tomorrow."

"Maybe we should collect your royalty," Derrick said.

"Wouldn't that be a hoot?" Artemisia said with a giggle, slipping her arm through Derrick's. "Just stomp up there and say, 'Pay me.'" She held her hand out, palm up.

We were almost at Zeke's booth when I realized Scott Kelly was coming toward us, with a soft drink and a sandwich in his hands, trying not to get jostled by the crowd. When he saw me, he stepped to the edge of the crowd, up against a building "Hey, Maureen. Can't resist, eh?"

We moved over to stand close to Scott. I was relieved to get out of press of people. "Scott, hi. We're just getting supper for some guests." I hadn't foreseen this possibility. "These are ... some friends of my agent."

Artemisia's mother nodded to Scott. "Hi, I'm Fran Johnson and this is my daughter ... Janis." I remembered that was her first name.

"Yeah," I said. "They were coming this way, so we invited them to stop by and sample FoodFest. Fran, Janis, this is Detective Scott Kelly."

"Welcome to Lawrenceville," Scott said. "Things are a little hectic right now, but I hope you enjoy your visit." His phone rang. "I've got to take this. Nice to meet you."

As Scott put his drink on a window ledge and reached for his phone, I said, "Could I call you later tonight?"

"Yeah, sure. Any time."

When our group approached Zeke's booth, his face, already glistening with sweat, brightened with a big smile. While we waited in line, I motioned for him to come over to the corner of the booth.

"Listen, Zeke," I said, keeping my voice down as much as I could, "I deeply appreciate your offer not to charge me for meals, but not right now, please. I've got company and you don't need for all these people to see you giving away food. Just let me pay, and we'll talk about the other business later."

Zeke nodded and surveyed the crowd. "Yeah, it might be better this time. But I'm not going to forget what you did for Dolores."

"How is she?"

"She's all right. She's been on that foot all day, so she needed to rest, but she's more comfortable than she was yesterday."

"Good. I'll try to get by to see her when things settle down."

It took half an hour but we got our barbecue and Rebecca's Thai food.

"Can we take a look at the store now?" Mrs. Johnson asked.

"Sure." For some reason I couldn't call her Fran, and she hadn't asked me to. "If Derrick and ... Janis can take the food back to the house, we'll be back over there shortly." I leaned in closer to Artemisia. "Don't you want to see where you'll be ... tomorrow?"

She shook her head. "Mama's the one who worries about all that. She always wants to 'check out the venue.'" She made air quotes. "I started singing on the tailgate of Daddy's truck when I was four. It doesn't matter to me."

I wished she would come with us. Spending half an hour alone with her mother was not a prospect I relished. If I agreed to write Artemisia's book, I wondered, how much contact would I have to have with her imperious mother?

"We'll see you back at the house," Derrick said. As they squeezed through the crowd, I wondered how people would react if they knew they were brushing shoulders—quite literally—with Artemisia.

CHAPTER 13

I unlocked the door to the store and Mrs. Johnson and I stepped inside. I made sure the door was locked behind us.

"Impressive," Mrs. Johnson said, running her eyes over the first floor and the mezzanine. "So, what did you have in mind for tomorrow?"

"Well, I thought Artemisia could sing from the mezzanine, use it like a stage. We can block the stairs and turn off the elevator. Robert and Derrick can help us, and we've got a young man, Joseph, who works part-time for us. He can be here, I think. My daughter will be here, and I believe my father-in-law will be also."

Mrs. Johnson shook her head. "When we contract with a venue for a concert, we always require at least two dozen security people. My daughter is extremely popular. We have five thousand or more people at her concerts. We've had a couple of scares lately with over-enthusiastic fans. I'm concerned that you haven't really thought this through."

"It wasn't my idea."

"That policeman you introduced us to, could you ask him for some officers?"

"I'm going to call him tonight, but you can see what a crowd we have here. Tomorrow will be even worse, since it's a Saturday. But I'll see what he can do."

"We'll have to manage, I suppose." Mrs. Johnson looked around like someone who expected to eat at an upscale restaurant but had been taken to a burger joint. "There's a back door, I assume."

"Yes. We can lock that." I hoped our rickety old locks would hold up to a crush of fans.

"All right. If we can keep a couple of guys at the front door, we might be able to let in a limited number of people at a time. Just the sight of a uniformed policeman or two would go a long way toward maintaining order."

I put my hands on my hips. "Look, it's obvious you don't want to do this. Why don't we just call it off? We haven't told anybody about it."

She shook her head. "You're right. I'm not at all eager for Artie to do a free concert, but she's set on it. I think we'll limit the number of songs she sings. She needs to save her voice for the concert in Atlanta on Tuesday. She'll get paid for that. Like our mothers always told us, nobody's going to buy the cow if you're giving the milk away for free. Is there any way we could limit cell phones in your store?"

"Short of searching everybody who comes in, I don't see how we could."

"I guess not. But people will record her and put it on the internet. We brought a bunch of CDs and DVDs for her to autograph and sell. I'm not sure why we bother. So many people just download the music these days."

"But you can't get her autograph on your iPod."

"I hope that will make a difference. We'll give you a percentage of the sales, of course. Would fifteen percent be all right?"

"Sure."

Mrs. Johnson laughed. "You're no businesswoman at all, are you, Maureen? We always give twenty-five percent of sales to the venue. Thirty percent if they insist. I'll give you that anyway."

"How is she going to perform? A cappella?" I was stung by being taken for a rube.

"We have audio equipment, just a CD player and the karaoke CDs that Artie uses to rehearse. We'll need some place for her to sign autographs—a table and chair and some way to keep people in line. We'll need a store employee to handle money at the table."

"I'm sorry this is turning into a big deal. You know, Artemisia called me and made the offer."

"I know. Artie is convinced it will be fun to do something 'spontaneous.' Like most people in the public eye, she has no idea how much planning it takes to do something spontaneous."

Her cell phone rang. She checked who was calling and said, "I have to take this."

I stepped away from her to allow her some privacy, but she didn't lower her voice. After listening to someone for a moment, she said, "How serious do you think it is?" She listened some more, then said, "Okay, let me know what you decide to do."

When she hung up she leaned against one of the display cases, put her hand to her head, and stared at the floor.

"Fran, is there anything I can do?" It didn't seem appropriate to call her Mrs. Johnson at that moment.

"What?" She looked up as though she'd just realized I was there. "Sorry. That was my husband's caregiver. He's having a rough day. He and Artie usually Skype around dinner time, but he's not going to be able to tonight. They may have to put him in the hospital."

"I'm sorry. Is it his legs?"

"He has some pretty bad back pain, in addition to losing his legs. And he has trouble with the prostheses." She ran a hand over her face. "Maureen, people think I am the quintessential Stage Mom. I'm pushy, overbearing, and I think the world revolves around my talented daughter."

"No, I'm sure—"

She held up her hands. "Guilty on all counts. You know my husband was badly injured in Iraq. You don't know that my twenty-year-old son has been in and out of drug rehab since he was thirteen. I failed to protect either of them. I'm not going to lose Artie."

I leaned against a display case, facing her. "Your son made his own choices, Fran, and you couldn't help what happened to your husband. At least he's still alive." *And he didn't divorce you and cheat on you.* "Artemisia said he's doing pretty well."

"That's what he wants her to think. I've heard him curse God and wish he could die. He puts up a good front around Artie because he knows it would crush her to see how he really feels. It helps that we're on the road a lot. His caretakers deal with him better than I can. He manages to pretend long enough to Skype with Artie for ten minutes every day. Tonight, though, he just can't do it. She'll be really disappointed."

These people were hardly more than strangers to me. Meeting Artemisia and watching her laugh and enjoy herself with Derrick, though, had endeared her to me. She really was as sweet as the image she projected. I knew I wanted to write a book with her.

"Look," I said to Fran, "I've only known you for a couple of hours, so I probably don't have any business saying anything, but I think we're going to be getting to know one another very well while Artemisia and I work on a book."

"Do you mean that?"

"Yes, so, as a newly adopted member of the family, I'm going to stick my nose in here and say, don't you think you should tell your daughter what the situation really is?"

Fran shook her head slowly. "I don't want to worry her. It might affect her performance at the concert in Atlanta. She might even cancel it. We would disappoint an awful lot of people and lose a lot of money."

I moved over to stand beside Fran. "From something she said to me the first time we talked, I think she suspects more than you realize. If anything happens to her dad and she's not there—"

"I know, I know." Fran shook her head. "She would never forgive me. You know, on one side, I'm glad you want to do the book. But, on the other side, this is why I'm hesitant about you—or anybody, not just you—writing a book about her. This is family business. The world knows too much about us already. Listening to Derrick reminded me of that."

My clients routinely bemoan their loss of privacy. I want to tell them to give the money back and they can have all the privacy they want. When you try to achieve fame and popularity, you have to give up something. "Sadly, that's part of the price of celebrity."

"Some days I wonder if it's too high a price." Fran crossed her arms over her chest and turned to me. "What would you write about my son and his drug problem?"

I shrugged. "I listen to what my clients tell me and try to understand what's important. I've never set out to malign or embarrass anyone. Showing how your family deals with a difficult situation like that could be a positive, not a negative."

"Well, I'm not sure what's going to happen tomorrow." Fran rubbed her hands on her slacks. "But right now supper's getting cold, and it smelled awfully good."

While we were eating on the porch, under the witch's hat, Fran got another phone call. She went to the other side of the porch and sat in the swing to talk. After she hung up she explained to Artemisia that her father was not feeling well and would not be able to Skype with her that evening.

"Is he okay?" Artemisia's eyes, more than her voice, betrayed the depth of her concern.

"He's having some pain," Fran said, taking a sip of her tea. "The doctor said for Chris to increase his meds a little, and he's sleeping now. You can talk to him in the morning." She patted her daughter's arm.

Most of our conversation was about Robert and Derrick's venture into parenthood. They showed us a picture of their surrogate, an attractive brown-haired woman in her mid-twenties.

"You hear about surrogates who back out on the deal," Fran said, "and try to keep the baby. I hope that doesn't happen to you." Her voice held an edge that made her words sound almost like a threat.

"We're lawyers," Robert said. "We've got an iron-clad contract. And we met her through another couple for whom she was a surrogate two years ago. They didn't have any problem."

After supper Artemisia pitched in to help my kids and Derrick clean up while Fran and I sat in the swing and sipped a little more tea.

"I could get used to this," Fran said, turning her head to survey the yard and the historic homes on the other side of the street. Her phone buzzed and she read a text and typed a short reply.

"Is your husband really doing okay?" I asked.

"He seems to be. I might put a positive spin on things, but I wouldn't lie to Artie. You're right, though. I need to give her a better idea of where things stand. Given what John, his caregiver, just texted, I think we're good for tomorrow. John will call me if there's any change." She stood up. "I guess we need to get things set up in the store."

"Let's do it this way," I said as the swing slowed down. "The food booths closed at eight, so a car can get to the front of the store now. We won't be able to tomorrow morning. I'll take your car over there and unload the stuff you brought, just to get it in the store. We can set it up tomorrow. You and Artemisia can stay here and talk. I'll ask my kids to look through some of their dad's stuff up on the third floor. They need to get a start on that. That'll give you two some privacy."

"Sounds like a plan. Thank you for being so understanding." She turned toward the front door, then turned back to me. "You know, Artie was right. Being around real people—not the show business phonies we have to deal with—renews your sense that there is some good in the world."

"You sure that's not just the sweet tea talking?"

Fran smiled and raised her glass in a toast. "It does give you a buzz, doesn't it?"

After the kitchen was cleaned up, Robert and Derrick went up-stairs to unpack and Rebecca was in the bathroom. Before leaving for the store, I went into my bedroom to put away some clothes but didn't bother to turn on the light. Artemisia and her mother were sitting in the swing, which hangs outside one of my windows.

"Well," Mrs. Johnson said, keeping her voice down, "I guess we'll have a 'gay ol' time' this weekend. Yabba-dabba-do."

"Mama, don't start that." Artemisia sounded tired. "They're nice people. Derrick's really funny. He and Robert are gonna have a baby. They're *so* excited."

"Artie, I didn't work this hard to get you this far just to have you become a laughing stock because of all your gay male fans. You're not singing in a Turkish bath. Or is that the next step down from singing in a damn antique store?"

"Mama—"

Fran's voice got sharper. "If you had checked with me before you talked to that woman, I would never have let you do this. You're sup-posed to check with your manager before you commit yourself to anything."

"Mama, I heard all this in the car. Several times. Can't we just do one thing that's fun?"

"This isn't about 'fun,' Artie. It's a business, and I'm your *business* manager."

"But I want Ms. Cooper to write my book. She's the best. Mr. Siegler says so. As my business manager you should see that having the best person possible write the book would be good business. You need to be nice to her and her family." Artemisia got up and stomped inside and up the stairs.

Still seething over the "that woman" remark and the disparage-ment of my son and his partner, I drove Fran's rental car over to the square and was able to squeeze in between the Thai food booth and the front door of Palmetto Antiques. I unloaded the boxes of CDs and DVDs and the CD player, dropping them in the office so no one could see them through the big plate glass windows. With enough ambient light from the square, I didn't bother to turn on the store lights.

After unloading the last box, I looked around the store before locking up, trying to visualize how we could control the crowd tomorrow. That's when I noticed the light under the doors leading to the work area in the rear. Not just a light, but a moving light! I stepped back into the office and called 9-1-1. The operator told me they would get somebody there as quickly as possible but they were dealing with a major disturbance north of town.

Now what should I do? I certainly couldn't barge into the work area and surprise whoever was there. What if he had a gun? Troy kept a gun in his desk in the office. I hate guns. That was always an issue between us. I knew he wanted to protect himself, but I didn't want the things in my house. I couldn't see any option in this situation, so I took the gun out of the desk drawer and removed the clip. I just wanted to scare somebody, not injure or kill them.

Cursing every creak in the old wooden floors, I made my way to the swinging doors that lead to the work area. Peeking through the crack between them, I saw a short man on his knees in front of one of the pieces of Lemand furniture. His back was toward me, but I could see that he was wearing a ski mask, on a warm, muggy night in June in South Carolina. The mask was pushed up so he could see better. He had pulled out a drawer and was inspecting it carefully, glancing down at a piece of paper next to him and then back up at the drawer. At least he was wearing latex gloves. But he was using our shop light! I put my phone up to the crack and switched on the camera. If the guy would just turn around—

My phone rang.

The guy pulled the ski mask down and jumped to his feet, snatching up the piece of paper he'd been looking at. He grabbed the drawer he'd pulled out and started for the back door. I didn't see him reach for any weapon.

I had no choice. If he got away with that drawer, he might as well take the whole dresser. "Stop or I'll shoot!" I shouted, shoving through the swinging doors.

The man had reached the back door, but he didn't know the little trick of pushing up on the handle when you're trying to open it from the inside. Thanks goodness I hadn't gotten around to calling a carpenter yet.

"Freeze! Right there!" I said.

Still holding the drawer, the man raised his other hand. I saw a tattoo on the lower part of his right arm—maybe a number with a ribbon wrapped around it. "Hey, take it easy, lady. I don't want to hurt anybody." His muffled voice sounded educated, not like some hooligan, and he wasn't any bigger than me.

I waved the gun slightly. "What the hell are you doing here?"

"I'm just checking on something. I haven't taken anything or damaged anything."

"You're on your way out with that drawer." I waved the gun again.

"Be careful with that thing," he said, bending as though he was going to set the drawer down. "Look, this is just a drawer. It's not worth killing anybody. In fact, if you want it—"

He flung the drawer at me, hard. I fell back, trying to avoid it, and hit my head on a piece of furniture. As I fell to the floor, I squeezed the trigger.

CHAPTER 14

"She's coming around, Detective," I heard a woman's voice say. I don't know about coming around, but my head was spinning around. And splitting. I opened my eyes to see an EMT on one side of me, checking my pulse, and Scott Kelly kneeling on the other side. I made an effort to sit up.

"Why don't you just stay where you are for a minute?" Scott said, putting a firm hand on my shoulder. "You took a pretty nasty crack on the head."

"Her pulse is okay," the EMT said. "I need to check her for a concussion. Do you feel like doing that, ma'am?"

I nodded and immediately regretted it. When I had satisfied the EMT that I knew my name, where I was, today's date, the president's name, and several other bits of information, she said, "She seems to be okay. Her eyes look all right."

"Can I sit up?" I asked. "This floor's cold, and dirty. Tell the owner to clean up back here."

The EMT nodded and Scott helped me to sit up and slide back until I was resting against a dresser. I became aware of several police officers in SWAT gear—Kevlar vests, helmets, and all the rest of it—behind Scott. "Thanks for getting here. How did you know where I was?"

"The GPS in your phone."

"The operator said you were trying to handle some mess north of town." I figured that was why they were fully decked out.

"What? Oh, I wasn't involved in that. I called you a few minutes ago. You answered your phone but didn't say anything. I heard some shouting and then a gunshot, so I called in these guys and we dashed over here."

"The vests and all this gear for a break-in?"

"When we hear a gunshot, this is what we do. Of course, I didn't know you were the one doing the shooting." He held up my pistol in a plastic bag. "Where did you get this?"

"It was Troy's. He had all kinds of permits."

"He did. You don't."

"He had one as a gun dealer for the store, and I'm co-owner of the store." Robert had assured me that I was covered for any weapons in the store. The guns in Troy's apartment were another matter. Pain shot through the back of my head. I put my hand on a lump. "Was it loaded?"

"There was one bullet in it. You didn't know? You didn't put it in there?"

"No." I started to shake my head but stopped just in time. "I took the clip out. Oh, God! Did I shoot him?"

"With an automatic like this, there can be a round in the chamber, even if you remove the clip. But I don't think you shot anybody. There's no blood anywhere. We dug the bullet out of that wall, by the door."

I looked in the direction he was pointing to see the back door smashed in.

"We had to break it down," Scott said apologetically.

"It sticks. You just have to know how to turn the knob."

"We'll pay to replace it." He handed the gun to one of the officers. "You're lucky you *didn't* hit the guy, Maureen. People have been charged with assault for shooting a burglar."

"Assault? Me?" I sat up straighter, righteous anger overriding the pain in my head. "*He* broke into *my* store!"

"But did he have a weapon?"

I slumped back down. "I didn't see one."

"Were you in fear for your life? Did you feel threatened?"

It dawned on me that he was coaching me for any inquest that I might face. "I certainly did. Troy was killed back here. Now I find somebody messing around with this furniture. And he threw that drawer at me."

"It's pretty substantial," Scott said. "We're going to have to take it in as evidence."

"You won't find anything. He was wearing latex gloves."

Scott shook his head. "We still have to let the forensics people check it out. Maybe we'll see why he was so interested in that particular drawer."

"Please be careful with it. It's part of a very valuable piece of furniture."

Leaving two officers to guard the store, Scott drove me home in Fran's rental car. He would walk back to the store and pick up his car. On the way I told him about Artemisia's planned performance the next day. He stared at me in disbelief.

"Maureen, that's going to create a massive crowd control problem. You didn't think about giving me some advance notice."

"I just found out about it on Thursday. It won't be announced until tomorrow morning, on social media. I thought, if she's in the store, we could have some control over the crowd."

"Look, this kid is enormously popular right now. My niece is a huge fan. I'm imagining thousands of people pressed up against those plate glass windows at the front of your store." He twisted his mouth and chewed on his lip. "I'll call the state police tonight and see if we can get some help."

"Scott, I am sorry. I'd never heard of her until a couple of days ago and, given everything else I'm dealing with right now—"

"It's okay. We'll work it out." His words were kinder than his tone.

When we pulled into the driveway, Artemisia, Rebecca, Derrick and Robert were sitting on the porch, singing. Artemisia and Derrick sat in the swing, with her hand resting on his shoulder. Robert and Rebecca had pulled up chairs from under the Witch's Hat. Pepper was settled between them, with Rebecca scratching his head.

"They'd better watch out," Scott said. "If your neighbors get any idea of who she is, you'll have a mob scene right here."

As we were getting out of the car, Fran came out of the house, holding her phone. The smile she tried to flash didn't convince me at all. I climbed the steps and stood behind Robert's chair.

"There you are," Fran said. "I was wondering what was keeping you." She looked at Scott as though waiting for an explanation.

"Good evening, Mrs. Johnson," Scott said. "Maureen ran into a slight problem at the store, but everything has been taken care of. I've got to get back, so I'll see you in the morning."

From the fact that she didn't ask what Scott meant by "a slight problem," I could tell that Fran had something else on her mind.

"Artie, could I talk to you, privately?" she said.

I massaged Robert's shoulders. "Kids—and that includes you, Derrick—I need your help upstairs. I've got a bunch of Troy's stuff in the family room. Let's see if we can start to make some sense of it."

Each of us had been working on a box of Troy's papers for about half an hour when Fran's voice floated up the stairs.

"Hello?"

I stepped to the head of the stairs. "Yeah, Fran, come on up."

Artemisia was right behind her mother. As soon as they reached the top of the stairs I could see the deep distress on their faces. I held my arms out to Fran and she stepped into them and started to cry. Artemisia ran to Derrick.

"What's the matter?" I asked.

"My husband tried to kill himself."

"Oh, God! What—"

"He got some of his pain meds and took a bunch." She stood back and blew her nose on the wad of tissues she was carrying.

"Is he—"

"His caregiver found him in time. They got his stomach pumped and he's in the hospital now." She sighed heavily. "Artie and I need to get home."

"Of course. Can we help you get on a plane?"

"I made some calls. The best we can do is a flight out of Columbia after lunch tomorrow. With the connections and layovers, we won't get to Tulsa until midnight, but at least we'll get there."

"Could you charter a plane?"

"I've called a couple of places to see about that, but I haven't found anything available until Sunday."

"I'll take you," Derrick said.

"What? How—"

"I'm a licensed pilot. Four other guys and I bought a plane last year. They love to go to Alabama football games." With one arm still around Artemisia, he looked at something on his phone. "Nobody has it reserved for this weekend." He typed a few keystrokes with his thumb. "Now I do."

"Oh, Derrick, we couldn't ask you to do that," Artemisia said.

"You didn't. I volunteered."

Artemisia threw her arms around his neck and kissed him on the cheek.

"He's a very good pilot," I offered. "I've flown with him a couple of times. And it's a nice-sized plane. A Learjet that seats six."

The next few hours were incredibly busy. Artemisia, Fran, Derrick, and I went back to the store so Artemisia could autograph the CDs and DVDs. The pictures—and there were over a hundred of them—she had already signed.

"We'll deduct our percentage of these sales," I said, "and send you the rest."

"Oh, goodness, no," Artemisia said before Fran could open her mouth. "Keep it all. And I am gonna sing," she insisted, turning to her mother, "even if it's just a couple of songs. I promised I would do that. You said Daddy is doing okay."

"Yes, hon," her mother said. "John says they've got him stabilized. He's sleeping a lot right now, so there's no real emergency. I told John to call me if there's any change."

"Okay. So, with Derrick taking us, we've got a little time to work with. I won't post anything on social media. It would complicate everything. Ms. Cooper, is there any way you could arrange for me to appear on the steps of the court house in the morning, like that band did? That might be the simplest way to do it."

"Let me talk to a couple of people."

I stepped into the office and called Scott first. When I explained the change of plans to him, he was relieved, to a degree.

"The lack of publicity on social media will make our job easier. The state police are sending six officers."

"Do you know who's in charge of the acts that appear on the court house steps?"

"That would be Georgia Ann Wilson."

"The woman who runs that artists' co-op on the west side of the square?"

"That's her."

"All right, I'll give her a call. Thanks for your help, Scott. I am sorry I dumped all of this on you. See you tomorrow." For some reason

I added, "Maybe we could get something to eat tomorrow evening, when things wind down a little."

"I'd like that, Maureen. I really would."

I didn't know Georgia Ann well, but I did know what a publicity hound she was. The front of her co-op is painted purple and yellow and she often stages contests on the sidewalk in front of it. I decided to call her in the morning. If I called her tonight, she would notify media all over the Upstate, and it might take more than six state troopers to get Artemisia out of Lawrenceville.

I rarely have trouble getting to sleep or staying asleep, but on this night I could hardly even get my eyes to stay closed. When I did close them I kept seeing things—the store, the spot where Troy died, knowing now that Dolores had been raped somewhere in there. It didn't seem like the same cozy place. And I hated seeing the Lemand furniture huddled in the work area, like a family of refugees uprooted from their home and powerless to control whatever was going to happen to them. Where would they end up? Would they ever see one another again?

Spending time in my grandparents' house as a child, I had never paid much attention to the furniture, any more than I did to the doors and windows. It was all just part of the place. I don't know how many times I got my grandmother's good china out of that sideboard, and one of the armoires—one with only two drawers at the bottom and room for hanging clothes—made a perfect place to conceal myself when my mother played hide–and–seek with me.

Yeah, that's how much of a loner I was. My mother was my primary playmate.

I closed my eyes to get a clearer image of myself sitting in that armoire, knees drawn up to my chin. My grandfather's clothes smelled of his pipe. I imagined myself looking around the interior of the armoire. What was there about it that had somebody poking around, pulling drawers out?

As I thought she might be, Georgia Ann was skeptical when I got her at breakfast the next morning. "Maureen, I've got a solid line-up of performers, starting at 10," she said, "and you expect me to create space for somebody when you won't tell me who it is?"

"I don't want to create a mob scene, Georgia Ann."

"She's that popular?"

"That popular and then some. I promise you she won't take up much room. She's not very tall, and she's only got one name—"

"Wait a minute! Are you serious? Are you talking about ... Artemisia?"

"There's a strong likelihood—"

"Oh, my God! I've got to call—"

"You've got to call *nobody*. That's the main part of the deal, Georgia Ann. Her dad's in the hospital, so she's got to get out of here as quickly as possible this morning. If we see so much as one reporter or camera, she won't appear, and you'll look pretty foolish." Fran had insisted on setting that limit.

Georgia Ann didn't say anything for a moment. "Well, you can't stop people from recording her on their phones."

"No, we can't. But she'll be gone by the time they can post anything and anybody hears about her being here."

"Maureen, I'm excited about this, of course, but if I can't make any publicity out of it, what good does it do us? She'll be gone before anybody knows she's here."

Fran had foreseen this objection. "I can make this promise, Georgia Ann—if you don't publicize her appearance today, she'll come back next year as the featured performer at Food-Fest, with all the publicity you want to generate."

Georgia Ann gasped. "You can guarantee that?"

"I've got it in writing." Fran had given me one of their standard performance contracts, signed but with her note that details were to be negotiated.

"That'll make us the biggest event in the Upstate—the whole state, for that matter."

"Yes, it will. But only if you don't publicize her appearance this morning."

Georgia Ann bowed to the inevitable. "All right then. Bring her to the basement of the court house a little before ten. I'll have one of our bands there to see what they can do to accompany her. I think anybody today knows at least three or four of her songs."

"She'll do two songs. *Two*." I even held up my fingers. "Then she's going to see her dad."

At 9:40 Derrick, Fran, and I left Robert, Rebecca, and Wyatt in the store and hustled the disguised Artemisia across the street, into the basement of the court house. The band that had performed her first hit song yesterday was tuning up. Georgia Ann hovered in the background, camera at the ready, twisting around like she really needed to go to the bathroom.

"Hey, guys!" Artemisia said, pulling off her wig and shaking her hair loose. "Thanks for helping me out on such short notice."

"Holy crap!" the drummer cried. "She looks ... just like Artemisia."

Artemisia smiled and patted him on the shoulder. "And you look ... just like a drummer." She turned to the girl who sang lead. "You're Sarah, aren't you?"

The girl could only nod. I wished she would close her mouth.

"You did a nice job on 'Misty Rainbow' yesterday. You might try it in a lower key, though. I think it would suit your voice better."

"We only know two keys," the bass guitarist said.

Georgia Ann stepped forward. "I know we couldn't do any publicity and there aren't any media people here, but do you mind if I take a couple of pictures?"

"Sure, go ahead," Fran said.

Once the group realized that Artemisia actually was who she appeared to be, they got down to business and settled on two songs from her most recent album. As they ran through the second one, Artemisia turned to Sarah, who was leaning against the wall, her arms over her chest and her head down. She clearly realized she was about to be upstaged in spectacular fashion.

"This one needs some background harmony," Artemisia said. "Can you do that?"

Sarah stood up and rubbed her hands on her jeans. "Yeah, sure."

Scott appeared in the doorway. "My guys are in position at the bottom of the steps. Any time you're ready."

"Are there any other entrances?" Fran asked.

"There are two," Scott said. "We've got them both locked and guarded."

Fran nodded her approval.

"We'll go up in the elevator," Georgia Ann said, "and come out the main door. It'll take two trips."

The band went first, with their instruments. Then Fran, Derrick, Artemisia, Georgia Ann, and I made the second trip. The drums, amps, and microphones were set up on the landing. When we got out of the elevator, the band was plugging in their guitars and doing sound checks. Georgia Ann stopped us just inside the main door.

"If you'll wait here, I'll introduce you."

The glass in the court house doors was heavy and there were ten steps from the doors down to the landing. We propped one of the doors open, so we could hear Georgia Ann's introduction. She was trying to draw people away from the booths to the steps, putting all her peppy personality into it.

"She was a high school cheerleader," Derrick said. "I'd bet on it. Head cheerleader."

Artemisia appeared disinterested, even sending a text before slipping her phone into a pocket of her pants. As introverted as I am, I couldn't imagine stepping out in front of that crowd, which was growing larger by the minute. When Georgia Ann finally raised her arm toward us and shouted her name, Artemisia gave Derrick a peck on the cheek and stepped out through the doors. The crowd erupted as the band started playing one of her more energetic numbers and she grabbed a mike and launched right into it.

Fran hardly seemed to see her daughter. Her eyes were on the crowd. "Be sure to thank your friend Scott for the extra security. Artie is so oblivious. She thinks everybody loves her."

"It looks like they do," I said.

"Some of them love her too much. They're the ones who can be so dangerous."

"Well, you're in a small town in South Carolina. I don't think we've got any really strange types out there."

"There are some crazies in every crowd." She ran her eyes back and forth again. "Remember Selena and that poor Grimmie girl. A lunatic shot her while she was signing autographs. Sometimes I'm sorry Artie won 'America's Icon.' Maybe I shouldn't have pushed her the way I did."

Derrick moved closer to us. "She's a natural talent, Ms. Johnson. I don't think you or she could have suppressed it. It would have found its way to the surface. And I'm so thankful it did. She's amazing."

The second number, one I didn't know, was also upbeat. Artemisia stood next to Sarah for part of it, while they harmonized. Then she hugged her. I could see hundreds of phones pointed at the stage. Sarah and her band would find their reputations made today.

When they finished the second song, Georgia Ann started to step out and thank her, but Artemisia held up her hand. Fran tensed, a frown spreading over her face. "The deal was for two songs, Artie," she muttered.

"I'm sorry I can't stay any longer," Artemisia told the crowd. "I had planned to spend the whole day here, but my daddy's in the hospital and I've got to get home today. I'll be back next year, though! That's a promise. Before I go, I need to tell you two things. First, get over to Zeke's barbecue stand today. I have never, and I mean *never*, eaten any better barbecue. And I want you to stop in at Palmetto Antiques, right here on the corner. Ms. Cooper has some pictures, CDs, and DVDs that I've autographed. They'll be on sale as long as they last. While you're there, take a look at the stuff she's got in the store. It's an amazing place.

"And now, the second thing. We haven't rehearsed this, but I want to sing the first song my daddy taught me when I was four." She turned to the band. "I can do it a cappella, but if you know that old hymn 'In the Garden,' I do it in G."

"Hey, that's one of the keys we know," the band's bassist said.

"Great!" Artemisia turned back to the crowd. "I know people are recording and posting stuff. That's okay. In fact—" She took out her phone and took a picture of the crowd. "Please be sure you post this next song, so my dad can see it." She took a deep breath. "Daddy, this is for you. I love you, and I'll see you later today."

As she began to sing, Artemisia closed her eyes, as though all she could see was her father's face. By the third bar the band came in softly behind her and Sarah improvised a haunting harmony.

Derrick put his arm around me as we watched the crowd's reaction. "I wish I had the Kleenex concession here today," he said, his voice unsteady.

"I wish I had a few more in my pocket." I dabbed at my eyes.

The state police had pulled a car up as close to the basement door of the courthouse as they could, but there were several food booths in the way. It took all six troopers and a few of Scott's men to get

Fran, Artemisia, and Derrick through the surging crowd and into the car. I could see why Fran was so afraid of adoring fans. People seemed to have no sense of the danger they posed to someone they claimed to admire.

The plan was for two of the troopers to take Fran, Artemisia, and Derrick to the airport in Greenville. I couldn't believe my eyes when several people ran for their cars, clearly intending to follow them. But the trooper driving turned on the lights and siren and roared off while the others blocked the main roads leading out of town long enough for Artemisia to escape.

We sold out of our supply of pictures, CDs and DVDs within an hour. The CDs and DVDs had a price and a bar code on them, so that was set. I was going to ask a dollar for the pictures, but Rebecca had priced them at five dollars. Nobody blinked an eye.

Fran was right: I wasn't much of a businesswoman. My daughter clearly was. She'd had Artemisia's performance playing on her phone and even had Pepper, with the cast on his leg, sitting beside her. "People were so distracted," she said, "they didn't even think about how much they were paying. Damn, I should have asked ten."

I was beginning to think about lunch—barbecue, of course—when Joseph walked into the store.

"Oh, hey," I said, "how's the crowd at Zeke's stand? Can I get something to eat?"

"Sorry, Ms. Cooper. After what that girl said, we couldn't keep up with the orders. We had to go back to the store for more supplies and the police had to keep people in line. We're completely sold out. There were about fifty people still in line when we had to close. Who was she?" He sounded like my dad imitating the guy at the end of an old "Lone Ranger" episode who gazes at the departing cloud of dust and asks, "Who was that masked man?"

I explained Artemisia to him and Rebecca played one of her songs from that morning on her phone.

"Hmm. Cute, but definitely not my style," Joseph said. "She must be really popular, though. She liked us on Facebook last night and now we've got five thousand new followers. We'll need to go to the store Monday morning just to get enough stuff to hold us until our suppliers can get to us. All we've got is scraps." He held up a bucket for Pepper.

I laughed. "Great! I can't get any barbecue, but my dog scores a feast."

"Hey, he's lucky to get it, Ms. Cooper. On my way over here somebody saw our label on the bucket and offered me twenty dollars for it."

The rest of the afternoon was busy enough that sometimes I even forgot about Derrick and his passengers. The Day the Music Died kept popping into my head. February 3, 1959— Buddy Holly, Richie Valens, and the Big Bopper died in the crash of a small plane in Iowa. But, I reminded myself, the weather had been awful that day and the plane much smaller than Derrick's.

About three-thirty Robert stuck his head into the office. "Just got a text from Derrick. They've landed. Artemisia wants him to meet her father. He'll be back later tonight."

"He doesn't want to stay over?"

Robert shook his head. "We've got to get that bedroom painted before we go to bed tomorrow night. I told him he'll just have to leave the little tart and haul himself back home. He could fly without the plane, I think."

"You're not jealous, are you?"

He waved his hand dismissively. "Pssht. Of course not. I'm delighted for him. How many of us get to have a once-in-a-lifetime experience like that? He will be your slave forever, you know."

I chuckled. "She blew through here like a tornado, didn't she? And look how many people she's affected—Zeke, Derrick, me."

Robert sat down and petted Pepper. "Don't forget Sarah and her band."

"Yeah, I'm sure they'll get lots of attention."

"They already have a dozen offers, including the State Fair in August. And they're going to open for Artemisia at one of her concerts in Cincinnati in the fall."

"How do you know that?"

"Because I'm now their agent. We signed the contract right before lunch."

I gasped. "Even though they only know how to play in two keys?"

"They have to learn one more by August. That's in the contract."

"Robert, you don't know anything about the music business."

"But I do know contracts."

Albert A. Bell, Jr

FoodFest closes on Saturday night with a concert. I didn't plan to stay for it, even though Robert's new clients—who had decided to call themselves Sarah and Her Band—would be the headliners. Scott felt things were calm enough and he had been on duty long enough that we could slip out and go somewhere quiet. Somebody from his department brought a big piece of plywood to cover my bashed-in back door, so I decided just to close up.

"Nobody's going to buy antiques while the concert's going on," I told him, "and I don't have any more Artemisia merchandise."

"Shoot, I was hoping to get a picture. You know, for my niece. ... Like I said, she's a big fan."

I picked up a manila envelope with Scott's name on it, from my desk. "They left one, autographed, in appreciation for your help with the security."

I turned off the lights in the front of the store. While the back door was being covered, Scott went to his car and brought in the drawer from the Lemand dresser. I looked it over and was relieved to see it was undamaged by whatever his technicians had done to it.

Before I could slip the drawer back into place he said, "There is one thing I need to show you." He held up a large white envelope he'd brought in with the drawer.

"What's that?"

"It's an x-ray of the drawer." He took out the image and held it up to the light. "It looks like it's got a false bottom."

CHAPTER 15

I picked up the drawer and held it up as though the light would let me see through it. "A false bottom?"

"Yeah. If you measure the depth inside and then outside, there's about a one-inch difference. The wood is heavy and the drawer's deep, so you don't notice it until you actually measure it."

"Did the x-ray show anything in it?"

"It looks like some pieces of paper, probably envelopes of some kind. There are several of them, packed pretty tight so you don't hear them rustling around."

I shook the drawer but couldn't hear anything. Then I turned it in several different directions. "How do you open it?"

"The tech guys couldn't figure that out. It may have something to do with the dowels that hold it together, but they were afraid to mess with it."

"Can't we just push some things and see what happens?" I put a finger on one of the corner dowels.

Scott pulled my hand back. "I wouldn't do that, Maureen. With some of these secret gizmos, you have to push or turn things in just the right order or it locks up and you'll never get it open."

"We could always cut it open."

Scott chuckled. "Yeah, I'm sure you want to take a saw to a piece of furniture that's worth, what, several hundred dollars?"

I shook my head. "Couple of thousand, probably."

Scott's eyebrows arched and he looked at the Lemand pieces with a new respect.

I turned the drawer over one more time but couldn't see any hint as to how to open a secret compartment. "So we need the plans that the maker was working from."

"That, or some document from him that explains how the mechanism works. You said the guy you scared off last night had a piece of paper with him, right?"

"Yes. He was looking at it and poking around on the drawer."

Scott took the drawer from me and looked at it from several angles. "He must have had some instructions about opening the thing."

"But I thought you said all of Lemand's stuff was destroyed when his plant burned."

Scott shrugged. "Who knows? He could have kept papers at home. Something might have gotten passed down to his family."

I took the drawer back and slid it into its place in the dresser. If it wasn't going to give up its secret, it might as well go back where it belonged. "I did a little checking on the family. His grandson, Christopher the third, had two daughters. One of them lived in Greenwood and died about a year ago. She had a son, according to her obituary."

"And I'll bet her son went through her papers. Do you think he might have been your intruder?"

"We didn't exactly have time for introductions, and he was wearing the ski mask."

"Well, it might be worth having a chat with him." Scott got out his phone and I gave him Christopher Lemand Proctor's name. He repeated it and asked someone in his office to gather whatever information could be gleaned about the man. "Call me with anything you get."

"Finding a place to eat tonight is going to be a pain, isn't it?" I said as Scott and I looked over the crowd outside the front door of Palmetto Antiques.

"Yeah. With every restaurant in a twenty-mile radius staffing a booth at FoodFest, there won't be a lot of options for places to eat." He shrugged. "We could always hit one of the booths."

Contending with the throng had no appeal for me. My introvert soul craved quiet. "How about going over to my place? We can have one of those 'whatever falls out of the fridge' dinners."

Scott ran a hand over his face. "You know, as tired as I am, that sounds great. As long as a beer is part of what falls out."

"There should be a couple. You want to just walk over there and pick up our cars later?"

As we skirted the crowd I slipped my arm through Scott's, mainly so I wouldn't get separated from him. When we turned down South Arbor Street, though, and the crowd thinned out, I didn't let go. We walked slowly, the way couples do in greeting card commercials, and I leaned into him. In spite of any reservations I had about him, I told myself that I needed Scott's solidity to reassure me because I didn't know what was going on or who was prowling around my store.

Without thinking about it, we were walking on Suellen Gillespie's side of the street, opposite my house. She and some of her family were sitting on her porch. Suellen waved to us to come up her sidewalk. Southern gentility does not allow such an invitation to be refused. As we climbed the steps, I slipped my arm out of Scott's. I recognized Suellen's daughter, Virginia, and two grandsons, who were exercising their thumbs on computer games on a phone and an iPad. With their earbuds in place, they might as well have been on the other side of the world.

"Well, I hear there was a surprise guest at FoodFest," Suellen said, "and you had some-thing to do with it."

"Do you really know Artemisia?" Virginia asked, leaning forward in her chair.

"I just met her yesterday. It looks like I'm going to be writing a book with her."

"That will certainly be interesting," Virginia said. "We didn't get here until this afternoon. I'm so sorry we missed her."

"She'll be back next year for the whole festival."

"Wonderful! Will she be staying with you?"

"We haven't made any plans." But I had just decided that we would have to find some other place for Artie to stay. I did not want my house under siege for three days. I wondered if Scott could put her into some kind of protective custody.

"Well, it's nice to see you," I said, taking Scott's hand. "We're going to see what sort of supper falls out of the refrigerator."

"Oh, that's one of my favorites," Virginia said as her old-fashioned Southern mother frowned. I hoped she wouldn't offer to feed us.

There were lights on in my house, and Robert's car was still in the driveway. He was sitting in the porch swing when we walked up the steps. He and Scott nodded to one another. Robert has never warmed up to Scott. I guess he doesn't like to see a man replacing his father, even though Troy was distant toward Robert once he realized his son was gay.

"I was hoping you'd get here before I left," Robert said. "I'm going to the airport to meet Derrick and we'll go home from there. But I wanted to give you this." He picked up a manila folder and handed it to me. "I went through another box of Dad's stuff this evening and found this. I was going to take it with me and show it to you later, when I could be here, but I'm glad Scott's here. I think you'll need somebody with you when you read it."

"What is it?" I asked as a knot tightened in my stomach.

"It's something Dad wrote after he got back from his second tour in Afghanistan." He hugged me and patted Scott on the shoulder, then headed for his car.

When we entered the kitchen I laid the folder on the counter without opening it.

"Do you want me to stay?" Scott asked.

I nodded. "Definitely, but I think I could face this better if I have something to eat. I probably won't feel like eating anything after I've read it." I opened the refrigerator. "Hey, here's some of my wild rice and seafood salad. Looks like enough for two. You know where the crackers are."

Scott retrieved a box of crackers from the shelf and some napkins. "You know, it might not be something horrible in that folder," he said.

I put two beers on the table and Scott opened them. I rarely drink beer, so I hadn't planned on having one, but now it seemed like a good idea. I suspected that a glass of sweet tea just wasn't going to do it. "These last few days I've learned there were things about Troy that I didn't know. And none of them have been good."

We sat down at the table. I dipped a couple of crackers into the salad and took a swallow of the beer to wash them down. "Okay, here goes," I said as I opened the folder.

What I found was four pages of notebook paper filled with Troy's handwriting. Some words were underlined. My breathing slowed as I read, and I took Scott's hand. He sipped his beer, ate some salad and crackers, and waited for me to finish. I looked back over the pages and closed the folder before I looked up at him.

"Do you want me to read it?" he asked.

I shook my head. "It's really personal and really intense."

"Can you tell me about it?"

I pushed a strand of hair behind my ear. "Long story short, there was an Afghan boy who hung around their base. His name was Hamid. He was nine. Troy became a kind of big brother to the boy. He gave him a soccer ball. I remember him asking me to send it to him. During a fire-fight Hamid was killed. Troy was pretty sure he killed him. He was firing while he ducked for cover."

"Oh, God!" Scott whispered.

"Why wouldn't he tell me?" I asked.

"Hon, I've only known a couple of police officers who were involved in shootings," Scott said. "One of them told me, if he didn't talk about it, he could almost convince himself it hadn't happened."

"You've never killed anybody, have you?" Maybe he was talking about himself.

Scott shook his head. "No. I shot a guy once but just wounded him." He touched my shoulder.

"Did you feel guilty?"

"Not really. Scared as hell, yes, but not guilty. He had drawn a gun on me and my partner. But I was put on desk duty for a couple of weeks and had to talk to a counselor. That's standard procedure when an officer is involved in a shooting. I wonder if Troy ever had that opportunity."

"I don't know that he ever went to a counselor, or that he would go. He used to say, 'It's the army. You shoot people.' And he'd been hunting and killing things since he was ten." Wyatt had cultivated Troy's love of the woods, guns, and hunting.

"Maureen, I don't care how many deer or rabbits you've shot. Nothing prepares you for pointing that gun at another human being and pulling the trigger. And to accidentally kill a child—I cannot possibly imagine how a sane person would react to that."

"Or how he could stay sane."

I didn't ask Scott to spend the night. Having him with me when I read about Hamid being killed had been reassuring, even though I had not told him how much anguish Troy had revealed in those four pages. He had even contemplated killing himself.

I stayed up until after one, going through other boxes of Troy's papers. With some black garbage bags at my side, I began dumping stuff when, after at least two readings, I could not see any significance to it. Just because Troy kept a piece of paper, I reminded myself over and over, that didn't mean it was worth keeping. My mantra became: Hoarders keep everything, but not everything is worth keeping.

After a few hours of sleep I got a quick breakfast, fed Pepper and cleaned up after him in the back yard. He seemed content to go back to sleep on the back porch, so I walked over to the store to retrieve my car.

Some of the food vendors had packed up after the closing concert last night, others were stirring now. Music—if that's what rap actually is—drifted from a booth across the square. The clean-up crews wouldn't start until all the booths were out of the way, so garbage cans over-flowed and food wrappers floated on a soft breeze across the courthouse lawn. A couple of homeless people scrounged through the trash, looking for things they could sell to the recycling center. At least I hoped that was what they were after.

I made sure the store was locked up. One of the officers that Scott had left on guard told me they would be there only another hour or so. In full daylight, with people around, they didn't think anyone would bother the place. I couldn't argue with their reasoning, but I knew I would check in at least a couple of times during the day. The walk over from the house would do me good.

Without thinking much about it, I turned my car toward the southeast side of town, where the cemetery is. One Sunday out of each month, as early in the morning as possible, I visit my parents' and grandparents' graves. Real flowers can be put on a grave for a few days after the funeral, but, once they've been cleared away, the city doesn't allow real flowers on the graves because they get droopy and messy. I keep "fresh" artificial flowers on my parents' graves, changing them with the seasons. I did that last month, so today would just be a visit, a few minutes for reflection.

When the cemetery came into view, I had to admit to myself something I had tried to forget: this would be my first visit since Troy was buried there. He had wanted to be cremated—as I intend to be—but he had never put anything in writing, and Wyatt had insisted that his son be buried next to his mother. Since I was no longer

Troy's wife, I had no legal standing in determining what was done with his body. And Wyatt paid for the funeral.

I parked my car in one of the few shady spots I could find. My parents' graves are close to a big tree, at one end of a row of graves. They bought the plots when this section of the cemetery was opened, so they had their pick. They had also bought ones for me and my kids. I would eventually sell mine, unless one of the kids wanted it for a spouse. Mom used to joke about "location, location, location." For some reason she liked the idea of having shade over her grave for at least part of the day. I had to admit that did make it more comfortable standing in front of the graves during the summer.

My phone buzzed and I glanced at it to see a text from Artemisia. Her father had gotten through the night and they were going to meet with his doctors today to discuss treatment options. She closed with a smiley emoji and "My love to you all. We owe you so much." I replied with good wishes.

I paid a short visit to my paternal grandparents' graves. My mother's parents were buried in a church cemetery north of town. I did not get out there as often as I felt I should. I'm not even sure why I feel the obligation—why anybody does.

My grandparents had not died at the same time, and my grandfather had died a hero's death. His headstone had been paid for by the city, which also took care of placing flowers on the grave regularly. Guys who had served with him sometimes placed something on the grave as well, on his birthday or the anniversary of his death. That anniversary had been last week, so I wasn't surprised to see several vases and bouquets. One that did surprise me was a small bouquet, all the more noticeable among the larger arrangements. I looked at the card and read, "Rusty, in my heart always." I had never heard my grandfather called Rusty, although it was a natural enough nickname for a man named Russell who, in his prime, had reddish brown hair.

As I turned back to my car I decided I would take a look at Troy's grave, just to see if everything had been done as it should be and whether the flowers had been removed yet. His family's plot was located on the other side of the large mausoleum which dominates the center of the cemetery. When I turned the corner of the building I was startled to see someone standing beside Troy's grave.

It was Dolores.

My first instinct was to turn back, but Dolores was facing in my direction and saw me before I could make a move. Southern gentility required that I walk over to her.

She spoke first, softly, almost shyly. "Hi."

"Good morning." I matched her quiet tone, not friendly but not rude either. For two women who had known each other only a couple of days, we had shared some deep secrets, but I couldn't forget that we had also shared Troy.

"I thought I would get out here before anybody else came around," Dolores said. "I hope you don't mind."

I kept my eyes focused on the grave, surrounded by at least a dozen vases and wreaths. "I haven't been his wife for the last five years. I don't have any claim on him." *If I did*, I thought, *he wouldn't even be buried here.* "Finding you beside his grave is better than finding his current girlfriend here."

"Well, actually ... ." She pointed to one of the bouquets beside the temporary headstone.

I knelt to examine the large arrangement and the tag attached to it, which read, "I wish I could have told you. Love, Anna."

Told him what? I wondered.

I stood up, ready to leave, but Dolores said, "You got time for a cup of coffee?"

I wasn't really in a mood for any more bonding, but I knew Dolores didn't have anybody else to turn to. Relations with her mother and her son were apparently tense. Even as little contact as I'd had with her, I had the odd sensation that I could sense what she was thinking, as though I had known her all my life. She wanted to talk about Joseph. But maybe that was just obvious.

Lawrenceville doesn't have a Starbucks and Pam's place isn't open on Sundays, so we went to the McDonald's just down the road from the cemetery. I like their vanilla lattés, but I settled for a plain small coffee because Dolores insisted on buying.

"Zeke paid me for working at his booth during FoodFest." It obviously meant something to her to be able to pick up the tab. "I can't pay you back yet for all you did for me at the emergency room, but at least I can do this."

We found a booth in the back where she could put her injured foot out to one side without tripping anyone. As I expected, the conversation centered on her efforts to establish a connection with her son. She and Joseph had talked and she felt they might have taken a tentative step or two.

"Have you told him ... the whole story yet?" I asked.

She shook her head. "I've been close a couple of times, but ... ."

"I think he would understand. What happened to you was not your fault." I reached across the table and took her hand. "You're not the first woman to have a strong reaction like that. Women who are raped often suffer PTSD."

"Isn't that what soldiers get when they're in combat?"

"Yes, some of them do. But it can happen to anybody who's been through a really bad experience. They can't stand to be in the place where it happened or to see or hear things—or people—that remind them of it."

She leaned over the table and lowered her voice, even though there was no one sitting close to us. "But how's he going to feel when he learns he was born because I was raped?"

"What has he been told?"

"My momma just told him that his father and I had some problems and had to go away for a while. You know, in our part of town, missing parents and kids being raised by grandmothers are pretty common, I'm sorry to say."

When we got to our cars Dolores asked me what I was planning to do for the rest of the day. The introvert part of me needed some time alone, so I said, quite truthfully, "I've got a lot to do at the store. I'm trying to figure out Troy's accounting system. And Joseph is supposed to come by this afternoon to show me the new web site he's creating for us. It's going to be a busy day."

Dolores hugged me. "If I can do anything for you, just let me know. And thank you for all you've done for my boy. You and your family have been so good to him."

Half an hour later I heard someone knocking impatiently on the front door of the store. I came out of the office, expecting to find some left-over tourist from FoodFest who thought we would open just for her, even though the lights were off and the sign hanging on the door was turned to the **CLOSED** side. But I saw Dolores, waving for me to come let her in.

I opened the door but remained standing in it. Dolores pushed her way past me. She seemed excited.

"What's up?" I asked.

Dolores limped into the office, motioning for me to follow her. That was all I could do.

"Look," she said, turning to face me, "I went back to the cemetery after we talked."

"Okay." That still didn't explain why she was here or why she was breathing so hard.

"I took the tag off of Anna's flowers and put them on another grave, a long way from Troy's."

I gasped. "You shouldn't have done that."

"You were thinking about it, weren't you? You're just too nice to do it."

I sat down at my desk. "Okay, the thought did cross my mind, but my mother would have been horrified. 'It's not what a lady would do.' That's what she would have said."

The corner of Dolores' mouth turned up. "Fortunately no one has ever accused me of being a lady."

"But the grounds crew is going to remove them tomorrow. That's the cemetery's policy."

"Screw the policy. I wanted that bitch's flowers off of Troy's grave. Yesterday."

"Well, I can appreciate that. But why are you here telling me this?"

"When I was moving the vase I noticed this stuck down in the flowers."

She pulled something from a pocket of her jeans and dropped it on my desk—a little teddy bear, no bigger than the palm of my hand, wearing a diaper.

"What—"

Dolores stamped her good foot impatiently and pulled Anna's tag from the flowers out of another pocket, slapping it down on my desk. "Oh, come on, Maureen! Don't you get it? Anna's pregnant."

❖❖❖

CHAPTER 16

When Dolores left I made sure the door was locked and returned to the office. The little bear lay on my desk, taunting me. I picked it up and just held it. Could Dolores be right about Anna's pregnancy? *I wish I could have told you.* Put together with the diapered bear, what else could that mean? Anna must have brought the flowers to the grave herself. She hadn't attended Troy's funeral and I couldn't remember noticing her bouquet among the flowers at the funeral home or at the grave site.

I suppose I could feel some sympathy for her—an unmarried woman with two young children and now expecting a third at age thirty-five. And everybody in this small—and small-minded—town would know about her situation. They would have rolled their eyes at Mary when she started telling that Virgin Birth story. To a large degree Anna relied on her personal reputation to bring in clients to her accounting and insurance business. She told me she hadn't attended Troy's funeral in order to avoid embarrassing encounters with people—potential customers—who knew about, or suspected, her affair with Troy. Robert had threatened to remove her if she did show up. What would he do when he found out she was carrying his father's child?

Damn you, Troy! Why do I even care anymore? I've got Scott. He's as sweet and loving a guy as any woman could want.

I slam-dunked the bear into the trash can beside the desk. Or I would have if it hadn't hit the rim and caromed off. I dropped to my knees to retrieve it from under the work table where it landed and started crying—harder than I cried when Troy told me he was leaving me, harder than I cried when they told me he was dead.

Shuddering with the last sobs, I dropped the bear into a desk drawer, got a wad of tissues and blew my nose. I had to get up and do something. Anything.

I tried to focus on business. Without consciously saying it, I had decided to keep the store and to work with Rebecca and Joseph to create a website and generate more business that way. My agent has told me that I sell more books on-line and as e-books than I do through bookstores. I make most of my writing income from my initial fee, but Dave always gets me one percent of the cover price on top of that, so how many books sell and where they sell matters to me. As much as I can get sentimental about bookstores and antique stores, that's not how people shop these days. If Palmetto Antiques couldn't establish a web presence, we might as well shut down.

For an hour or so I browsed websites of other antique stores and made notes of what we might do and what we should avoid doing. Dark backgrounds and lots of flashing/blinking stuff definitely belonged in the latter category. Then I found a store in Bristol, Tennessee, that had a Christopher Lemand nightstand. The asking price took my breath away. The store's posted hours were 10-5 on Sunday. It was 10:30 now, so I called them.

When I explained where I was calling from and what I was interested in, the owner, a woman named Natalie, chuckled.

"Honey, if you're in Lawrenceville, you're at the source of it all, as I'm sure you know."

"Yes. We've just bought several pieces of Lemand furniture at an estate sale."

"Christopher 150?"

I had to recall Wyatt's explanation that the first Lemand had played with the idea that his initials, CL, were 150 in Roman numerals.

"That's right. From a house built in 1892. It was Lemand's own house, in fact."

"Oh, honey, that's like finding a gold mine. What do you have?"

After I described what was sitting in my storeroom, Natalie said, "Whew! Do you honestly realize what you've got? Forget the gold mine. You've found the lost Ark of the Covenant. Do you have somebody to help you price it and sell it?"

"My father-in-law has been in this business for a long time."

"Okay, then, what can I help you with?"

I wanted to lead up to the real purpose of my call. "Well, first, pricing. I think my father-in-law has a good sense for that, but, frankly, I was surprised to see what you're asking for the nightstand on your website."

"Honey, it's all supply and demand. Christopher 150 made such a limited number of pieces. All of them by hand. There's not more than a dozen of his pieces on the market right now in the entire country. The nightstand I've got is the first one I've seen in years."

"But you haven't sold it."

"We just put it out in the store and on the site yesterday. It'll be gone by Tuesday, I guarantee it. You know, let me check something." She fell silent for a minute, then said, "Maureen, are you still there?"

"Yes."

"I was wrong about Tuesday. The nightstand has sold."

"In less than twenty-four hours? For your asking price? To somebody who just saw a picture?"

"Yes, ma'am. Now, is there anything else I can help you with?"

This was going to be the trickier part. I tried to sound casual. "I've been told that the elder Lemand sometimes put secret compartments in his furniture—false bottoms in drawers, that kind of thing. Do you know anything about that?"

"Just that he did it. Oh, my! Have you found one?"

"No, I've just heard the stories." I hoped I could lie convincingly. I never could deceive my mother.

"Well, a couple of them have been found when pieces were damaged. They're devilishly difficult to open if you don't have the instructions. And you're aware, I'm sure, that the factory burned."

"In 1950, yes."

"As far as anybody knows, his papers were destroyed then, too."

I didn't disabuse her of that notion. The fewer people who knew what I knew about the possibility of some of Lemand's papers still being in existence, the better. "What was in the pieces that have been opened?"

"Deeds, stock certificates, that sort of thing. The owners used them as safe deposit boxes, I guess. Then their descendants forgot they were there or didn't know how to open them."

"So, no first editions of Shakespeare or anything like that?"

Natalie chuckled. "No, but the furniture itself is almost in that category. It's such a shame that it's been taken out of the house."

"I agree, but there's nothing I can do about that."

"There is an argument to be made that, this way, more people can enjoy these treasures. Just be sure you've got your stuff secured, hon. When you start publicizing what you've got, you're going to be swamped."

"So you think it might be better to just put a couple of pieces on the market at a time?"

"That's what I would do. You won't drive the prices down that way. I'm really serious, though, about keeping things locked up securely. I don't like to make jokes about it, but this is, quite literally, furniture that some people would kill for."

My conversation with Natalie convinced me that I had to find out who had broken into the store Friday night and what was on the piece of paper he had been looking at. I was willing to bet it was Christopher Lemand Proctor. I went back to the information I had found about him online, downloaded a picture and sent it to my cell phone.

I was about to leave the store when the office phone rang. I found myself talking to a man with a good-ol'-boy accent.

"Ms. Cooper, my name is David Woodward, in Knoxville," he said. "I just had a call from my friend Natalie Parker up in Bristol. She says you have some Lemand furniture for sale."

Damn that woman! "No, Mr. Woodward, that's incorrect."

"You mean you don't—"

"Oh, I have some Lemand furniture, but it's not for sale yet."

"I see. Well, I'm willing to pay whatever you want."

"Mr. Woodward, we're assessing the furniture. My husband ran this store. He died a week ago, and I'm still figuring out how to do this."

That slowed him down for just a moment. "I'm very sorry to hear about your loss, Ms. Cooper." He took a breath. "Could you possibly send me some pictures of the furniture?"

"Not right now. We're setting up a website. When we're ready to proceed, we'll put up some information about the furniture."

"Well, could you take my number and call me before you make any decisions? I will pay top dollar."

I took his number just to get rid of him.

By the time I made a bathroom stop and got back to the office the phone was ringing again. I didn't recognize the number, so I let it go to voice mail. I typed and printed a document and locked up, with Natalie's advice about security ringing in my ears. A determined person could get past my ancient locks, even the piece of plywood the police had fastened into place over my busted back door, with hardly any effort. At least the locksmith was coming tomorrow.

After a quick stop by the house to check on Pepper, I drove over to the Boyds' house. I hoped they were home from church by now, and they were. Mrs. Boyd was ensconced in her spot on the front porch with a blanket over her lap, even though the day was already warm. Her small, frail body just didn't have enough meat on it to insulate her. Her daughter, whose name I couldn't remember, was sitting beside her. Their greeting wasn't exactly cordial, and I could hardly blame them. They didn't offer me a seat, so I stood in front of them, leaning against the porch railing.

"Mrs. Boyd," I began, "I'm really ... embarrassed. My ex-husband and my daughter did not treat you fairly when they bought those pieces of Lemand furniture last week."

"No, they didn't, but that Maxwell woman played her part in it, too."

I nodded, happy to lay some of the blame off on Anna. "I had nothing to do with it, I assure you."

"I know, dear," Mrs. Boyd said.

"But I want to make it right." I reached into my purse and pulled out the document I'd printed before I left the store. "What I'm proposing to do is treat the furniture as on consignment. We'll split the profit from the sale of it fifty-fifty. If that suits you, you can just sign there and your daughter can witness it." *And Rebecca can have a hissy fit when she finds out.*

"Why, that's very gracious of you," Mrs. Boyd said as she signed and passed the document to her daughter. "It's what I would expect from Walter and Martha's granddaughter."

"I'm sorry their great-granddaughter took advantage of you. Even though Rebecca was *not* working for me on that day, I don't want anyone associated with me or my store to have that kind of reputation."

"Are you going to run the store then?" her daughter asked as she handed the agreement back to me. Before returning it to my purse, I glanced at it to remind myself of her name.

"It looks that way, Barbara. I don't plan to be there day-to-day, but I will keep an eye on overall operations, and I'll have a serious talk with Rebecca about how we treat the people we do business with. Now, before I go, I have one question to ask you." I took out my phone and pulled up Proctor's picture. "Have either of you seen this man before?"

Mrs. Boyd shook her head, but Barbara nodded. "I think he was here the day of the sale. I don't remember much about him—he had on sunglasses—but I did notice a tattoo on his right forearm."

"A tattoo? Of what?"

"It was a number—150, I think—with a ribbon winding around it. He showed a lot of interest in the Lemand furniture. I even saw him take a couple of drawers out and look them over, like he was examining how they were made. I told him to be careful with them."

"Did he say anything to you?"

"He said he would check back at the end of the sale and see about buying things we had left over. Several people did that. He gave us a business card."

"Do you still have it?"

"We had a jar by the door for people to drop business cards in. Do you know where that is, Momma?"

"It's in the kitchen," Mrs. Boyd said, "by the phone."

Barbara made a quick trip inside and came back with a jar containing several dozen business cards, which she handed to me. "I have no way of knowing which one is his, I'm afraid."

I started scrounging through the cards. "I think I know his name. I just need to verify the address that I have. I'm not sure the information I got off the internet is up-to-date."

Anybody can print a business cards these days, but Proctor's was a particularly amateurish job. It gave a post office box number, a phone number—which I assumed was a cell—and an email address. The card identified him as "Christopher L. Proctor, Antique Furniture Buyer." But I knew he didn't always buy the furniture. My research on him had turned up his prison record—three convictions for burglary and several more for passing bad checks. Over the past twenty years he'd spent more time in jail than out. At least he didn't demonstrate a proclivity for violence, and his first reaction when I confronted him in my store had been to run. Scott says most B&E guys prefer flight to fight.

As I returned to my car and dropped Proctor's card on the dashboard, I thought what a shame it was to see how some creative people's families decline as the generations go on, or maybe fail to live up to the first generation's accomplishments would be a kinder way to think of it. Isn't each generation supposed to do a little better than the one before it? That's what I hoped for my children. Christopher Lemand's craftsmanship seems to have been passed down to his son but to have diminished in each generation after that, until it was distilled down into the genes of a petty thief.

A petty thief that I needed to talk to. I knew I couldn't go looking for him alone. But I couldn't call Scott because, every other Sunday, he takes his mother to Columbia to see her older sister—her only living sibling—who is in a care facility because of her Alzheimer's. Today was one of those Sundays. Scott asks that he not be disturbed during those visits, and I observe that restriction.

Still, I needed backup. I called Joseph, but it went directly to voice mail. I gave a quick thought to calling Rebecca but dismissed the idea just as quickly. I simply was not up for dealing with her right now. My next thought surprised me—Dolores. Even with her limited mobility, she was accustomed to dealing with people like Proctor. We would at least outnumber him. I called her mother's house. That was where I contacted Joseph if I couldn't get him on his cell, so I had the number in my phone.

Miz Maribelle answered. After a brief exchange of pleasantries that felt strained, almost brusque, she called Dolores to the phone.

"How would you feel about a little road trip?" I asked. "Down to Greenwood."

She lowered her voice. "I'd be happy to drive around the block, as long as it got me out of here for a while."

"What's the problem?"

"We can talk in the car. Are you going to pick me up?"

"Can you be ready in about fifteen minutes? I need to make sure Pepper's got food and water."

"I'll be waiting on the porch."

Dolores was true to her word. In fact, she was down the steps and on the sidewalk. The Hughes' house had a four-foot-high chain-link fence around the small yard and was badly in need of paint, as were most of the houses around them. The fence itself was bent in places, as though things had run into it. This section of town had originally been built for the workers in the textile mill that now stood boarded up two blocks away. My grandmother said she went to school with children who lived here, but since the 1960s "white flight" and the collapse of the Southern textile industry had turned it into a ghetto.

Dolores sighed heavily as she settled into the car. Her mother, wearing an apron over what my grandmother used to call a house-dress, stood inside the screen door, arms folded over her ample chest and her lips pursed tightly. There was no disguising her displeasure about something.

"What's the problem?" I asked as we pulled away from the curb.

"You, apparently, and your daughter."

"What—"

Dolores fastened her seatbelt. "I was telling Mama about us having coffee this morning and talking about Joseph. She got really upset. She says I shouldn't be talking to you about our family business. In fact, she says it would be better if I didn't have anything to do with you. And she's even more upset about whatever's going on between Rebecca and Joseph."

"Is there something going on between them? They've been friends for a long time. They hang out together."

"I think they're moving beyond that. Joseph hasn't come home the last two nights."

I checked the side-view mirror and tried not to give any outward sign of how much that news startled me. Since she was in high school Rebecca had been attracted to "bad boys." She probably got that from me. At least Joseph was one of the nicest bad boys you could want to meet. "Well, they're both adults. There's really nothing we can do about it."

"Just what I'd expect from a white liberal." Dolores shook her head. "Mama says she'll put a stop to it if it's the last thing she does."

"Where is that coming from? Your mother has never been what you'd call effusive or gushy with me, but she's never been rude."

Dolores leaned back against the headrest. "I hate to say it, but in her own way Mama's kind of a racist. She says blacks would be better off if we kept away from whites. She was going on this morning about 'four hundred years of slavery and Jim Crow in this country, and white cops still shootin' black men.'"

"But things have gotten better, don't you think?"

Dolores looked out the window as we drove through downtown, past my store with the policeman standing guard beside the boarded-up rear door, and turned onto the highway to Greenwood. "Better than what? Remember how Zeke and Joseph got here? And nobody ever got arrested."

"You said you never reported the rape. You don't know what might have happened if you had."

"I know exactly what would have happened—nothing."

My grip on the steering wheel tightened. "I have to say I resent that. My grandfather was chief of police here for a long time, you know. He would never—"

She held up a hand. "Let's stop talking about this. I like you, Maureen. You're a nice person, a little naïve maybe when it comes to how people like me live, but you're very generous. And I know you've had your own problems." She looked out the window and took a deep breath, signaling an end to that topic of conversation. Turning back to me, she said, "So, if we're playing Thelma and Louise, where are we going? Didn't you say something about Greenwood?"

I wasn't sure how the movie reference applied. I had no intention of driving off a cliff, although maybe that was an apt metaphor for what I was doing. It would fit in with all the other craziness in my life over the past week. "Yeah, I want to see if we can find a guy named Christopher Proctor."

"Who is he? What do you want with him?"

"I want to know what he knows about Lemand furniture and why he broke into my store."

"You're not planning some crazy-ass stunt, like a citizen's arrest, are you?"

"No, I just want to find him and see if I can talk to him." I handed her the business card that was lying on my dashboard.

"There's no home address on here, just a p. o. box number."

"On the back." I had looked up his mother's address and made a note of it. "His mother died a few months ago. That was her address. I'm betting that's where Proctor will be."

"What do you know about this dude?"

"He's been in and out of jail for years."

"For what?"

"Burglary, writing bad checks."

"He ever whip up on somebody?"

"No, he's never done anything violent."

"And you think he'll, what, invite us in for a chat and a cup of tea?" She mimed drinking tea with her pinky extended.

"Okay, I haven't thought this all the way through. I just want to know where to find the guy. Then I guess we can turn it over to the police. Scott has told me, though, that a B&E ranks pretty low on their list of priorities, especially if nothing was actually taken."

"It probably ranks higher than a white man raping a black woman."

I decided to let that comment pass. I couldn't ease Dolores' pain. In truth, she was probably right about my naïveté. "All I know is that a piece of that furniture fell on Troy and killed him. I don't think it was an accident. Your fingerprints were on the furniture—"

"But—"

"But you have a solid alibi for the time when Troy died. I know. If I thought you had anything to do with his death, you wouldn't be in this car. This guy Proctor is the only other person who's been poking around in the furniture."

"The only other person you know about."

"Granted. I've got to talk to him."

"About what? 'Hey, dude, why'd you break into my store?'"

"That's part of it. I'm hoping I can bargain with him, tell him I won't press charges about the break-in if he'll tell me what he knows about hidden compartments in that furniture."

"This sounds like one of those movies my mama watches, with the woman playing amateur detective who gets into some really stupid situations."

I almost blushed because I like those movies, too. "Hey, I'm not meeting the guy at midnight in the old warehouse, and I'm not coming alone. I'm just going to try to talk with him. At the very least, I'll find out where he is and turn the whole thing over to the police, okay?"

"All right. But, whatever you do, don't say 'What could possibly go wrong?'"

❖❖❖

CHAPTER 17

Greenwood sits near, but not on, the Saluda River. It's not much bigger than Lawrenceville—fewer than 25,000 people. In early June the town hosts a Flower Festival and then a Festival of Discovery the second weekend in July, which emphasizes blues music and barbecue. When Lawrenceville started FoodFest ten years ago, we had to be sure we tucked it in between those two events.

The town is struggling. A big newspaper article a couple of years ago pointed out that Greenwood County had experienced the sharpest economic decline of any county in the entire United States, due largely to the closure of several plants and outsourcing of jobs. That could explain—though not excuse—why someone like Christopher Proctor resorted to crime.

My GPS took us to the Proctor house, in what might generously be called a lower middle-class neighborhood. All of the houses were small and made of red brick, probably constructed in the suburban boom right after World War II. For the Proctor house, which sat on a corner, a narrow sidewalk led from the street to what could barely be called a stoop, much less a porch. Two windows to the left of the front door—one smaller than the other and frosted—suggested a bedroom and a bathroom. A picture window to the right indicated the living room. Given the square shape of all the houses in the neighborhood, there couldn't have been more than three rooms behind what we could see—probably a kitchen, a small dining room, and another bedroom. The driveway, on the right side of the house, was unpaved and empty. One overgrown bush was the only element of landscaping. "Dingy" and "depressing" were the first two words that popped into my mind.

"Cute little place," Dolores said, and, when I saw her expression,

I realized she wasn't being sarcastic. "Nice big yard. And they don't need a fence."

What do the Germans say? *Alles ist relativ?*

"So, what's the plan, Thelma?" Dolores asked.

"Well, Louise, it doesn't look like there's anybody at home. He must have access to a car. He's come to Lawrenceville a couple of times."

"Probably using his mother's car. Are we just going to sit here waiting for him?"

"I don't want to attract attention. That church parking lot in the middle of the block is empty now. We could see the house from there and be less conspicuous."

"How about a bathroom stop first?"

We found a McDonald's near the house and used the restroom. I bought a small drink because I feel like it's cheating to use a business' restrooms without buying something. I certainly don't want people doing that in my store.

"Do you want something?" I asked Dolores.

"Nah, it would just make me have to pee again."

I pulled into the church parking lot and positioned the car so we could see Proctor's house. The driveway was still empty.

"Let me make sure I've got this straight," Dolores said. "This guy is some grandson of the guy who made all that ugly furniture you've got in your storeroom."

Alles ist relativ, indeed. "Yeah, he's the fifth generation from Christopher Lemand, one of the great Arts and Crafts designers of the late nineteenth century."

"But this guy Proctor is a jailbird. Not exactly bringing glory to the family name. Funny how that happens sometimes. Somewhere I read that Shakespeare's three children left nothing of any importance. Of course, the son died when he was eleven."

"He gets a pass then," I said.

Dolores chuckled. "But his twin sister was illiterate. Think about that. The greatest writer in the English language, and his daughter couldn't read or write."

I must have let my amazement show too openly on my face.

"I'm not stupid, Maureen. Prisons have libraries. I had time to read a lot. You may not believe it, but I would've been class salutatorian in high school if old man Martin hadn't given me a C- in biology 'cause I wouldn't let him get in my pants." She picked up my drink out of the cupholder. "Do you mind? Just a sip?"

"Help yourself. If I drink much more, I'll have to pee again. Remember when we were twenty and had to remind ourselves to go once in a while."

Dolores' face turned grim. "You learn to hold it when you're in a jail cell. It was hard for me because one of my kidneys doesn't work so hot. Coupla hard punches during a fight."

"I'm sorry. I keep saying things—"

"Hey, look." Dolores pointed over my shoulder. "Somebody's pulling into Proctor's driveway."

The car was a Cadillac, probably fifteen years old, dark gray and four-door, unmistakably an old lady's car. It was easy to imagine Mrs. Proctor and several of her widow friends going to lunch at Denny's in that car. The man who got out of it, who hadn't been wearing a seatbelt, was the man whose picture I had on my phone and I was pretty sure he was the man who had broken into my store. In the daylight he looked smaller, less intimidating. He wore black jeans and a T-shirt with some Goth-looking design on the front. I couldn't see enough of his arm to spot a tattoo. A cigarette dangled from his mouth and his thinning brown hair was overdue to be trimmed and washed. As he unlocked the front door, he glanced around nervously, like a man in the habit of looking over his shoulder.

"Are we just gonna sit here watching him?" Dolores said.

"Well, I—"

"Pull into the driveway, block his car." She waved her hand. "He parked right up against the garage door."

I started my car and drove out of the church parking lot, wondering how Dolores had taken charge. Maybe because I had no plan. Somebody ought to have one.

I pulled into the driveway and noticed the vanity license plate: CL 150. We were definitely in the right place. As I turned off the engine, Dolores got out and headed for the back of the house, putting a finger to her lips. The gesture wasn't necessary. The hum of an aircon-ditioner window unit would cover any sound she might make. I gave her a minute before I stepped up to the front door and rang the bell.

When Proctor opened the door a crack, he didn't recognize me at first. "What … . Hey, what the hell are *you* doing here?"

"I just want to talk to you, Mr. Proctor."

"How do I know you're not going to shoot me again?"

"I didn't shoot you. The gun went off. I didn't know it was loaded."

"Yeah, like I'm gonna believe that."

"Honestly, I had taken the clip out, but there was one bullet in the chamber."

He was still blocking the door. "Okay. Apology accepted."

"I'm not apologizing, just stating a fact. You had broken into my store—"

Proctor snorted. "With those crummy old locks, 'breaking' is hardly the word."

"It's the word the police would use. And you threw the drawer at me. I've still got a knot on my head." I put my hand on the spot. "That's assault."

"I'd call it self-defense, since you were pointing a gun at me. Now get out of here."

I put a hand on the door to keep him from closing it. "Listen, Proctor, I've done some checking on your background. You've been arrested several times for B&E and bad checks. You're out on parole now. If you're arrested again—and there's an assault charge on top of the B&E—how long would you be in jail?" I tried to push the door open. "I don't want to get you in any more trouble. I just want to talk to you."

"Screw you!" He slammed the door and I could hear him running. Then I heard two people yelling.

"Let go of me!" Proctor shouted, as his voice came closer to the front door.

"Open the damn door!" Dolores' voice boomed.

The door opened and I saw Dolores twisting his left arm behind his back. As I stepped into the house, she pushed him down on the sofa in the living room.

Entering the house was like walking through a time portal back to the 1980s. The walls were taupe. The room was dominated by a sofa and chair with what was once a subdued paisley pattern on them and wood strips down the arms and across the bottom of each piece. A pile of newspapers filled up one end of the sofa and spilled over onto the floor. The only modern piece in the room was a flat-screen TV sitting across from the sofa in front of the window, which was covered by closed drapes. Several cords hung from the TV but didn't seem to be attached to any plugs.

What nearly forced me out of the house, though, was the cigarette stench. There were no ashtrays on the coffee table or the end table by the sofa, but cigarette butts floated in unfinished cups of coffee and smoldered in empty bowls.

"What do you bitches want?" Proctor worked his shoulder as though Dolores had actually hurt him.

"Let's talk about Lemand furniture," I said.

"What about it?" He picked up a pack of cigarettes off the coffee table, pulled one out and lit it, blowing the smoke right at me.

"You're very interested in it, and I want to know why."

"My family made the stuff. What's it to you?"

"A piece of that furniture fell on my husband and killed him. I know you were sniffing around it at the Boyds' house, and you broke into my store to have another look at it. I think the police would be interested in talking to you."

"Wait! Your husband was killed?" He dropped the cigarette into the nearest coffee cup. "I didn't have nothing to do with that. I swear to God. When did that happen?"

When I told him, he relaxed. "I was right here in Greenwood then. And I can prove it."

Dolores snorted. "I'm sure you've got some first-class witnesses to give you an alibi."

From the way his face darkened when he glared at her I wondered if he had a Confederate flag somewhere in the house. "The great state of South Carolina can vouch for me, bitch. I bought a lottery ticket that afternoon over at the Quik-Pik. I played 150 straight, like I always do. And I won five hundred dollars. That's how I got the TV. It's a 40-inch." He gestured toward it with pride. "Haven't even got it hooked up yet. I've still got a copy of the ticket, for luck. The time and the place where I bought it are printed right on the ticket."

Alibis don't get much tighter than that, assuming he bought the ticket himself and didn't have someone else do it. Surveillance cameras could verify that. "150?" I said.

"Yeah. Family tradition. Family joke's more like it. You know, from

CL. I've even got it tattooed on my arm." He stuck out his right arm to show us the tattoo. "In prison you have to get a tattoo or you'll be somebody's bitch." He looked up at Dolores. "Ain't that right?"

"What makes you think I've been in jail?" she said.

"I can see it in your eyes, practically smell it on you. Where's your tattoo?"

"Some place you'll never see."

"Hey," I said, "you guys can reminisce some other time. Right now we need to focus on furniture." I turned to Proctor. "We both know there's something special about that furniture, don't we? That's why you're still trying to get at it."

"Yeah. I knew the first CL made the furniture in that house. I thought maybe I could buy something. When I saw the ridiculous prices they had on it, though, I figured they didn't really want to get rid of it. Everybody in the antiques business knows that people have a 'don't-really-want-to-sell' price."

"Are you in the antiques business?" Dolores asked.

"In a manner of speaking," he said with a smirk.

"But you had found out something about the furniture, hadn't you?" I said. "Probably in your mother's papers."

"Yeah, yeah." He waved a hand in disgust. "Secret compartments and all that shit."

"Look, I won't press charges against you for breaking into the store, if you'll tell me what you know about those compartments."

"Okay. I can show you. There's a nightstand in that bedroom. Take a look at it." He lit another cigarette as he stood.

Dolores and I stepped into a small back bedroom that opened off the living room. Proctor stopped at the door because there wasn't space for all three of us in the room. A window a/c unit blocked the light and made the room feel even smaller, almost cell-like. An un-made single bed and a dresser from the 1970s took up most of the floor space, but next to the bed sat a Lemand nightstand.

"This was my room when I was a kid," Proctor said from behind us. "I spent hours trying to figure out if there was a secret compart-ment in that nightstand because I'd heard my mother and grand-mother talk about it."

"Did your mother have any other pieces?" I asked.

"She had a dresser, but she sold it and bought the car."

The door closed and we heard a key turn in the lock.

"I had a lot of time to think about that nightstand," Proctor said through the door. "My mother used to lock me in there whenever I pissed her off. And I pissed her off a lot."

Dolores shook the doorknob and pounded on the door. "Hey, you asshole, let us outta here!"

"Don't panic," Proctor said. "I'll call the cops to let you out once I'm far enough away from here. I just need to put some distance between me and you bitches." Over the hum of the a/c we heard some bumping and then the slam of the front door.

Dolores' shoulders slumped. "Well, we walked right into that. What are we gonna do?" She started to sit on the bed.

I grabbed her arm. "Do you really want to sit there? I'm sure it's where Proctor's been sleeping and ... God knows what else."

She stood up straight and looked over her shoulder in disgust. "Oh, yeah. Good point. You've got a phone, don't you? Call somebody."

"My phone's in my purse, in the car." I kicked the door. "Damn!"

"You need to borrow my boot?" Dolores said.

"I guess we've got no choice. He did say he would call the cops."

Dolores shook her head in disgust. "Girl, you are too naïve to live. He's not gonna call any cops. He just wanted you to relax and give him some time to get away."

I rubbed my hands on my jeans, a nervous habit of mine. "I'm not used to being locked up and sitting and waiting." As soon as the words were out of my mouth I could see how much they had hurt Dolores. I hugged her. "I'm sorry. I just can't stand the idea of being locked in a small space like this. I know I sound ridiculous saying that to somebody who's been locked in a jail cell, but I'm feeling kind of panicky."

"I'm kinda freaked, too," Dolores said. "Jail cells have bars. You can see through them, stick your hand through them." She put her arms around me. "It's okay. We'll get out of here. We just need to take a minute and consider our options."

I crossed the room and examined the air conditioner. "There's a frame around this thing. It looks pretty solid, but the two of us together might be able to knock it loose." I hit the frame with the palm of my hand and immediately regretted doing so.

"The a/c in the window on the other side of the house had a brace under it," Dolores said. "If this one does too, it's gonna be really hard to move it."

"Do you have any better suggestions?" I snapped.

Dolores drew herself up to her full height. "Hey, don't get testy with me. This wasn't my idea. Let's consider our options."

"Okay." I smacked my fist against the door. "It just bugs the hell out of me that Proctor's getting away."

"Well, we're not gonna catch him. That's for sure. But we know where he lives. We can let the police know. Right now let's just focus on staying calm. We've got time."

I sniffed. "What's that smell?"

We looked at the bottom of the door to see smoke drifting under it.

CHAPTER 18

"Oh, shit!" Dolores cried. "He set the place on fire!" She grabbed the doorknob and jerked on it. The house might have been small, but it was solid.

"Why would he set it on fire?"

"That's a question you ask *after* we're out of here," Dolores said.

"We need a tool." I opened the closet door. "If this was his room when he was a kid, maybe he had, I don't know—boys always have sticks and crap like that."

I hated to touch the clothes hanging in the closet, but I shoved them out of the way and, among several pieces of sports equipment, found the answer to an unspoken prayer—a dinged-up old aluminum baseball bat.

"Seems like boys always have their porn collections, too," Dolores said, looking over my shoulder at the box of magazines on the floor of the closet.

I pulled out the bat and swung at the door. The bat bounced back at me.

Dolores grabbed the bat out of my hands. "Here, give me that. You swing like a girl. Get back."

I retreated to stand by the air conditioner. The door had two panels in it. Dolores broke through the top one on her third vicious swing.

"Go, girl!" I shouted.

She looked over her shoulder at me. "Lot of time in the prison weight room." A couple of more swings gave her enough space to reach through, find the key, and unlock the door.

The smoke was coming from the pile of newspapers on the floor in front of the sofa. They hadn't burst into flames. From the way they were smoldering, I didn't think they were going to actually burn.

"Son of a bitch just tossed his cigarette on the papers," Dolores said.

"No, look. That bowl that he was using as an ashtray—I think he knocked it over when he was picking up his TV." I pointed to the spot where Proctor's prized over-sized TV had sat.

"He took what mattered to him, I guess," Dolores said.

We stamped on the smoldering papers and shuffled them around with our feet. Dolores opened the front door and I saw that my van had been moved to the street and Proctor's car was gone.

"How did he move your car?" Dolores asked.

"I left the keys in it. And my purse. Damn!"

"Well, I hope the keys are still in the car," Dolores said. "Let's get outta here."

"Wait, we can't leave the nightstand," I insisted.

"What—"

I started back toward the bedroom. "It's a Lemand. We can't just leave it."

"It's not yours," Dolores said as she fell into step behind me.

"Somehow I don't think Proctor's going to protest. Give me a hand, before the neighbors notice us."

The nightstand was heavy enough that it took both of us to carry it out to my van. Once we had it in the back and the tailgate down, I got in the driver's seat and reached for the ignition. "Damn!"

"What?" Dolores asked.

"The keys aren't here. He must have taken them."

"Maybe he stuck them in your purse."

I looked in my purse. "Nope. My credit cards are here, and my phone. He did take my cash, though." Two hundred dollars in cash, but I didn't want to mention that.

"He didn't take anything that would leave a trail," Dolores said. "That's what I would have done—I mean, hypothetically. What are we gonna do without your keys? You got a spare hidden somewhere?"

"No, but I've got an app on my phone that will find my keys, if they aren't too far away." I turned on my phone, activated the app, and was relieved to hear my keys chirping from the ditch across the road. I retrieved them and, as we pulled away from the house, I handed the phone to Dolores. "Call 9-1-1. Tell them about the fire. I think we took care of it, but you never know."

"And why do you care? Why should we do anything for that little weasel?"

"Karma's a bitch, Dolores. I don't want to poke her in the eye."

We had gone about ten miles up highway 72, a four-lane road with moderately heavy traffic that would take us to I-26 and back to Lawrenceville, when I glanced in my rearview mirror. "Is that Proctor's car behind us?"

Dolores looked over her shoulder. "Yeah, that's the granny-mobile. He must hate driving that thing, the way it ruins his tough-guy image."

"I thought he was trying to get away from us."

"Looks more like he's tailing us. And gaining on us."

Proctor must have realized that we'd seen him. He increased his speed and was soon close enough that we could see him mouthing what I was sure were obscenities at us.

"Call the police," I told Dolores.

Proctor was right on my bumper now. Dolores told the 9-1-1 operator that we were afraid of a road rage incident. I saw a Burger King ahead of us.

"I'm going to pull in there. At least there will be people around."

Dolores told the operator what we were doing. Proctor pulled in to the space beside us, got out of his car and ran over to mine. "Keep your window up," Dolores said.

"Don't worry about that."

"You crazy bitches!" Proctor shouted, pounding on my window. "I come back to get a piece of cable for my TV and there you are stealing stuff out of my house."

People in the restaurant were watching us and I noticed a couple of them picking up their phones. I hoped they were calling the police and not just recording some video to put on the internet. I was wondering how long I should wait for the cops when I saw flashing red and blue lights pulling into the parking lot. Proctor turned toward his car, but the patrol car parked so that it was blocking both of us. Then a second car pulled in from the other direction.

An officer got out of the first car. "Step away from the vehicle, sir. Keep your hands where I can see them."

Proctor raised his hands enough to show he was unarmed, a gesture I suspected he was familiar with. "These bitches stole something out of my house," he said, jerking his head toward us.

"All right, sir. We'll get it all straightened out. Just step back and calm down."

An officer got out of the other car, his hand resting on his gun. His stocky build reminded me of the cartoonish policeman in a Jackie Gleason movie. The first officer, who looked like he could be July in the policeman's calendar—tall, tan, and muscular—leaned down toward my window as I lowered it. The image of him in a Speedo flashed into my head.

"Are you ladies all right?"

"Yes, we're fine."

"Could I see some ID, please? Driver's license, registration and insurance."

"ID? But—"

"It's just procedure, ma'am. I need to know who I'm dealing with." He turned to the chubby cop. Maybe he would be Santa for December in the calendar. "Bud, would you check him out?" Proctor dug out his driver's license. Officer Santa walked with him to his car so Proctor could get the other documents.

I gave Officer July the things he'd asked for. Dolores wasn't carrying a purse, and she made no move toward a pocket.

"Ma'am," the officer said, "I need to see some ID."

"I don't have a driver's license," Dolores said.

"What's your name and date of birth?"

Dolores told him, and he returned to his patrol car. I've seen the computers and equipment that Scott and his men have in their cars— almost like the cockpit of a jet plane—so I knew he was checking on our records, as the other officer was doing with Proctor.

"They're gonna slap the cuffs on me," Dolores said mournfully.

"You haven't done anything."

"Maureen, I'm an ex-con, I'm black, and, oh, yeah, we just stole a valuable piece of furniture out of that man's house."

"He's also an ex-con, and he stole money out of my purse, in addition to locking us in that room."

Dolores shook her head. "How much money, by the way?"

"Two hundred dollars."

"That's your walking-around money?" Dolores whistled and her eyebrows arched.

"Not all the time. I just happened to have that much on me today." Actually I am uncomfortable if I have less than two hundred dollars in my purse. What Robert calls one of my endearing little eccentricities.

After a couple of minutes both policemen got out of their cars and conferred. Then Officer July leaned down to my window again. "Can you tell me briefly what's going on here, Ms. Cooper?"

I'm not one of those writers who has to sell her work to agents or editors, so I've never mastered the elevator pitch—that two- or three-sentence description of a book that's supposed to sell it before the elevator doors open. And I hate writing synopses. I did try to keep my explanation within limits, but I could tell the moment I began to lose Officer July.

"So, that piece in the back of your vehicle," he said, "is that the Lemonade furniture that you took out of the house?"

"It's Lemand. And yes, that's it. But we thought the house was on fire, and it's too valuable a piece to just let it burn."

"How valuable, ma'am?"

"A thousand dollars, maybe twelve hundred." As soon as the words were out of my mouth, I realized that he was now thinking of a felony.

He stood back from the car. "Ms. Cooper, Ms. Hughes, would you step out of the vehicle, please?"

I could see the fear in Dolores' eyes. I took her hand and whispered, "Do not run! Whatever you do, don't run."

"If I didn't have this damn boot on ... ."

"It's just a misunderstanding. We'll get it straightened out."

"For you it's a misunderstanding. For me it's more jail time." She leaned back against the headrest. "I should've listened to my mama."

Officer July let his hand rest lightly on his gun and Officer Santa came to attention. "Ladies, exit the vehicle, please."

We got out of the car. Dolores had her hands raised. I saw all the phones from the restaurant pointing at us and motioned for her to put her hands down.

"Come around here, please," Officer July said.

I read his name tag. His name was Bensal. I liked Officer July better.

He turned to Proctor. "Mr. Proctor, I'd like to hear your account of what's happened."

Proctor didn't veer too far from the truth, but he emphasized how we had "burst into" his house and created concern for his safety.

"Is that why you locked them in the room?" Officer Santa asked.

"Yeah, just till I could get out of there. I was gonna call the cops to let 'em out. I told 'em that, but I never got the chance. I came back to get something I'd forgotten and there they were, hauling my nightstand out the front door."

"Why didn't you call the police?"

"Because he forgot to mention the two hundred dollars he stole from my purse," I said. "Did you do that because you were concerned for your safety?"

Officer July raised a hand. "Ms. Cooper, let us ask the questions." He turned to Proctor. "Mr. Proctor, Ms. Cooper says you stole two hundred dollars from her purse. Did you?"

"What proof's she got?" Proctor's lip curled. "Serial numbers on the bills?"

"I had four fifty-dollar bills in my purse. See if he has them in his pocket." I wished we could get this settled or go down to the police station. I saw at least four phones inside the Burger King pointed toward us. Damn technology!

"Mr. Proctor, I have probable cause to search you," Officer July said.

"Yeah, okay. I took the money." He made no movement to fish it out of his pocket. "And she stole my nightstand."

The two policemen stepped away from us to confer, but we could still hear them.

"What do you think, Bud?" Officer July said. "How do we handle this?"

"I don't know, Kurt. Nobody's been hurt. It's kind of like a domestic dispute, except we've got two ex-cons with extensive records, breaking and entering, robbery—"

"Could I make a suggestion?" Dolores said. We all turned toward her. "A compromise?"

"Compromise?" Officer July asked.

"Yes. We could drop all charges, on both sides—breaking and entering, unlawful imprisonment, robbery, whatever. If Ms. Cooper is willing, she could let Mr. Proctor keep the two hundred dollars to pay for the door we had to break down when he locked us in. Then, also if Ms. Cooper is willing, she could buy the nightstand."

"Sure, I'd be happy to," I said. "That all sounds good."

"How much?" Proctor demanded.

"I'll give you ... five hundred dollars." I wondered if this was how Rebecca felt when she scammed old Mrs. Boyd.

"It's worth twice that. I heard you say so."

"At retail, probably. But I can't pay you the retail price and then expect to make any money on it. And you didn't pay a dime for it, so it's all profit for you."

"All right, eight hundred."

"I'll give you seven hundred. That's the best I can do."

Proctor screwed up his mouth.

"That'll buy a bunch of lottery tickets," Dolores said.

"You got a checkbook with you?"

"You know I do, since you've been through my purse."

Officer Santa's radio crackled and he went off to answer another call. Officer July hung around while I wrote a check and Proctor signed a statement, witnessed by the officer, making me the legal owner of the nightstand. Then he left. Before I handed Proctor the check, I said, "One more thing."

"Aw, come on, lady!"

I waved the check in his face. "You've got to show us what you know about the secret compartment."

Scott shook his head as I finished recapping my afternoon while we ate supper at my kitchen table. "You know," he said, "there's a reason you leave police work to policemen."

"Yes, I know it wasn't a smart thing to do, but you weren't available. I still don't understand why Proctor reacted the way he did, though. Right from the start I told him I wouldn't press charges about the break-in at the store, if he would just tell me what he knows about the furniture. That was all I wanted. We weren't threatening him in any way." I didn't mention Dolores twisting his arm, literally.

"Guys who've been in jail are easily spooked."

"We weren't police. He knew that."

"Well, he may know more than you suspect, maybe about Troy's death, in spite of his alleged alibi. I want to talk to him."

"But I promised him we'd drop the charges."

"For the B&E and unlawful imprisonment. I want to know what he might know about Troy's death. I'm not going to arrest him, just talk to him."

"He's got an alibi for the time when Troy died."

"Yeah. I have to give him credit. Time stamp on a lottery ticket. That's the first time I've heard that one. It should be easy enough to verify. I'll call the state police and have them put out a BOLO on him. The vanity plate will help. CL 150, you said?" Scott picked up his phone and made the call.

I nodded. "His family is fixated on that 150 thing."

"So," Scott said, putting down his phone, "the nightstand is in your store."

I poured us both some more iced tea. "Dolores and I are going to take a good look at it tomorrow and compare it to the other pieces."

"And you're letting her stay in Troy's apartment." He picked up another piece of barbecue, the last of my leftovers from Zeke's generosity. "Do you think that's a good idea?"

"I don't think it's a *bad* idea. She was a big help today, and she really needed to get away from her mother. Troy wasn't paying rent, so it's not like I'm losing anything."

On the drive back from Greenwood Dolores and I had talked about her mother's reaction to her burgeoning relationship with me. Neither of us could understand why Miz Maribelle objected so vehemently to us getting to know one another. "You'll both regret it," she kept telling Dolores. I decided to offer the apartment to Dolores if she would help me clean it out and would take Troy's place as the super in the house. We had stopped at Walmart to buy some sheets and towels and milk and a few other basics to get her settled in.

"The Ellison garbage people are going to drop a dumpster over there tomorrow. I told Dolores to start making piles of what looks like it could go out. I'll look things over before we actually toss anything, of course."

"What if she finds something and doesn't show it to you? She has done time for burglary, you said."

I sat up straighter. "We've already got everything personal out of Troy's study. It's all in boxes upstairs here. You saw the letter about the child he killed in Afghanistan. The rest of the stuff in the apartment is just ... stuff. I trust her to sort through it for me. I think she really wants to make a new start and reconnect with her family. She's a smart woman. She would have been salutatorian of her class in high school if old man Martin hadn't given her a C because she wouldn't sleep with him."

"How do you know that?"

"She told me."

"And you believe everything she tells you?"

"When I put it together with what I've heard Martin say—just the way he talks about girls and about blacks—yes, I do."

I've never been one of those people who believes I have an infallible "gut instinct" about others, but the work I do requires me to make judgments about people. Over the years I've found that I can get a pretty good sense of someone's character after talking with them for a relatively short time. I've turned down a couple of assignments from Dave because I got a bad "vibe" from the person he wanted me to work with. As things panned out in those cases, I was very glad that I did. Now, for reasons I couldn't explain to myself, Dolores and I seemed to be connecting on some level. I like her, and I trust her.

"You know," Scott said, "she's lived for years by tricking people and preying on them."

"I have yet to see her try to deceive me."

"How would you know, hon?" Exasperation crept into Scott's voice. "You've known her for less than three days, and you met her because she broke into Troy's apartment."

"We've gotten beyond that. She's been very open about a lot of things."

Scott leaned back and laughed. "Why shouldn't she be? You've been *very* generous to your ex-husband's ex-girlfriend—medical expenses, rent-free place to live—"

"Scott, she was raped. Do you have any idea how traumatic that can be for a woman?" I didn't give him time to answer. "For years she's had no support system, cut off from her family, just struggling to survive. Sometimes it can make all the difference in the world if just one person shows you they care."

Scott got up and got more ice from the fridge. "But does caring have to involve buying her a phone?"

"If she's going to do her job as the super in that house, we need to be able to communicate quickly."

As he sat down again Scott shook his head and took another sip of tea. "Maureen, I agree with every word you're saying. But would you mind if I ran a check on her, to see exactly what kind of record she has?"

I shrugged. "Suit yourself. You're going to do it, no matter what I say."

"I just want to make sure you don't get hurt." He reached across the table and I let him take my hand. "If you're letting someone that you know is a convicted felon live in that apartment, you could have some liability for your other tenants. You remember John Tinker, don't you?"

"That poor guy. We always used to say his name rang a bell. Math teacher, wasn't he?"

"Yes, but he also owned a four-unit apartment building on the north side of town. Ten years ago he rented one apartment to a guy who was a registered sex offender, but John didn't check and so didn't know about it. The guy molested a child who lived in one of the other apartments. I was one of the arresting officers. The tenants sued John. They claimed he was negligent and had endangered them."

"I don't see what—"

"Maureen, the court found for the plaintiffs. Tinker lost the building and just about everything else he owned."

CHAPTER 19

"Knock, knock," I heard Dolores say through the screen door on the back porch on Monday morning. "You up?"

"Oh, hi. I thought I was picking you up this morning."

"I felt like walking." She opened the door and came into the kitchen.

"Even with your foot?"

"It's a lot better. I'm thinking about taking this boot off today."

I put the orange juice back in the fridge. "Why don't you wait and see what the doctor says? You've got an appointment tomorrow, don't you?"

"Okay, yes, Mother," she said with a laugh.

"Have you had some breakfast?"

"Yeah, I'm good."

"All right. Just let me brush my teeth and I'll be ready to go." When I came out of the bathroom I picked up my purse and keys.

"Would you be interested in walking over?" Dolores asked. "I'd like the exercise."

"If you feel like it, that would be fine. Pepper will probably want to go with us."

"We'll look like a coupla gimps."

"Did you sleep all right?" I asked as we started down the steps with Pepper between us.

"Better than I have in a long time. Thanks again for everything. In case I haven't said it enough times already."

"Please, don't say it again. You're helping me out a lot by keeping an eye on things in that house. I called my tenants last night and told them you would be there."

"Yeah, Connie and her husband came down and introduced themselves."

As we reached the street and turned toward town, Dolores said, "I started going through some of Troy's stuff last night."

"Still looking for that letter you wrote him?"

She nodded. "No luck, though."

"Did you find anything worth keeping?"

"Nothing yet. I've made a few piles for you to look through and put the rest into garbage bags."

"I'll want to take a quick look through those, too."

We had reached the town square. With the back door of my store boarded up, we had to go in the front. As I found my key, Dolores said, "Would it be all right if I went up to Zeke's place for a little bit? I want to see how he's recovering from FoodFest and how Mama's doing."

"You don't have to ask my permission," I said.

"Well, you've done so much for me—"

"And not one bit of it has made you obligated to me. In fact, I'm obligated to you for all the help you're giving me. I'll see you later. Give my best to Zeke."

Dolores gave Pepper a parting scratch between his ears and set out for Zeke's, another five-minute walk. Without Pepper to slow her down, she really did seem to be moving more comfortably.

As soon as Pepper and I entered the store he stopped, his ears up. "What's wrong, boy?" He took a few steps.

I headed straight for the office and got Troy's gun out of the desk drawer. This time I made sure the clip was in it.

"Is there somebody in here, boy?"

Pepper barked several times. I heard someone in heavy shoes trotting down the stairs from the second floor. *It must be Joseph,* I thought. *He must have spent the night here for some reason. I'll have to make sure he tells me when he's going to do that.* I opened the drawer to put the gun back but kept it in my hand because I didn't understand why Pepper was still growling. He knows and likes Joseph.

Then I heard a voice, "Hey, mutt. It's okay. Be cool."

Christopher Proctor was in the store. Again!

Proctor stopped at the door of the office and raised his hands when he saw the gun pointed at him. "Geez, lady! What is it with you and that damn gun?"

"What is it with you and breaking into my store, Proctor? Did you come to steal your nightstand back?"

"No. I came to ask for your help."

"My help?" I laughed. "Don't move. I'm going to call the police."

"Thank you. That's exactly what I want you to do."

Scott and a uniformed officer arrived in less than five minutes. I put my gun away and Proctor lowered his hands. He told Scott he just wanted to talk. I suggested we go to the employee lounge on the second floor, where there would be room for all of us.

"Yeah, that sofa's pretty comfortable," Proctor said. "That's where I spent the night."

Scott glared at me. "The locksmith is coming tomorrow," I said, "and the alarm guy will be here today." That seemed to mollify him.

Pepper stopped at the foot of the stairs. "You guys go ahead," I said. "Pepper and I will take the elevator."

"All right," Scott said, when we were settled in the lounge and a recorder had been turned on, "what do you want to talk about? And why couldn't you go to the police in Greenwood?"

"Because they're after me. Or, one of them is after me."

"Does this have anything to do with our run-in yesterday?" I asked. "I thought we settled that."

"No, this is something else. But it does have to do with the Lemand furniture."

"Why don't you just tell us what's going on?" Scott said. "We'll hold the questions." He looked straight at me and I sat back and made a zipping motion across my lips.

"Okay," Proctor said. "I don't suppose I could smoke in here." When I shook my head he said, "Figures. I did smoke in the bathroom last night. Kept the exhaust fan on, though." He clasped his hands on the table in front of him, almost as though he was about to pray. "Okay. Three months ago I get out of jail and come home. This guy shows up at the door. Big guy. He's a cop, a lieutenant. Name's Dunmoore, Brian Dunmoore."

I gasped so loudly that both men turned to stare at me. Pepper's ears went up.

"What did he want?" Scott asked.

"He says he wants me to do him a favor. And when a cop wants a favor from a guy like me, I listen. He says he knows I'm related to Christopher Lemand. There's this house in Lawrenceville that's full of Lemand furniture, and he was interested in it. I said, yeah, my great-great-grandfather built that house and lived in it."

"That's where your grandparents lived, isn't it, Maureen?" Scott asked.

I nodded. "The whole time I was growing up, until my grandfather was killed twenty years ago."

Scott turned back to Proctor. "Okay, so what was so interesting about this house?"

"Dunmoore said he had heard that Lemand sometimes put secret panels and stuff in his furniture. Did I know anything about that? I told him I did. Did I know how to open them? I showed him the nightstand in my room and how I could open that. He almost pissed himself."

"Did he tell you why he was so excited about that?" Scott asked.

"He used to be on the police force here, when he was just out of high school. He said the chief then was on the take."

Scott held up his hand to stop me. I was about to explode. Pepper sat up, alert to my anxiety. "Maureen, stay cool," Scott said. "Let me handle this."

He turned to Proctor. "Did he say he *thought* the chief was on the take?"

"No, he was definite. He said the chief was on the take from drug dealers, and he thought he was hiding the money in his house, the house my great-great-grandfather built. He had seen an ad about a big sale at that house. He wanted to hire me to see if I could figure out where the panels were and how to open them. If I could, he would buy the furniture and he would give me a share of whatever was in there. I told him I didn't want to take the risk. If I got caught, I would be back in jail and probably wouldn't get out for a long time. It wasn't worth it, just to go looking for chump change."

"How did Dunmoore react to that?"

"He called me a stupid little turd. He said he'd been getting five hundred a week, and he was sure the Chief had it hidden in his house."

"But you didn't find anything?"

"No."

I was glad to hear that. My grandfather could not have been a dirty cop.

"The problem was, I didn't find anything because I couldn't open any of the panels I found. The trick that opened my nightstand didn't work on any of the furniture in that house."

"You're sure there were panels."

"Yeah, I could see where the mechanisms were. I think maybe the old man rigged them one way for that set of furniture but differently for other pieces. The nightstand I had didn't come from that house. I couldn't figure out anything about the furniture from that house."

"You certainly tried hard enough," I said. "You went to the sale, you broke in here twice, and you broke into Mrs. Boyd's garage."

"That garage door was open," Proctor said. "I didn't break into anything, and Dunmoore gave me a key to this place. Not like I really needed one, not with these crappy locks."

I couldn't help myself. "Dunmoore had a key?"

"Yeah. He said he worked here when he was in high school. The owner then gave keys to all of his employees and never took them back." He took the key out of his pocket and laid it on the table. I grabbed it.

"And nobody *ever* changed the locks," Scott said slowly. With that scolding done, he turned back to Proctor. "So, why have you come here now?"

Proctor scratched his chest. "Dunmoore doesn't believe that I didn't find anything. He thinks I'm holding out on him. He made me come back in here a second time. He was outside, waiting on me that time. He had the car. When he heard Annie Oakley here shooting at me, he took off. I was expecting him to be there, but I had to run like hell. Now he's threatening to kill me. I sure can't go to the Greenwood police."

"Did he say why he was so sure Chief Cooper was taking money from drug dealers?" Scott asked.

"He said he was in on it. Like he told me, he got a cut."

I jumped up from my chair and Pepper stood up with me. "That's a bald-faced lie! My grandfather would never do that." I loomed over Proctor.

Proctor drew back. "Lady, all I know is what Dunmoore told me. You want to know more, you gotta talk to him."

"Maureen, sit down, please," Scott held out his hand as though he would push me down. "We'll certainly try to talk to Dunmoore."

But I wasn't going to be shushed. I leaned forward, my face as close to Proctor's as his cigarette stench would let me get. "If he was getting money from the Chief, why did Dunmoore leave?"

Proctor ran a trembling hand through his thinning hair. His craving for a cigarette was growing stronger by the minute. "He said him and the chief got into a big argument and the chief told him to get out of town and not come back."

"Did he say what the argument was about?"

"No." Proctor screwed up his mouth and his tone turned sarcastic. "It's not like me and him are best buds. He told the chief he would go if he got some money. He met the chief at his house and the chief gave him $20,000."

"That's impossible." My voice rose to a squeak. "Where would my grandfather get $20,000?"

Proctor smirked. "I don't know, but you don't just walk up to an ATM and take out that kind of money. Believe me, I've tried. He said the chief handed him an envelope with the money in it."

An envelope. That's what the x-ray of the drawer showed.

"So what do you want?" Scott asked.

Proctor turned serious, holding out his hands to plead. "I want to get out of South Carolina. I've got an aunt in Ohio, outside of Columbus. I could go there, but I'm sure Dunmoore has put out a BOLO on my car. I wouldn't get to the state line. I drove every back road I could think of just to get here last night. I'll never make it to the airport without getting stopped."

"Before we can do anything for you," Scott said, "I'm going to have to check out your story. I think I should take you into protective custody, just until tomorrow."

Proctor drew back, his hands raised in protest. "No way. You put me in a jail cell, and you'll find me hanging in it tomorrow morning."

"Here in Lawrenceville? I don't believe—"

"Dunmoore's got connections all over the place. I've talked to a coupla guys I was in jail with. That's why I locked this broad and the other piece of jail bait in the bedroom and ran. I figured they was gonna call the police, and that would mean handing me over to Dunmoore."

"I can't just let you walk out of here," Scott said.

"Why not? You've got my statement. Print it and I'll sign it. You've got a witness." He pointed to me.

Scott shook his head. "Not until I can verify some things. But, if I can't put you in protective custody at the jail, where are you going to stay for a day or two?"

Proctor spread his hands, palms up. "How about here?"

"What?" I sputtered. "Here? You can't be—"

"It's not such a bad idea," Scott rubbed his chin. "We can put an officer in here—"

"But my family will be in here. I'll have customers in and out." *I wished.* "You want me to expose them to whatever Dunmoore might do?"

"If Dunmoore knew where Proctor was, he'd probably be dead by now." He turned to Proctor. "No offense intended."

"None taken. You're absolutely right. One reason I came here was because I didn't think it would occur to him that I would. I mean, why should you people help me?"

"I can't think of one good reason." I sat back and folded my arms.

"Maureen, I believe we can make this work," Scott said. "We often keep people in safe houses. I think we can manage it for one night. We'll have an officer inside and a couple on surveillance outside."

"Bad idea." Proctor shook his head. "Dunmoore's a cop. He'll spot your guys outside, and he'll wonder why you're watching this place. And I don't want just any of your guys in here with me. You don't know who you can trust."

"Then who—"

"You, Detective. I want *you* to stay here overnight."

Scott rolled his eyes. "All right. If it'll help bust a crooked cop ... ."

"And somebody needs to put my car out of sight." Proctor laid his key on the table. "It's parked behind that coffee shop across the street."

Scott picked up the key. "There's a service station a couple of blocks from here. I know the owner. We can park it in one of the bays. We'll get you to the airport tomorrow. What about a plane ticket?"

When Proctor hesitated, I said, "I paid you $750 for that night-stand yesterday."

"I haven't exactly had a chance to get to a bank, even if one was open on Sunday night. Hey, what'll you give me for my TV set? You know it's brand new. I haven't even got it hooked up yet. It's in the trunk of my car. In fact, I'll sell you the stinkin' car."

"I can't believe this." I was fuming as Scott, Pepper and I took the elevator downstairs, leaving Proctor ensconced in the employee lounge. "The guy breaks into my store twice and now he's a ... a house guest. What next? Will he make me remove all the red M&Ms from the candy dish?"

Scott blinked. "You have a candy dish?"

"That was sarcasm, dear. Just sarcasm. The guy's acting like some prima donna."

"I don't think he'll give you much trouble. You heard me tell him that I'll throw him in jail if he does. That's his greatest fear right now."

We went into the office, and I closed the door behind us, my hands shaking. "Could he possibly be telling the truth? Could my grandfather have been taking money from drug dealers?"

"Yeah, I find that hard to believe. Every day I walk past that memorial to him in the Justice Center. He might as well have a halo over his head."

Scott was right. The foyer of the Justice Center is dominated by a large bronze plaque that memorializes my grandfather. The image of him is a good likeness, surrounded by a circle of stars, with his name and the dates of his life and his service under the image. How could the kind, generous man I grew up loving as Papa have betrayed everything he stood for?

I sat down on the small sofa that Troy kept in the office and looked up at the ceiling in utter disbelief. I would have been less shocked if that ceiling fell on me, like so many facets of my life seemed to be crashing around me. Pepper must have sensed my anxiety; he laid his head on my knees. I petted him without thinking. The questions swirled. Had my grandfather been a dirty cop? Had my ex-husband been murdered? Had he really gotten his girlfriend pregnant? One thing I knew for a fact: he and our daughter had scammed an old woman out of thousands of dollars.

Then it hit me—what if Troy knew, or suspected, that there was money hidden in the Lemand furniture? Once he had it in his store, he could have taken all the time he needed figuring out how to open the panels. And he wouldn't have to report anything he found to anyone. I put my hands on my head, as if I could keep it from spinning or exploding. I felt like it could do either at any moment.

Scott was on the phone to his office. He asked someone for information on Brian Dunmoore, then listened and made notes. "Okay, thanks. I'll be back over there in a half hour or so." Hanging up, he swiveled his chair to face me. "So, Dunmoore was on the force here for four years after he finished high school. Exemplary record. Made sergeant in record time. Couple of letters of commendation—from your grandfather. Then he left with no explanation. He's been in Greenwood ever since."

"When did he leave?"

When Scott gave me the date, I gasped.

"What's the matter?" he asked.

"Look, I don't know how much I should tell you. Dolores told me some things, and I feel like it was in confidence—"

Scott rested his arms on his knees and leaned toward me. "You're not a priest or a lawyer, Maureen. You can't claim confidentiality. If you know something that might help us understand what's going on, you need to tell me."

"Okay. Just don't say anything to anybody else, please." I took a deep breath and scratched Pepper under his chin. "She told me that Brian Dunmoore raped her, right here in this store. That's when she got pregnant with Joseph. I don't know the exact date, but I do know that Troy found out and beat Dunmoore up. That all happened just a couple of days before Dunmoore left here."

Scott leaned back in the chair. "So it sounds like your grandfather made him leave and he demanded some money to keep quiet."

I took the piece of paper Scott had been writing on and studied the dates. "But why? If he and Dunmoore were involved in drug trafficking, what difference would it make if Dunmoore raped Dolores?"

"Assuming the worst," Scott said, "that your grandfather was involved—and it pains me to even think that—maybe he was worried that, if Dunmoore was accused of rape, there would be an investigation that might stumble onto the drug business. Or Dunmoore might throw your grandfather under the bus to save himself. Your grandfather had to shut Dunmoore up—short of killing him—and get him out of here."

Suddenly a distant memory thrust itself forward in my brain. "Who was chief of police in Greenwood at that time?"

Scott checked. "A guy named Parker. Why?"

"He was one of my grandfather's best friends. When I was a kid, my family used to rent a place on Lake Murray for a couple of weeks in the summer. All kinds of people would come and stay for a few days. One of them was the chief of police from Greenwood. My grandmother talked about what great friends they were, how he and my grandfather would do anything for one another."

Scott rubbed his chin. "For your grandfather, sending Dunmoore to Greenwood was the next best thing to putting him in jail. Dunmoore would know that his every move was being watched."

"Couldn't he just get a job somewhere else?"

"Not without a recommendation. And I'll bet he would never get—"

The bell over the front door jingled and a man's voice said, "Hello?"

I opened the office door and saw a young man in a khaki uniform that identified him as coming from the security company I had contacted.

"Hi," he said. "Ms. Cooper? I'm Mark. I'm here to assess your security situation."

CHAPTER 20

We ran into a traffic jam at the front door, made even more cumbersome by Pepper trying to check everybody out. Mark was unloading his equipment. Dolores, Joseph, and Rebecca came in as Scott was leaving. He promised to be in touch later in the day. "If Proctor gives you the least bit of trouble," he said, "just call me."

"Or I could sic Pepper on him."

Scott petted the dog's broad back. "This ol' sweetheart? Nah."

I told Mark to look at whatever he needed to while I talked to the Three Musketeers. Rebecca was wearing a pair of black jeans and a gray blouse, reasonable attire for the manager of an antique store, I suppose. Joseph looked ready for work in a pair of jeans and a blue T-shirt.

"They were at Zeke's," Dolores said, "helping him get set up after FoodFest."

I didn't want to think about where Rebecca and Joseph might have spent the night. They were adults, and it wasn't any of my business. I took the three of them—four, if I counted Pepper—through the swinging doors to the work area at the back of the store, out of Mark's hearing. As I explained who Proctor was and what he was doing here, everyone's eyes got bigger and bigger.

"Take money from drug dealers? Grandpa Cooper wouldn't have done that." Rebecca was as adamant as I was. "Not in a million years." She was just a toddler when my grandfather was killed, but she knew the legend.

Dolores' expression showed the conflict she was feeling. "Dunmoore? He's around here?"

"That's what Proctor says. I'm sorry you have to hear that."

"Who's Dunmoore?" Joseph asked.

He's your father. I wished it could be said that simply, but there was nothing simple about this situation. *You've got a crooked cop and a rapist for a father. For part of that at least, I can feel your pain.*

"He's a guy I had some trouble with in high school," Dolores said quickly. I was impressed with how level she kept her voice. "He left town a long time ago."

"Is this Brian Dunmoore you're talking about?" Joseph asked.

Dolores gasped. "What do you know about him?"

"He coaches the Greenwood team in my Wooden Bat League. We've played them a couple of times this summer. He coaches third base, so we've talked some." Joseph plays third base and still has aspirations of getting a professional contract.

"Talked about what?" Dolores' voice grew tense.

"When he heard my name, he said he knew you and Mr. McKenzie when you were all in high school. He played football and baseball with Mr. McKenzie. He seems like a nice guy. He knows a scout for the Braves. He said he'd tell him about me, get him to come see me play. I can't believe what you're saying about him."

"Maybe it's a ... different Brian Dunmoore," I said lamely.

Dolores, with her hand over her mouth, turned and ran toward the office.

"What's wrong with her?" Joseph's look of consternation seemed genuine. I couldn't detect any sympathy, though.

In the awkward silence that followed, Rebecca looked around at the Lemand furniture. "So you're saying there might be money hidden in this furniture?"

I nodded. "Sadly, that looks like a real possibility, so we can't sell even one piece of it until we figure this out. I want you and Joseph to move all of this stuff up to the third floor, to get it as far away from potential thieves as possible." *Ignoring the fact that a very potential thief was comfortably lodged in our employee lounge at that moment.*

Rebecca rolled her eyes. "That'll take all morning!"

I patted her cheek a little harder than I needed to. "If you're going to manage the store, dear, you have to put in the effort. Get Proctor to help you. He's got nothing to do but go in the bathroom and smoke."

Scott had told Proctor not to show himself outside the building for any reason. I would have to fumigate the restroom, but I had to agree with Scott.

I ticked items off on my fingers. "Ask him what tricks he's tried to get the panels open. Get him to show you where the mechanisms are—anything he can tell you. Put blue tape at the right spots. Make notes. If we know where to start looking and can eliminate things that don't work, that'll save us time when we're trying to figure it out."

Leaving them to start working, Pepper and I set out to find Dolores. As we got close to the office I heard muffled sobs coming from the women's restroom. The door was locked, but I tapped softly.

"Dolores? Hon, can we talk about it?"

After a moment of hesitation, the door opened. I stepped into the restroom, closing the door in Pepper's face. "Sorry, boy. Ladies only. Unless you identify as—"

Dolores threw her arms around my neck. "My God, Maureen!" she managed to get out between sobs. "That son of a bitch ... is talking to Joseph ... like they're ... great friends!"

I returned her hug. "I know, I know. It's not Joseph's fault. He doesn't know."

"What if ... Dunmoore knows?"

I hadn't thought about that. Realizing how old Joseph is and when Dolores had been raped, Dunmoore could have done a little figuring and come to the conclusion that Joseph might be his son. As a police officer, he would have access to birth records and any other information about Joseph that was available. "If he does, then he's just sick. He's playing with you. Don't you think you'd better tell Joseph everything before this goes any further?"

"No!" She took a deep breath. "No, no. I will not. What I'll do is kill that bastard if I ever get the chance. It's what I should have done years ago."

I took her firmly by the shoulders. "Look, there's no need for that kind of talk. What can I do to help you get through this?"

"I need to keep busy." She clenched her fists. "And I want to hear anything else Joseph says about Dunmoore."

"Okay. I want to do some serious rearranging in the front of the store. Are you up for that?"

"Physical labor. Yeah, that sounds like just what I need."

As Dolores, Pepper, and I walked past the office, Mark waved a hand, signaling for us to come in. He held up the tablet on which he'd been making notes.

"I've finished looking over your video monitoring equipment and I've got some recommendations." He was admiring the recording device in the office. The recorder was inside a storage cabinet on the back wall. Since I thought it didn't work, I hadn't even looked at it since Troy's death. "I haven't seen one of these in a long time," he said. "Talk about a dinosaur, but one that lives and breathes."

"If someone had offered to sell my husband a dinosaur, I'm sure he would have bought it." I made a sweeping motion with my arm around the store. "As you can see, he was fond of old things, even if they didn't work. He thought just having the cameras up where people could see them might make them think twice about stealing something. He meant to try to fix it when he had time."

"Excuse me, but you're talking about him in the past tense—"

"He was killed last Monday when a heavy piece of furniture fell on him."

"Oh, I'm so sorry," Mark muttered.

That's a real conversation stopper, and I regretted dropping it on the man. "Are you telling me that he fixed this thing?"

"Somebody did." He sounded relieved to get back to business.

"How can you tell?"

Mark pointed to a green light on the recorder. "It's working right now." He touched a button and the light went off.

"You mean it's been recording?" I looked at the thing in disbelief. "For how long?"

"I don't know. You've got a motion sensor out there, so it would go on and off." He punched a button and a VHS tape popped out of the device. "With these old machines, they record until they reach the end of the tape, then they rewind and start taping over whatever's on there. You do lose the older data."

"How long would it cover?" Dolores asked. I figured she was worried that her visit to the store on the day Troy died might have been recorded.

"Depending on the speed it's set on, you could have from two to six hours of recording. This one's set so that you should have six hours and it's almost at the end. Do you want to see what's on this tape?"

I wasn't sure I wanted to. What if it showed Troy and Anna Maxwell? But what if it showed something connected to Troy's death. "Maybe I should call Scott," I said. "This might have evidence relating to Troy's death on it." I hit my speed dial.

"Hey, Maureen," he said. "What can I do for you?"

"We just found out that Troy had gotten the security camera working. It looks like there's something on the tape. Do you want to see it?"

"Certainly. I'll be there in five minutes. Don't do anything with it until I get there."

"He's coming right over," I told Mark.

"We'll need a TV and an old VCR," Mark said.

"We've got a few of those, back in this corner." I led him and Dolores across the store, to where Troy kept everything from 1930s radios to TVs and stereos from more recent years.

Mark found a big, boxy TV with a VCR built into it. "This should do nicely." He plugged it in and we waited for Scott to arrive, which he did in record time. He looked the tape over and made a notation on it before handing it back to Mark.

"We had a lot of people in here during FoodFest," I said as Mark inserted the tape. "Most of this footage may be from the last couple of days."

"Do you want me to rewind?" Mark said. "Or shall we just play it to the end?"

"Just run it to the end. Nobody makes these tapes anymore. I'm curious to see where Troy got this one."

"I'll fast-forward it," Mark said.

The few remaining minutes on the tape were taken up by the end of an episode of "Friends," a show that Troy enjoyed but I never could get into. I guess every guy in that era was in love with Jennifer Anniston. Then the tape rewound itself and started to play. We watched a few minutes of customers in the store and Troy moving around. Seeing him, alive and active, brought a lump into my throat.

"Notice the time stamp on the bottom left," Mark said. "This was a pretty sophisticated piece of equipment for its day. Your husband did a nice job of fixing it."

"There are several cameras in the store," Scott said, "but all of these shots are from one angle."

"He had just the one camera hooked up." Mark pointed in the direction of the front door. "It picked up people right after they came in and followed them part of the way across the store."

On the screen the front door of the store opened and a large man wearing a plaid shirt, jeans, and a baseball cap entered. He went through the store and into the back. Dolores gave a quick gasp, but when I looked over at her she kept her eyes on the screen. The video stopped, then started again as the man came back through the store and left, with Pepper trailing him and barking. He grabbed the dog's collar, dragged him into the office, and closed the door. The entire time, the bill of his cap kept us from getting a clear look at his face. I noticed this time that he favored his left leg. He didn't exactly limp, but he did have what people around here call "a hitch in his git-along." The time-stamp showed the date and approximate time when the police said Troy had died.

Had I just seen the man who killed Troy?

I stopped the tape. "There's no way you can get a better look at his face?"

"No, ma'am. I can't punch a couple of buttons on a computer and magically run a facial recognition scan, like they do on TV. That is possible, but you need much more sophisticated equipment and software than I've got. And with a tape this old, recorded on this slow speed, it would be difficult to get high enough resolution to positively identify somebody."

"Do you have anything like that?" I asked Scott.

Before he could answer Dolores said, "I don't need high resolution. That was Brian Dunmoore."

"Are you sure?" Scott asked.

"I'd know that walk anywhere." She folded her arms protectively over her chest. "I need to sit down." She turned toward the office.

Mark took the tape out of the VCR and placed it in Scott's waiting hand.

"I'll have our techs look at it," Scott said. "We may be able to clean up the image, just to corroborate Dolores' identification, but we need to keep this as part of our investigation."

"It looks like you've got a lot going on here today," Mark said, and I wanted to compliment him on his sensitivity. "Should I come back some other time?"

"No. I need to get this done now. So, what kind of system would you recommend?"

Scott left and Mark had no trouble selling me a state-of-the-art security system, with cameras, motion sensors, and alarms covering the entire store, front to back and top to bottom—everywhere but the restrooms. No more video tapes, just a DVR that would record for what sounded like an infinite number of hours. Probably more than I needed, but I wasn't thinking clearly.

"I'll get most of the preliminary work done today and tomorrow," Mark said. "It'll be easier since there's not much wiring involved with these new systems and you don't expect me to hide it."

"It'll never be noticed in this place."

"If you'll call me when that busted rear door has been fixed, I'll come back to hook up an alarm there."

I knew he wanted to ask what had happened but didn't think he should.

"The last few days have been hectic around here," I said.

The whole rest of the day was just as hectic. Mark worked around us, between us, and over us, doing preliminary work for a new security system. He would not actually finish the installation until next week. Wyatt arrived and gave his blessings to the expense for the security system. "If you've got Lemand furniture in here, you need absolutely the best protection you can get."

He pitched in to help Rebecca and Joseph move the furniture to the third floor. Like the second floor, the third was open, with a railing running around it, giving the whole store the feeling of an atrium or the gallery after which it was named.

Joseph leaned over the railing and called down to me. "Hey, Ms. Cooper, this railing is really in bad shape." He wiggled a piece of it.

"Okay. I'll call a carpenter. Because of her foot, I told Dolores she should stay on the first floor and staff the register. We actually did have a few customers who had heard Artemisia endorse us.

The most requested item was one of the singer's autographed pictures. I didn't think we had any left, but Rebecca, coming out of the bathroom, heard what one woman was asking for as a birthday gift for her daughter and came to the front of the store. "Just a second," she said. She went into the office and returned with one of the pictures Artemisia had brought with her, signed in advance. It was protected in a plastic sleeve with the price tag on it. My eyes widened when I read "$50." That seemed to cool the woman's enthusiasm too.

"That's a lot," she said.

"It's what you would pay if you ordered it online," Rebecca countered, "and you would have shipping costs as well."

"How do I know it's real?"

Rebecca took out her phone and showed the woman a video of Artemisia signing items in the store on Friday evening. "And it comes with a Certificate of Authenticity," she said. "We guarantee that it's genuine." She pulled a sheet of paper from behind the picture. "There's a number on the back of the picture that matches the number on the certificate."

I picked up a marker and drew a line through the $50. "Since it's for your daughter's birthday, we'll discount it." Steam was practically spewing out of Rebecca's ears as I wrote $25.

After the woman left, quite satisfied, with the picture and the certificate in their protective sleeve, I took Rebecca into the office. "Fifty dollars? Certificate of Authenticity? Where did you get all that?"

"Mother, I'm *really* tired of you questioning my business acumen."

"To me it looks more like you have a gift for ripping people off."

She pulled a folder containing a dozen or so pictures out of a file drawer and slapped them down on the desk. "I held back a few of the pictures before I put them on the table for her. In that mob scene on Saturday nobody missed them. I printed the certificates last night at home. The signature is hers. That's no rip-off. This is the price you have to pay for an autographed picture of that ... that child. Just go online and look. No, wait, I'll save you the trouble." She picked up her phone and showed me several sites offering exactly what we had—even the same photograph—at fifty dollars.

"A lot of the people who paid five dollars here on Saturday are probably already selling their pictures online or congratulating themselves for ripping us off, but that's the highest price Artemisia would let me put on them."

"When were you going to tell me you had these?"

"I was going to put a poster in the window and put them out a few at a time. Maybe sell some on our web site, if you ever let Joseph set one up."

All I could do was shake my head. "Okay. I'm sorry, hon. I didn't realize—"

"There is *so* much about this business that you don't realize, Mother." She slammed the office door as she went back to help Joseph and Wyatt move the furniture upstairs.

I was surprised when Proctor bestirred himself from the sofa in the employee lounge and offered to help as well. Then I realized he just wanted another opportunity to examine the furniture. I couldn't entirely object. He probably had a better chance of figuring out how to open the panels than we did. After all, he'd done it once, we never had. We would have to make sure he wasn't left alone with it overnight.

After his first trip up in the freight elevator, though, Proctor refused to get back in it. "Listen to that thing. It creaks and shimmies like it could fall at any minute."

I had to chuckle. "You don't wear a seatbelt in your car," I said, "but you're worried about an elevator falling? I mean, how often does that happen, compared to a car accident?"

"It only has to happen once, lady. When was the last time that thing was inspected?"

"Actually, it never has been inspected," Wyatt admitted. "Because it's a freight elevator and not open to the public, we're not required to have it inspected. It's recommended, but the inspection costs a hundred dollars, so Troy and I decided to save some money at that point."

"I'll walk," Proctor said. And he did. He helped load the elevator while it was sitting solidly on the ground floor, then took the stairs up to the third floor, where he helped move the furniture once the others had gotten it off the elevator.

When all the pieces were safely stowed, Joseph watched while Proctor examined each one. Whenever he spotted what he thought was a mechanism to open a panel, Joseph would put a piece of blue tape on it. The job was completed by lunch time, but Proctor still claimed he couldn't open anything.

As we all sat around the table in the employee lounge, eating sandwiches from Pam's shop across the street, I thought, *Three of the five people sitting with me right now—working with me—have served time in prison. My daughter has done some decidedly shady things, and I have no idea what my father-in-law may have done. But why should I be surprised? My own grandfather may have been one of the most corrupt men in the history of this town.*

My gaze must have lingered too long on Proctor, who was sitting across the table from me. "Why are you looking at me?" he asked.

"Oh, I was just thinking ... that your great-great-grandfather was ... a clever man. All those secret panels."

"I guess." He took another bite of his sandwich. "Sometimes I wonder if my ability to open locks might have come from the old man. You know, in the genes."

"Not like it did you a whole lot of good," Dolores said from one end of the table.

After a few minutes of silence Wyatt said, "Maureen, I understand that you've worked out an arrangement with Mrs. Boyd to pay her a portion of whatever we make on selling the Lemand furniture." From Rebecca's glower I knew where his "understanding" came from.

"I felt like it was the fairest thing to do. We did get the furniture for a ridiculously low price." I glowered right back at her.

Wyatt tapped his finger on the table. "But, as I told you earlier, in this business the seller has to be aware of the value of what he or she is selling. *Caveat vendor* applies just as much as *caveat emptor.*"

"And 'do unto others' seems to me to trump any of your maxims, but I guess they don't teach that in business courses."

"If we do find something," Joseph said from the end of the table opposite his mother, "who will it belong to?" Dolores had not taken her eyes off him while we ate.

"That could be a complex question," Wyatt said. "We own the furniture now—"

"Except that Mom told Mrs. Boyd we would treat it as a consignment," Rebecca snapped. "Doesn't that give her at least part ownership? Maybe she'll make a claim. The stuff came from her house."

"But it was my grandparents' house when whatever's in there was put in there."

Proctor wiped his mouth on the back of his hand, ignoring the pile of napkins I had put in the middle of the table. "I hate to bust your bubble, but if it turns out to be money from drug deals that's hidden in there, the government'll swoop down on it. Probably take the furniture, too. They might even take your damn store."

"He's right," Dolores said. "Anything connected with drug money—even stuff you've bought with it—they'll confiscate." She took a sip of her drink. "At least that's what I've heard."

"We need to talk to a lawyer," I said. "I'll call Robert right after lunch. We need to have some idea of the consequences."

"Maybe we'd be better off," Joseph said, "just to sell the furniture and let the next owners deal with it."

"No, no, no," Proctor said as he chewed. "If Dunmoore's right, there could be an absolute boatload of money in there. If I can get the things open, I'll be happy with a finder's fee. Maybe ten percent? Okay?"

CHAPTER 21

After lunch we went back to various tasks. Dolores took Pepper out to do his business. As they returned to the office, I was settling in to call Robert. I had my phone in my hand when it buzzed. I quickly read a text from Robert and gasped. "Holy crap!"

"What? Is something wrong?" Dolores asked.

"No. He says he and Derrick went with their surrogate this morning to get an ultrasound of the baby. It's twins!" I turned the phone so Dolores could see the picture of the ultrasound.

"Cool." She paused. "You said 'he and Derrick.' So this is one of those same-sex arrangements?"

"Yes." I felt my shields going up. "Robert and Derrick have been together since law school. They got married right after the Supreme Court legalized same-sex marriages. They hired a surrogate and—maybe this is too much information, but what the hell—they both donated sperm. It was mixed together when the woman was impregnated."

Dolores wrinkled her nose. "So they won't know whose child it actually is. And you won't know if it's your grandchild, I mean by blood."

"It will be *their* child, regardless, and my grandchild—or grandchildren, it seems—no matter what. If they ever need to identify paternity, for medical reasons, I'm sure they could. Otherwise, it doesn't matter."

"Hey, what if she's having fraternal twins—one from each father?"

I rolled my eyes.

"It could happen."

"Well, yeah, it could." I called Robert but got his voice mail, so I tried Derrick.

"Hey, Mom," he said. "You must have gotten the news about the twins."

"Yes. It's amazing. Congratulations!"

"We're still trying to take it all in." He sounded like he was choking up, then fell silent. He is an emotional person. It's something I love about him. The other men in my life—my dad, my husband, Robert—were/are all such stoics.

"Derrick, is everything okay?"

"Robert didn't want to say anything ... that might worry you, with all you're going through, but ... ."

I sat up straighter. "But what?"

"They think there might be a problem with one of the babies' hearts. It's so hard to tell when there are two of them."

"Are you going to have some more tests?"

"We plan to, but we're not sure how much our insurance will cover. Or what we'll do after the birth if there is a problem. I guess I can sell my share of the plane."

"Listen, you do whatever you need to. I'll take care of anything your insurance doesn't cover." I was already thinking that I could sell my rental place—but, no, Dolores was living there. Well I could ask for a bigger advance on Artemisia's book.

"I wasn't asking—"

"I know you weren't, sweetheart. You don't have to ask. Just take care of those babies."

I ended the call, ran my hand over my eyes, and put my phone down. I looked up to find Dolores studying me, her head cocked.

"What?"

"Girl, you're amazing," she said softly.

"What do you mean?"

"The way you jump in and start taking care of people. You did it for me in the E. R., after I hurt myself breaking into *your* house. And you've given me a place to live."

"I'm not *giving* it. You're working for it. Just wait till you get a call at two in the morning that something's not working."

She waved her hand. "Okay, if that makes us both feel better. I don't think anybody else in Lawrenceville—certainly no other white person—would have done what you've done. They'd have had me arrested—"

"You know, I've been thinking about that."

We both laughed.

"And now," Dolores said, shaking her head, "your son and his gay partner. I'll bet most people in Lawrenceville have a problem with that."

I nodded. "That's why they settled in Greenville. And Derrick's parents aren't from here, but they've cut him off. They're very conservative people."

"They give you that line about 'God didn't create Adam and Bruce'?"

I nodded ruefully. "Exactly. That's why he calls me Mom."

"Maybe the babies will change their minds."

"I hope something will. But if the babies don't, that just means more grandma time for me!" We fist-bumped.

Dolores perched on the edge of the desk. "I'll bet Troy wasn't happy when he found out his son was gay."

"Why do you say that?"

"In high school he was always Mr. Macho. If anybody even made a joke about him doing something 'gay,' Troy would pound him. The guys I've known who acted like that were usually afraid they *were* gay and just couldn't admit it."

It was amazing how much I was learning about my family from someone I didn't know, except in passing, three days ago. "I think Troy was ... insecure about that. He didn't cut Robert off entirely after he came out, but he did turn more and more to Joseph."

"Yeah, football player, baseball star—I can see that attraction for a guy like Troy."

"He was even relieved when Rebecca started having sex with boys, like it absolved him of some responsibility or ... I don't know, proved something." I pulled a leg up under me. "Do you think she and Joseph—"

"I don't know, Maureen. I just don't know. Joseph and I aren't talking about stuff on that level."

About three o'clock Scott returned to the store. He and Proctor and I sat around the table in the employee lounge. Scott unfolded a map of the state that had an erratic black line drawn on it, leading from Lawrenceville to the Columbia airport.

Proctor snorted when he saw the map. "Did you have somebody in the drunk tank draw that?"

"This is the route you'll take tomorrow morning when you go to the airport. In return for the information you've given us, I found enough money in the department budget to buy you a one-way ticket to Columbus." He laid the boarding pass on the table. "From there you're on your own. There's an unmarked car behind the store. I did the paperwork and brought it over here so you can be ready to go first thing. Here are the keys. I'll have a plain-clothes officer here to drive you. Be ready at eight."

Proctor shook his head. "No way, man. You're the only policeman in this county that I can trust. Either you drive me or it's no deal. I'll just stay right here."

I slapped him on the arm. "You ungrateful, arrogant prick! We've gone through all sorts of contortions to help you. We ought to just kick you to the curb right now and send up a flare so Dunmoore can find you."

"Hey, take it easy. Take it easy. I appreciate everything you're doing. I really do. But you don't know who in this department is in Dunmoore's pocket."

"While I am flattered," Scott said with mock humility, "by your high opinion of my honesty, I have to be in court for the next two days to testify in a case."

"Then I'll wait here." Proctor folded his arms and leaned back in his chair.

"Like hell you will," I said. I turned to Scott. "There's no way I'm going to put up with him one minute longer than I have to. Give me the keys. *I'll* drive him."

"Maureen, I don't think that's—"

"You've given us an unmarked car and a route that nobody's going to expect us to follow. How hard can it be? It'll take forty-five minutes on these back roads, then half an hour back on the interstate."

Scott looked at the map, ran his hands over his eyes, and nodded. "All right. I don't see any alternative. He's not a prisoner, so it's not like we have to have an officer transport him."

"Could I at least handcuff him?"

Proctor flashed a nervous smile.

"Do you think I'm joking?" I slapped his arm again and he grabbed it.

"You've really got some anger issues, lady."

Scott spread his hands on the table. "You're right, Maureen. The sooner he's out of our sight, the better we'll both like it."

"Hey, I'm right here." Proctor brought his chair down hard on all four legs. "And this is no picnic for me either."

Scott ignored him and turned to me. "Let me load this route into your phone."

"Be sure you leave the map with me. I'm more likely to use it than anything on my phone."

For the rest of the afternoon Dolores and I worked at rearranging items on the main floor of the building to create wider aisles and try to diminish the feeling that customers had stumbled into somebody's hoard. Rebecca and Joseph selected items to photograph and upload onto the test version of our website. I couldn't shake the sensation that they looked like a young couple picking items for their wedding registry. I wondered if anybody had ever registered at an antique store or if an antique store had ever offered that possibility.

About four I decided to go home. Dave had emailed me the contract for Artemisia's book. I like to consider such things in the solitude of my office. I wanted to be sure her mother hadn't imposed any unusual conditions or limitations on what I could and could not write about. Only once in my career—early on—had I gotten stung because I didn't read every word in a contract. Dave and I both assumed it was all boilerplate. Never again. If I had the least doubt, I called Robert.

I stopped in the office door to survey my domain. Mark was finished with his security work for the day and would be back the next morning. Dolores was vigorously dusting shelves that hadn't had that much attention in a decade or two.

"Can you hang out here until Scott arrives to babysit Proctor for the night?" I asked her. "He said he'd get here by six."

"Sure, no problem." She seemed distracted.

"Are you still worried about Joseph and Dunmoore?"

She started to tear up. "Joseph's team is playing the team from Greenwood tonight. Dunmoore will be there. Joseph wants me to come out and say hello to him. He thinks we can all be friends, no matter what kind of problems we might have had years ago."

"Oh, my word, Dolores!" I put a hand on her arm. "I can't imagine how you could go through that. You aren't going to, are you?"

"I said I wasn't sure. He got all in my face about how I wouldn't even try to help him. If I don't go, he'll be mad at me. If I do go, I'll want to pick up a bat and bash Dunmoore's ugly head in."

"You've got to tell Joseph."

"I think it's too late. What if Dunmoore really does know a scout for the Braves? All Joseph's ever wanted was to be a professional ball-player. If I tell him what Dunmoore did—and who he is—it would ruin everything for him. I didn't come back here just to mess up my son's life all over again."

"How about if I go with you?"

"You don't have to do that."

"I know I don't."

I was almost out the door when Dolores caught up with me. She was carrying a large black purse with a shoulder strap and looked quite pleased with herself.

"Maureen, I found this while I was dusting. Would you mind if I have it? You can take it out of whatever you decide to pay me."

I took the hint, but I said, "Just take it. I've never seen you with a purse."

She wiped a little more dust off the bag. "I haven't had much to carry, but now, thanks to you, I've got a phone, the keys to a house, a little money. I don't have that much room in my pockets."

Especially as tight as she wore her pants. "Sure, you're welcome to it. And we'll talk about financial stuff soon. We need to get some things down in writing, especially about the apartment."

"Thanks." She slipped the strap onto her shoulder. The purse wasn't quite right with her jeans and T-shirt, but I was glad to see her picking up little traits of domesticity.

I went home for a while to review the contract for Artemisia's book, then drove back to the store to pick up Dolores at six-thirty. She was quiet, keeping her head down, her hand resting on her purse.

"Are you sure you're up for this?" I asked.

She nodded quickly, barely looking at me. "Absolutely."

I wasn't going to push her. I could understand why she was so distant. The prospect of confronting—in front of her son—a man who had done such a horrible thing to her would have tied any woman's stomach into knots. Forgiveness? Reconciliation? I couldn't see any such thing happening tonight. I resolved to stay as close to Dolores as possible. There was no telling what Dunmoore might do or say.

The ballgame would be played on the high school field. It had been rebuilt and modernized quite a bit since Dolores and I were students there. "They've done a lot to the place," I said, trying to lighten the mood as we made our way to the metal bench seats on the third base side.

"Yeah, they have," Dolores said.

The teams were waiting for a pre-game concert to end so they could take the field. Sarah and Her Band were capitalizing on their new-found celebrity. They sounded pretty good singing their own songs instead of covering Artemisia's. Robert knew what he was doing when he signed them. Joseph's team was standing in front of their dugout, so we waved at him. He gave a furtive wave, as embarrassed, but pleased, as any kid when his mother waves at him in a public place. Dolores smiled but remained quiet.

The Greenwood team was in their dugout and I didn't see any sign of Dunmoore. "It's really hot this evening," I said. "Do you want a drink?"

"Root beer, please. Thank you."

Attendance was light and everybody was listening to Sarah's band. Like any baseball field, the stands for this one followed a loose U-shape, with the concession stand at the bottom of the U, behind home plate. The concession stand was almost deserted.

Some quick research had informed me that Wooden Bat Leagues are made up of players out of high school and college who weren't drafted by major league teams. These leagues gave them one more chance to try to impress scouts with their ability to hit with the type of bats used in the majors instead of the metal bats that high schools and colleges use. Making money wasn't their purpose; getting exposure to scouts was. Sarah and her guys were doing the same thing, and probably not making any money either. Even the promise of a fireworks display after the game didn't seem to be drawing a crowd.

On my way to the concession stand I decided to make a bathroom stop. When I came out, a burly man in the Greenwood team's uniform was leaning against the wall opposite the door to the restroom, arms crossed over his chest.

"Well, Maureen Cooper," Brian Dunmoore said. "I thought I recognized you. Long time, no see."

"Not nearly long enough." I told myself if he took so much as one step toward me I would scream.

"You know, that's just rude, Maureen. I remember you as being so polite. Troy always said you were such a nice person." He straightened up, dropping his arms to his sides, and stood away from the wall but did not move toward me. "What have you got against me?"

The gall of the man! I kept my voice low. "Where should I start? Oh, I know, let's start with you raping Dolores Hughes."

His eyes bugged. "What? Is she still saying that was what happened? Why, that lying—"

He stopped when a woman and two young girls came around the corner and toward the restroom. It was Anna Maxwell and her daughters. We nodded at one another as I stepped away from the door.

Seeing that we would still be visible to passersby—even though there weren't any at the moment—I motioned for Dunmoore to follow me into an area in front of the concession stand, where tables were set up so people could stand and eat. The cleats on his baseball shoes clicked on the concrete floor.

When we were standing on opposite sides of the farthermost table, he took a deep breath. "Maureen, I did not rape Dolores. She came on to me, in those white shorts and that red top cut practically down to her waist. Yes, we had sex—I think she wanted to make Troy jealous—but I did not rape her. I swear it. She was all over me."

I made sure the table stayed between us. It was bolted to the floor, so I couldn't use it as a weapon, but as long as it stood between us, I felt it provided some degree of protection. "Her blouse was torn and she had a black eye and some scratches. My father-in-law can testify to that."

"Oh, c'mon, Maureen. Do you realize how easy it is to tear a blouse and hit yourself in the eye?" He jerked his fist toward his face. "I'm a cop. I can't count how many times I've seen women do stuff like that after they've been with a guy and then have second thoughts about it."

"Why should I believe you? Troy beat you up because of it, and you left town two days later."

"Troy did that because he was still hot for her." He raised his hands and lowered his head. "I'm sorry to say that. I know you were married by then, but Dolores meant the world to him. He told me he'd kill me if I didn't leave town."

Great! One more person telling me how little I knew about my husband. I looked beyond Dunmoore to collect myself. The two kids working concessions had stepped out from behind the counter and were looking down a passageway to see the band.

Dunmoore went on. "I couldn't believe it when he told me Dolores was claiming that I raped her, and he obviously believed every word of it. But you can't prove anything in a situation like that. You know, 'he said, she said.' No witnesses. I could see Troy was mad enough to kill me, though. I figured I could take him, but it might be safer for me to get out of sight for a while."

Son of a bitch! Everything he said could be true. But everything Dolores said could just as easily be true. "You went to see my grandfather, Chief Cooper, right before you left town. Why?"

He looked almost amused. "You've been doing your homework. I had to turn in my letter of resignation and explain to the chief that he would probably be hearing stories and I wanted him to know the truth."

"What did he say?"

"He asked me what had happened and I told him that Dolores came on to me."

I winced. "What was his reaction?"

"That's when things got weird. He looked at the scratches and bruises on my face and my broken nose and asked me if she did that. I had to laugh. I said, 'Do you think Dolores could have done this?'"

"'Well, who did?' he said."

"I told him Troy did it."

I held up my hand to stop him as Anna and her girls came out of the restroom. When I was sure they were out of earshot, I said, "What happened then?"

"Then the Chief smiled. When he was getting mad, he had this creepy expression, what we called his mad-scientist smile. When you saw that smile, you knew you were going to catch hell. 'My granddaughter's husband did this?' he said, like he was real proud. 'Well, he saved me the trouble of whipping your ass.'"

"And, before I could react, he grabbed my shirt and slammed me up against the wall. 'Listen, scumbag,' he said. 'There are two girls in this town that you must *never* mess with—that *nobody* must ever mess with. One is my granddaughter—'"

"'Hey, Chief,'" I said, 'I would never—' But he just tightened his grip. 'And the other is Dolores Hughes.' He backhanded me across my nose and slammed my head against the wall again. I'd never seen him so mad."

I stepped closer to the table. I couldn't believe what I was hearing. "Why Dolores?"

Dunmoore nodded. "That's exactly what I said. 'Why Dolores Hughes?'"

"'You don't have to know why,' was all the Chief said. And he told me to get out of town that night. I figured I could handle Troy, but not the Chief."

Gripping the edge of the table to steady myself, I asked, "How much money did he give you to leave?"

"Money? What money? What are you talking about?"

Before I could say any more, I saw Dolores come into the empty food court, looking for me. When Dunmoore noticed me glancing over his shoulder, he turned and spotted her. Quickening her pace as she walked toward us, she reached into her purse and pulled out a gun.

CHAPTER 22

Dunmoore ducked under the table and I rushed at Dolores, grabbing her hand and forcing her arm toward the ceiling. I heard the gun click as she pulled the trigger several times before I hit her hand on the metal table and made her drop the thing. Dunmoore cowered like a child under the table, with his hands over his head.

"Duck and cover never was a very effective strategy, dumb ass," I sneered at him. I scooped up the gun and pushed Dolores toward the exit.

"Why wouldn't it fire?" she cried as I hustled her to the car. Apparently no one had noticed what happened because the band was playing their raucous finale. I shoved her into the car and tore out of the parking lot, with no thought of fastening any seatbelts.

"I had him." Dolores slammed her fist into the door and grimaced. "I could've killed the bastard. Why wouldn't it fire?"

"Because I keep the clip locked in a separate drawer. You didn't notice that the gun was empty?" I was so thankful I had made sure there was no bullet in the chamber. I took several deep breaths, trying to stop my heart from racing.

Dolores leaned back against the headrest, shaking her head. "I just knew you had a gun in that drawer. That's where Troy and Wyatt kept it twenty years ago. They always kept it loaded. I had to grab it while Scott wasn't looking." She put her head in her hands and began to sob.

So the purse was just a big holster. "What were you thinking, Dolores? What in God's name were you thinking? Do you want to spend the rest of your life in jail?"

Dolores looked over at me, her face contorted by her weeping. "That man has had me in a kind of jail since the day he raped me,

Maureen. When I knew he was going to be here tonight, all I could see was his ugly face. I could feel every place he touched me. If I could kill him, I thought, I would be free, even if I was behind bars."

All the way to my house I expected to hear sirens and see red and blue lights in my rear-view mirror, but all I heard was Dolores' crying. When I pulled into the driveway and she realized where we were, she looked over at me. "Why are we here?"

"I want you to stay here tonight. And I'm going to call Scott."

Dolores sat bolt upright. "You're going to call a cop? I thought I could—"

"I'm not going to say anything about what just happened. I mean, nothing happened, right? Let's just say we—how do they put it?—we punked the guy."

We got out of the car and went in through the back door, to be greeted by Pepper's wagging tail and slobbering tongue.

"Do you think Dunmoore will try to do something?" Dolores asked.

"I have no idea, but I'd feel a lot safer if Scott was here." I picked up my phone.

Dolores sat down at the kitchen table "I never did get my root beer."

"Yeah. Well, attempted murder does kind of disrupt what you were doing." I reached into the fridge and pulled out one of the beers that Scott keeps stocked there. "How about a non-root beer?"

Dolores' hand trembled slightly as she took the cold can. "Perfect. Are you going to have one? You must be as shook up as I am."

"I am, but I'll get myself some tea." When Scott answered, I asked him to come to the house.

He sighed heavily. "I'm supposed to stay here all night with Proctor. I'm not supposed to leave him alone, or have you forgotten?"

"Oh, crap." I rolled my eyes. "Okay, bring him with you. It might be helpful to have him here anyway. Try to keep him as much out of sight as you can. Dunmoore's out at the ballpark, but we don't know if he's got somebody watching the store." Or my house, I thought.

"You gals didn't stay for the fireworks?"

"We almost set off some of our own."

"What—"

"Let's just say that Dolores' encounter with Dunmoore didn't go so well and leave it at that. Okay?"

When I hung up, Dolores said, "I've got to do something. I can't just sit here. You said you have a bunch of Troy's stuff upstairs. Do you mind if I look through it? I'd really like to find that letter I wrote him last month."

This was a fork in the road for me. To this point I had heard only Dolores' story and I believed her. Now I had heard an alternative version, one that explained the facts just as well—up to a point. But, if Dolores had seduced Dunmoore to make Troy jealous, why would she try to kill him? And why was Proctor claiming that Dunmoore had hired him to look for money in the Lemand furniture? Could I trust having these people around me? What might Dolores find in Troy's papers that she might hide from me? Well, as Hemingway said, "The best way to find out if you can trust people is to trust them."

"Hello." Dolores waved her hand in front of my face. "Earth to Maureen. Do you mind if I look through Troy's stuff upstairs?"

I nodded. "Sure. Just put things back when you're done with them. I want to see everything in context when I get around to going through it."

"No problem." She started up the stairs and groaned a bit. "Whew, too bad you don't have an elevator in this place. Any place over two stories high ought to have an elevator."

"Is your ankle still bothering you that much?"

"More than I want to admit. I'm going to stay off it as much as I can the next day or two."

"Make yourself at home. There are four bedrooms on the second floor. The sheets are clean on all the beds. Pick one."

"So you really do mean for me to stay here tonight?"

"I think that would be safest, don't you? I think Proctor and Scott should stay here, too."

She rolled her eyes. "You got any dip? We'll just have a party."

"I know the guy is a pain, but he'll be in Ohio this time tomorrow. He won't be our problem anymore."

While waiting for Scott to arrive, I sipped my tea and thought about what Dunmoore had said. I wasn't ready to discuss it with Dolores, or anybody else. I know from interviewing people for my books that they often create their own narrative about critical moments in their lives. The farther removed they get from any incident, the more they convince themselves that their version is truth. Or they learn how to tell a lie with conviction. But, when they do that, it has a canned quality to it. The gestures, the pauses—they all feel rehearsed. That was the sensation I got from listening to Dunmoore. My question about the money disrupted his narrative. He'd stumbled like an actor who had lost his place in his script. I hadn't gotten to hear what he would have said about the money because of Dolores' ... intrusion.

When listening to Dolores, though, I felt raw emotion, anger, deep pain. With Christopher Proctor, too, I did not have the sense of a man reading from a script. Ironically, the ex-con came across as more believable than the cop. And he seemed genuinely afraid of Dunmoore.

Scott and Proctor arrived in the car from the impound lot that I would drive to the airport tomorrow. I stood and looked out the window as Scott pulled all the way around to the back of my house and he and Proctor got out. Apparently not even a policeman could make Proctor wear a seatbelt. I met them on the back steps.

"So, I'm being moved to another jail," Proctor said without even a hello.

"I told you," Scott said, "I can put you in a real jail." He playfully punched Proctor on the arm. I couldn't believe what I saw. Was he joking with him?

"All right, all right." Proctor raised his hands. "I assume this place has TV."

Scott pointed toward my den. "Through the dining room. *Big* screen TV."

"Cable?"

"Premium cable," I said. "Knock yourself out. Just don't order any pay-per-view."

"Sports channels?"

"There are a bunch of those. I don't know anything about them."

"A snob, eh?" He raised his hand with his pinky up. "Oh, I only watch PBS. That's what all you intellect'als say. I'll bet you binge-watch 'Real Housewives.'"

The man was half-right. After spending all day working on a book, I need to hear a human voice other than my own. I get into my pajamas and curl up in the den to watch a little news or go back to a few episodes of "West Wing," my all-time favorite, which Troy never could stand. "They all talk too fast," he used to say.

Just before Proctor disappeared from sight, Scott called, "Hey, Chris, you want a beer?"

"Sounds good. Thanks."

Scott opened my fridge and scrounged a couple of beers. He grabbed a bag of chips off the shelf and started toward the den.

"Where are you going?" I asked in disbelief.

"Braves' game. They're already in the second inning."

I grabbed his arm. "My God, are you bonding with that man?"

"We've been talking." Scott shrugged and looked toward the den. "He's not that bad a guy, Maureen. His life has not been easy. His mother was so rough on him that he was placed in foster care a couple of times. She used to lock him in his room. One time she left him in there for three days. A neighbor called Protective Services because they hadn't seen the boy for a while."

A shudder went over me as I recalled what it felt like to be locked in that room for just a few minutes.

"With all you've written about people's lives," Scott reminded me, "you know how much something like that can traumatize a child. Chris is a survivor."

"But he's a felon! He broke into my store. He threw that drawer at me."

"Hey, Dolores is a felon, too. She broke into your rental house. And she broke Pepper's leg. You don't seem to have a problem with any of that."

"But—"

He put down one of the beer cans and shook a finger at me. "You know, it wasn't too long ago that somebody told me people just need someone to believe in them."

"No fair quoting me against myself!" I waved him away. "All right, I give up. You guys enjoy your bromance."

"And our beer." He picked up the can and raised it in a salute.

Scott was right, of course. As I climbed the stairs to the third floor, I wondered why I had felt such an immediate bond with Dolores. She and Proctor—I could never call him Chris—shared a lot of life experiences. I didn't think Miz Maribelle would ever be as abusive to Dolores as Proctor's mother was, but there didn't seem to be a strong father figure in either of their lives. The trauma that so damaged Dolores was inflicted by one person in one incident, instead of over a period of time. The effect, though, was very similar. They both "acted out" by turning to crime.

I reached the family room to find Dolores looking over some piles of paper that she had set out on top of the waist-high storage cabinets on one side of the room.

"You get the children settled?" she asked over her shoulder.

I snorted. "They're bonding over beer and a baseball game. They're on a first-name basis now."

"So are we, and I'm enjoying my beer."

I didn't want to pursue this any further. "It looks like you're organizing stuff. What have you found?"

The next morning was busy. I was glad for all the bathrooms in my house and Pepper was happy to have so many people to pet him and sweet talk to him. Scott and Proctor had gone to sleep in their recliner chairs in the den. I had to laugh when I went in to turn off the TV and wake them up. "I never thought of this as a man-cave," I said as I shook Scott's shoulder.

"It has all the makings." He rubbed his eyes and tapped Proctor on the leg. "Hey, Chris, time to get up. We've got to get moving."

"Do I have time to shower?" Proctor asked.

"Yes," I said, "but we'll need to get something to eat on the road."

"I can live with that."

While Proctor showered, Scott made a phone call, then reported to me. "The guys who had your house under surveillance say they didn't see anything. Pepper seems to have been aware of them, though."

"I heard him moving around during the night. Where were your guys?"

Scott shook his head. "Need-to-know basis, and you don't need to know. They were at the store, but I moved them when Chris and I came over here."

"So nobody was watching the store last night?"

"Maureen, we have only so much manpower. I made sure everything was locked up. This was what I had to do."

"I'm not criticizing, hon."

"Then why does it feel like you are?" He rubbed his hands over his face. "Can I use your bathroom to shave and shower? You'll need to drop me off at the store so I can pick up my car, go home, change clothes, and get to court." He checked his watch. "I've got about an hour." He hustled off toward my bedroom.

My bedroom is by far the largest in the house. Originally it did not have a master bath, but my parents added a good-sized one when they did some remodeling. I updated it a few years ago, after Troy left me, to give me something to do and to give it less of a masculine feel. Scott keeps a toothbrush and a razor here, just like I keep a few things at his apartment.

Dolores came down the back stairs into the kitchen, running her hands through her hair. "Who's that singing in the shower upstairs?"

"That's your favorite ex-con. My favorite cop is in the bathroom down here. Do you want some coffee?"

She shook her head. "I'm going to head back to my apartment and get to work sorting Troy's stuff. Do you think Rebecca and Joseph will want me in the store today?"

"You'll have to ask them." I added some milk to my coffee and took a sip. "Dolores, when are you going to talk to Joseph? Everybody has a right to know where they came from. Our biological heritage is such an important part of who we are."

"I've tried that argument with Mama, but she doesn't buy it. She says I've gotten along fine all my life not knowing who my father was. And I guess I did until Dunmoore raped me."

"You know, they say with adopted kids, the worst thing that can happen is for them not to be told they're adopted. If they find out accidentally or if somebody tells them to spite them, it can be devastating. I think the same principle applies here. You need to control the circumstances under which Joseph learns what Dunmoore did to you."

"What did the bastard tell you yesterday?"

I decided to lay everything on the table. "He admitted to having sex with you, but he said you came on to him."

Dolores snorted in derision. "And did I beat myself up and tear my clothes?"

"He said you did. Women do it sometimes, he claimed, to shift blame onto the man."

"Do you believe him?"

"No, not at all." I didn't hesitate or waver in my answer. "I felt like he was reciting a story he had made up. And why would you try to kill him if—"

She looked straight at me. "Maureen, you've got to believe me. I thought the gun was loaded, and I wanted, with all my heart and soul, to kill that bastard. Maybe that's who I really am, and maybe you need to be aware of that."

Before I could even begin to process what she was saying, Scott came back into the kitchen, his hair still damp around the edges. "What about a loaded gun?"

"Hypothetical question," I stammered. "Don't we need to be getting out of here?"

"Yeah, we do." He was turning to holler up the stairs when Proctor appeared. "All right," Scott said. "Are we ready?" He tossed the car keys to me.

I grabbed my purse. "Talk to Joseph," I told Dolores, "and to your mother. Please."

We got into the car, with Scott in the back seat and Proctor riding shotgun. I took a moment to familiarize myself with the instrument panel before turning to Proctor. "I don't suppose I could ask you to fasten your seatbelt."

"You could ask," he said. "Do you know how many people get killed every year because they can't get out of a car after an accident?"

"Probably only a fraction of those who're killed when they're thrown from the car."

"I tried, Maureen," Scott offered from behind me. "I think we're just going to have to let this one go."

When we got to the store Scott gave me a quick peck and hustled to his car. He does not like to be late. I looked over my shoulder in surprise when Proctor followed me into the store and into the office.

"I'm not going to be a sitting target," he said.

I had put the gun into my purse last night when I took it away from Dolores. Now I unlocked the desk drawer where I kept the clip and loaded the gun with a satisfying click.

"Good idea," Proctor said. "You want me to hold it?"

"Not on your life." I put the weapon back in my purse and scanned the desk.

"What are you looking for?" Proctor asked. "We need to get out of here."

"I don't see the map with our route on it."

"You've got it on your tablet, don't you? I saw Scott put it in there."

"Yes."

"Then let's go. I've got a plane to catch." He chuckled. "First time I've ever said that."

I ran my hand through the papers on the desk one more time. I was sure this was where I had left the map on which Scott had marked our route, but Proctor was right. There wasn't time to waste.

I wedged my purse between my seat and the door, but I did let Proctor hold my tablet as I followed the directions. The Columbia airport sits on the southwest side of the city. The most direct route for us would have been to follow US 378, which runs along the west side of Lake Murray. In 1930, when the earthen dam that created the lake was finished, it was the largest man-made lake in the world. With a little time I could probably find the cabin on the northern end of the lake that my family used to rent. At the age of ten I wrote my first book there.

Today, though, our convoluted route took us along deserted two-lane roads, past run-down farms, their barns collapsing, and stretches of pine forest planted by the CCC during the Depression. The northwestern part of South Carolina boasts mountains, forests, lakes, and rolling countryside. The closer one gets to Columbia, in the center of the state, the drier, flatter, and more barren the terrain becomes. The land, over-farmed for centuries, just seems tired.

As the annoying voice on the tablet gave me directions, Proctor noticed the icon I had put on there to mark the pictures I'd taken of the Lemand furniture. I had focused on the one drawer that Scott's tech people had x-rayed, one that I knew contained a panel and something inside it. I had photographed it from every angle and as closely as I could.

"These are great pictures," Proctor said. "It's like looking at the stuff with a magnifying glass."

"Thanks, I guess."

"If I had these and the drawer itself, I'll bet I could figure out how to open it. You know, it can't be that hard. Your grandfather must have figured it out, if he was hiding money in the furniture. He had to be able to put it in and to know he could get it out easily."

"I'm still not ready to admit that's what he was doing."

Proctor pointed to a spot on one of the pictures. "It has something to do with the dowels on the back end of the drawer. At least it did with the drawer in my nightstand that I opened. But I tried what I knew when I was in your store, and it didn't work. I don't understand what's different about these pieces."

Glancing at what he was pointing to, I hadn't paid attention to what was going on around me. When I checked the rearview mirror, I saw a car gaining on us. It was unmarked, but it had a push-bumper on the front of it—what I had called a "cow-catcher" until Scott corrected me. Police officers use the things to push cars out of their way without harming their own vehicles.

Proctor looked over his shoulder. "Oh, God! It's Dunmoore. Step on it!"

I wasn't sure what he expected me to do on a narrow road in a car built for comfort, not speed. I saw nowhere to turn or pull off. At this point the road was slightly elevated above the farm land on either side. The car behind us made up the distance quickly, and I could see Brian Dunmoore driving it. When he hit us the first time, the jolt bounced me in my seat. I had to fight to maintain control. He crunched my rear bumper again and then roared into the other lane. As he drew up alongside us he turned his wheel to the right. Metal ground against metal. I couldn't keep my car on the road. As it lifted into the air, I heard a scream.

CHAPTER 23

I don't know how many times the car rolled over. When it came to a stop, it was sitting upright. I was in my seat with the airbag deployed. I didn't feel any intense pain, just shock, and I could move my arms and legs. Looking to my right, I saw the car door was open and the seat was empty.

I was trying to unfasten my seatbelt when I saw Dunmoore turning around and driving back in my direction. I reached into my purse and pulled out the gun. The glass in my side window was shattered but still in place. Using the barrel of the gun, I knocked it out of my way. Dunmoore stopped on the side of the road. As he started down the embankment, I raised the gun.

"Not gonna fall for that again, Maureen," he said with a smirk.

When I pulled the trigger the bullet struck right at his feet. My hand was shaking too much to make an accurate shot, and I wasn't even sure what I was trying to hit. Dunmoore looked to his right and scrambled back up the embankment. As he screeched away in his car, another vehicle stopped.

I was trying to unfasten my seatbelt when Scott's face appeared in my busted window. At first I thought I was dreaming.

"Are you all right?" he asked.

"I think so. I just can't get the damn seatbelt loose."

With some difficulty Scott opened the bashed-in door and helped me get out of the car. "I'll take the gun," he said. "The cops will be here in a minute. You don't want to have to explain this." He took me by my elbow. "Can you walk? Does anything feel broken?"

"I'm going to have some beautiful bruises, but I can walk."

Scott helped me back to his car. "I'm going to check on Proctor," he said. In a couple of minutes he returned to tell me that Proctor was dead. "He slammed into a tree when he was thrown from the car."

I couldn't help but feel sorrow, but all he had to do was fasten the damn seatbelt. "Shouldn't you be going after Dunmoore?"

"I put out a BOLO. He'll probably ditch that car pretty soon, though. Are you sure you're all right? That's my main concern."

I stretched and checked the sorest places. "I think so. Just some bruises and I'm shaking pretty bad. How did he know where we were? He must have gotten into the store last night and found that map. It wasn't on my desk this morning."

"I've got the map," Scott said. "I took it when we came over to your house, just in case somebody got into the store." He walked over to my car, knelt down, and looked under the rear. He reached under the bumper and pulled something off. He stood up, holding what looked like a battery. "It's a tracking device," he said. "Poor ol' Chris was right. Somebody in the Lawrenceville department is in Dunmoore's pocket. They put this on here when I reserved the car."

Two police vehicles pulled up, followed by an ambulance, then a wrecker. Scott talked with them and accompanied them as they asked me what had happened. As I answered their questions I wished my hands would stop shaking. When they seemed satisfied, Scott shook hands and left them to clean up the mess.

"Now we've got to get you to a hospital," he said as he got into his car.

"What are you doing here? I thought you had to be in court?"

"Key witness didn't show. The judge issued a bench warrant for his arrest and postponed the trial. I decided I would check up on you."

The curtain pulled back and a nurse stepped into my bay, pushing a chest-high little table with a small computer on it. She couldn't have been any older than Rebecca. I could imagine her in a cheerleader's outfit more easily than in scrubs.

"Hi, my name's Beth. How are you doing, hon?"

"I think I'm okay, but you probably know better than I do."

She checked one of the monitors above my bed and entered something into her computer. "You're actually doing well enough that we're going to send you home. You've got a few bruises and scratches, but the airbag and seatbelts did what they were supposed to do."

I shifted in the bed and put my hand across my chest when I felt a stab of pain.

"That's where the seatbelt grabbed you," Beth said. "That's what'll hurt the most for a week or so. The doctor's going to give you a prescription for the pain. We've got some in your IV and a low dosage of a sedative right now. You were really agitated when they brought you in. Otherwise you're in good shape. Just push the buzzer if you need anything." She turned and wheeled her table out of the bay, leaving the curtain partly pulled back.

I took a deep breath and regretted it. Then I heard two male voices, one of which I recognized. A doctor appeared from behind the curtain, with Scott right behind him.

"I'm Dr. Nichols," the man said, offering me his hand. "I'm glad to see you doing so well. You had quite an experience."

"She's a tough one," Scott said.

I felt anything but tough. "The nurse said I could go home." I hoped I didn't sound as pathetic to them as I did to myself.

"Yes," Dr. Nichols said. "We'll have you out of here in about ten minutes. The nurse will disconnect your IV, and you'll be ready to go. The sedative will be in your system for a few more hours, so don't drive or try to do too much for the rest of the day."

It took closer to twenty minutes to get me unhooked, go over my follow-up procedures, and wheel me out to Scott's car. I could have walked, but as my adrenalin rush subsided and everything sank in, it actually felt pretty good to let someone take me for a ride.

"Why do you think Dunmoore came back?" I asked as we pulled out of the parking lot.

"Probably going to make sure you were both dead. It's a pity you didn't take him out right there. Would've saved us a lot of trouble."

"Scott, I've never pointed a gun at anybody before. My hand was shaking, and I couldn't will myself to kill him, no matter what he's done."

"Did he have a gun?"

"Not that I saw."

"That's not surprising. He couldn't have risked shooting you, if he wanted to make your deaths look accidental. He was probably going to bash your head in."

"But he did a lot of damage to the car. Nobody would believe that was an accident."

"It could have been road rage from some unknown driver. It's been known to happen. I had a message while you were in x-ray. They've found where he ditched the car he used. He must have had another one waiting for him."

"Then how are you going to find him?"

"I don't think he's ready to leave here just yet. He still doesn't know what's in that furniture."

Scott fell silent as I called Robert and Rebecca and assured them that I was okay. Dolores was expecting me back shortly after noon, so I called her to say I would be a little late. I talked longer with her than I did with either of my children. The threat of Brian Dunmoore was now one more bond between us, it seemed.

When all of that was taken care of, I turned to Scott. "What are we going to do about Proctor?" I knew I was talking slowly. Damn sedative. I hate being drugged, except when I'm having a baby. Then I'll take anything they've got.

Scott looked at me in surprise. "'We'? Why is it up to us? What is there to do? He's dead."

"He has to be buried, doesn't he?"

"I guess so. That could run into some money."

I waved a hand as my eyes started to close. "I don't want 'em to just throw him in a hole in the ground. I'll take care of it. Maybe have him cremated. See if his aunt in Ohio wants the ashes. Or put 'em some place that was special to him."

"Careful. They might end up on a shelf in your den. He loved that big-screen TV."

I slept until about seven that evening. When I woke up, Dolores was sitting in the easy chair in the reading nook in my bedroom. "Oh, hey," I said. "I didn't expect—"

She came over and stood by the bed. "I hope you don't mind. Scott was here for a while, but he had to leave. Rebecca came by. I told them I would be here when you woke up, to make sure you stayed put."

I sat up and pushed the blanket back. "I'm fine."

"No, you're not. You were in a horrific accident. You're scraped and bruised."

"It wasn't an accident. But I'm going to have one if I don't get to the bathroom." I put my legs over the edge of the bed and sat for a minute to steady myself.

"Do you need some help?"

"Not since I was four." With Dolores' hand on my arm I got to my feet and made sure I could stay on them. "I'm fine." But she walked beside me to the bathroom anyway.

After doing what I needed to do, I splashed some water on my face and studied myself in the mirror. The airbag had left some bruises, but none of them looked too bad. I didn't have any stitches on my face, so no scarring. I could see a couple of places on my arms and feel a few more on my chest and left side. Unbuttoning my blouse, I ran my finger along the purple stripe that the seatbelt had made from my left shoulder over my chest to the right side of my waist.

"Are you all right?" Dolores asked from the other side of the door.

I stood up straight and took a deep breath. "Yeah, out in a minute."

"Let's get you back in bed," Dolores said as I opened the door.

"No, I don't want to go back to bed. I'd like a little something to eat."

"Okay, get in bed and I'll bring you something."

I turned toward the kitchen. "I don't have time to lie around. Dunmoore's still loose out there."

"That's Scott's problem, not yours."

"Dunmoore's after whatever is in that Lemand furniture. It's in my store. That makes it my problem."

"Scott said he was leaving somebody in the store tonight. You don't have anything to worry about. Get back in the bed." She reached for my arm, but I pulled away.

"Dolores, Proctor was right. Somebody in the police department here is in Dunmoore's pocket. What scares the hell out of me is that it may be Scott."

Dolores' jaw dropped. "Why on earth would you say that?"

"It's a lot of things coming together. He always seems to know where I am and what I'm doing. After the accident this morning he took my gun and told me not to say anything to the police about knowing Dunmoore. He said Dunmoore or one of his stooges put the tracking device on the car, but I'm not so sure. He got me in and out of that hospital as quickly as he could." I dropped the pajama bottoms somebody had dressed me in and slipped into a pair of jeans. "I'm going to the store."

"Then I'm coming with you," Dolores said.

As we went out the back door I picked up the light jacket I keep hanging on the porch. The weather wasn't chilly, but I was. Pepper stopped licking his cast and looked up at me. "No, Pepper." I tapped him lightly on the nose and took out the small bottle of bitter apple spray that was in my jacket pocket. "Watch your eyes," I said to Dolores. When I sprayed it on the cast, she jerked her head back.

"That stuff is vile."

"It's the only thing that keeps him from licking the cast." I slipped the bottle back into my pocket because I knew putting it on the shelf above Pepper's bed would cause me pain in several places.

Dolores knelt and rubbed the dog's head. "Pepper, buddy, I'm so sorry for doing this to you. I will make it up to you, I promise."

As we got to the car I put on my jacket and took out my keys, but Dolores grabbed my arm. "You are *not* driving. You shouldn't even be standing up, but you are most definitely not driving." She took the keys and walked around to the driver's side.

"How are you going to manage with that boot on your foot?"

We looked at one another and, in spite of ourselves, laughed. "We're pretty pathetic, aren't we?" I said.

"What do you think we could do if Dunmoore did come to the store?"

"I really wish Scott hadn't taken my gun. I asked him to give it back after we left the hospital, but he said he wanted to check the permit. I was acting kind of trigger-happy, he said, and he didn't want me to shoot anybody illegally. That's one more reason I'm a little suspicious of him. He seems to want to disarm me."

Dolores pulled out her phone. "I'll call Joseph."

"Do you want to get him involved?"

"Our only strength is in numbers."

We parked on the square in front of the store, which was dark except for a few emergency lights. I assumed the officer that Scott had put on guard was patrolling or maybe sitting in the lounge. Joseph pulled up in his car as we were unlocking the door.

"How are you doing, Ms. Cooper?" Joseph asked.

"Not as well as she's trying to pretend," Dolores said. I couldn't argue with her.

We entered the store and I made sure the door was locked behind us. How I wished we had the new locks and alarms, but it would be the end of the week before all of that was installed and up and running. I called out, "Hello? Officer? It's Maureen Cooper. I'm just checking on things."

"Maybe he's up on the third floor," Joseph suggested. "That's where the Lemand furniture is."

Dolores and I hobbled toward the small passenger elevator while Joseph started up the stairs. When we reached the third floor and the door opened, we saw Joseph on his knees with his hands on his head. Behind him stood Brian Dunmoore, pointing a gun at Joseph and then at us.

So much for numbers, I thought.

"Nobody move!" Dunmoore said. "Damn! This just keeps getting more and more complicated. Maureen, I never figured you to be such a trouble-maker."

"What did you do with the guard who was here?" I asked.

Dunmoore chuckled. "He's trying on his handcuffs back in the storeroom. I don't want to kill anybody unless I have to."

"And you had to kill Christopher Proctor and me?"

"Proctor double-crossed me. He had it coming. You were going to be collateral damage—unfortunate but sometimes inevitable."

"Proctor didn't double-cross you. He honestly didn't know how to open these panels." I glanced around at the drawers pulled out from the furniture and scattered over the floor. Dunmoore had been here a while. At least he didn't seem to have damaged anything.

"I've been trying to figure these things out for the past hour," Dunmoore said, "but it's slow going. You three can work faster than I can alone. It has something to do with the damn dowels on the bottom and back of the drawers." Stepping away from us, he waved the gun to herd us toward the furniture. "Keep your hands where I can see 'em. First one that even looks at me funny or tries to get to a phone gets blown away."

For a few minutes we poked at dowels and turned drawers this way and that with no luck. "Since you're going to kill us anyway," I finally said to Dunmoore, "could you tell me what happened between you and my grandfather?"

Dunmoore leaned against the largest dresser. If he'd had a drink in his hand instead of a gun, he could have been at a cocktail party. "I'm not going to kill anybody, Maureen. I don't want to kill anybody. All I know is that one day I busted a dealer. He told me he was one of the Chief's guys, wink-wink. I had no idea what he was talking about. I went to the Chief and he told me the story. One night, during an arrest, when his partner was out of sight, he was offered a bribe to let the suspect dispose of a certain amount of drugs in order to reduce the charge. He realized this could be a source of income. He took the bribe and the drugs. Within a few years he was running the drug business in this area."

"You keep saying that. Show me proof."

"If I could get these damn panels open, you'd see proof."

"You tried to get Troy to let you look at the furniture, didn't you?"

"I wasn't—"

"Don't bother to lie about it. We've got video of you in the store at the time Troy died. You killed him, didn't you?"

The gun dipped for just a second, but not long enough for me to do anything about it. "It was an accident. Proctor told me Troy had bought the furniture. I wanted to talk to Troy about it, see if we could work a deal, but he was still on me about Dolores. Like it happened yesterday. We got into a fight. I hit his head on the floor. When I realized he was dead, I tipped that piece of furniture over on him."

I closed my eyes and winced, hoping Troy really was dead before the armoire crushed him. I wanted to keep Dunmoore talking, to buy time for ... something.

"So you killed my husband and you're telling me my grandfather was a drug dealer?"

"If it's any consolation to you, he did not sell drugs, but he convinced the major dealers that, if they kept drug violence under control—and out of the white parts of town—and let us arrest and prosecute some low-level dealers now and then, they could do whatever they wanted. He protected them and got a cut of their profits. He made me one of those offers I couldn't refuse. 'Now that you know,' he told me, 'you can either work with me or I'll have you killed.'"

I could not imagine those words coming from Papa's mouth. "But why would my grandfather do that? My grandmother inherited a lot of money. They lived quite comfortably."

"It was *her* money, though," Dunmoore said, "and she never let him forget it."

My God, was that what I did to Troy?

"You see, the sainted Chief Cooper had something going on the side and needed money that his wife didn't know about."

Dolores gasped. Dunmoore pointed the gun at her. "Did you find something?"

"No," she said.

Dunmoore stood away from the dresser and put the gun against her temple. "Then why did you react like that?"

"Because I think my mother was the something Chief Cooper had going on the side."

I reached out to her. "Dolores—"

Dunmoore slapped my hand away.

"I remember a white man," Dolores said, "coming to see her late at night, when I was a little girl and supposed to be asleep."

Bending over her, Dunmoore grabbed Dolores' hair and yanked her head back. "Of course! He told me there were two women in this town that nobody should ever mess with—Maureen and you. His granddaughter and—" He jerked Dolores' head again—"Damn! You're Cooper's daughter, aren't you?"

"Leave her alone!" Joseph growled.

Dunmoore turned his gun toward Joseph. "Oh, you haven't heard the best part yet ... son. Yeah, you're the Chief's grandson and my son. And Maureen is related to you, and sorta to me, I guess. We're just one big happy family here."

Dolores pulled free. "How do you know he's your son?"

"I've suspected it for a couple of years. He was born almost nine months to the day after our little ... encounter. But the connection to the Chief—man, I never saw that coming."

"Shut up, you bastard!" Joseph yelled and slung a drawer at Dunmoore.

The drawer bounced off Dunmoore's broad shoulder. He pointed the gun toward Joseph and fired as he stumbled toward me. I reached into my pocket and pulled out the bitter apple spray. Two squirts hit him right in the face. He dropped the gun, grabbed at his eyes and yelled. Spinning around in pain, he crashed through the rotten railing and fell. We heard him land with a splintering of glass on one of the display cases on the first floor.

CHAPTER 24

I've always led a quiet life, surrounded by books. The chaos that erupted in my store over the next couple of hours almost drove me into the fetal position—phone calls, sirens, ambulances, police. When it all calmed down, Dolores was in the hospital with a bullet wound in her shoulder. She had thrown herself in front of Joseph and had lost a good bit of blood. They asked for blood donors. Joseph was a match, but he couldn't donate because, he admitted, he has Hepatitis C.

"That's what's kept me and Rebecca from sleeping together. I couldn't tell her, but I didn't want to infect her."

Joseph, Rebecca, and I we were sitting in one corner of a waiting room down the hall from Dolores' room, which I was paying for. I had also donated a pint of blood because Dolores and I were both AB-. She could take Type O blood, but the hospital said that having an exact match from a relative greatly reduces the chance of any problems in a transfusion. I enjoyed the nurse's reaction when I told her Dolores was my aunt. Now we were waiting for Dolores to come back from surgery.

"Hepatitis?" Rebecca said. "So that's it. I'm really sorry, but I am kind of relieved to hear it. I thought you weren't all that interested in me."

"Oh, I'm very interested," Joseph said, "but it turns out we had another good reason not to ... cousin."

Rebecca sat up in her chair. "Is that what we are?" She turned to me. "Let me get this straight. Papa Cooper, your grandfather, was Dolores' father?"

"Right," I said. "So Dolores and my father are half-sibs. That makes her my aunt."

"But she's only, like, two years older than you are."

"That doesn't matter. She's my aunt, and that makes you and Joseph some kind of cousins, first or second, once or twice removed. I don't know exactly, but you are pretty closely related."

A nurse came into the waiting room. "She's awake and would like to see Joseph and then you, Ms. Cooper."

After Joseph came back to the waiting room, trying not to show his tears, I made my way into Dolores' room. She looked comfortable enough. I put a hand on hers and we looked into one another's eyes for a moment.

"You just keep savin' my sorry ass, girl," she finally said.

Dolores slept for a while. I ran home to take care of Pepper and returned to the hospital to find her mother in the room with her. I found myself thinking that, if Dolores was my aunt, her mother must be some kind of relation of mine. I needed a genealogy reference book.

Miz Maribelle stood up when I came into the room. "Ms. Cooper, I can't thank you enough for all you've done for Dolores and the rest of my family. I've said and thought some unkind things about you, and I want to apologize." She hugged me. "We'll never be able to repay your kindness."

"You don't even have to think about repaying," I said. "After all, we're family. You can do two things for me, though. You can call me Maureen, and you can tell me about this other life that my grandfather had."

We settled ourselves into the two chairs beside Dolores' bed. Miz Maribelle looked at her hands for a moment, then began. "I met Rusty when I did housework for him and his wife. You'd never know it now, but I was quite a looker then, if I must say so myself. Rusty was a police sergeant who had married above his station, and his wife never quite let him forget."

I did remember overhearing some sharp words between my grandparents, and I had known since I was in high school that my grandmother had the money—and a lot of power—in the relationship.

"Your grandmother was kind of a rebel herself," Miz Maribelle continued. "She married Rusty partly to defy her parents, he told me.

He wanted to take responsibility for supporting Dolores, but their money came from his wife's inheritance. He knew he couldn't siphon off any to support Dolores without his wife noticing."

"Did he ever tell you where the money came from?" I was still hoping there might be some other explanation than drug money.

"No, he didn't. I suspected it wasn't coming from the family bank account, but I guess I didn't really want to know. I had my kids to consider. We lived comfortably. My children had anything they needed and some of what they wanted. Rusty told me he regarded Zeke as a member of 'our family' as well, so I didn't have to worry about spending some of the money on him."

"But what about after he was killed."

"I saved a good bit of what he gave me. I lived modestly. I never wanted to draw attention to myself or my children. By the time Rusty was killed, Zeke had started his business, with some help from Rusty, and Dolores was out of high school. We got by all right. He was a good man, Maureen. Even if he did something wrong, he did it to take care of his little girl."

The next ten days were hectic. The first thing I did was call in a carpenter to replace the railing around the galleries on the second and third floor. He recommended installing metal rails that ran from floor to ceiling and I agreed. Sometimes at night I woke up to the sight of Brian Dunmoore tumbling over the edge and the awful sound when he hit that display case on the first floor.

Joseph figured out that certain ones of the dowels in the drawers were slightly flattened on one side. When those were pushed, the panels opened. We found a total of just over $50,000 in several of the drawers, along with the number of a bank account in the Cayman Islands and the password to access it. The account contained $500,000. Robert used the information and confirmed it.

"You know it's drug money," Scott said, as he and I and Robert and Derrick finished supper in my dining room one evening. "The government could seize it and any assets deriving from it."

"We don't *know* anything," Derrick said. "All we have is hearsay. Chief Cooper was never convicted, never even tried, for drug-trafficking. His wife came from a wealthy family. People from wealthy families sometimes hide money because they don't trust banks. This falls in the category of finding change under the sofa cushions, or buying a coat at a garage sale and finding a $20 bill in the pocket when you get home. It's yours. The problem could come from attracting attention to yourself by suddenly spending large sums."

"The fact that the bills are older," Robert said, "would also make people notice you. You can do whatever you want with the cash you found. Just do it in small amounts. The FBI and Homeland Security start to pay attention when you deposit or withdraw $10,000 or more."

"But I don't want the damn money. I don't know what to do with it. It doesn't belong to me. It doesn't belong to Mrs. Boyd. I talked to Miz Maribelle."

"Did you mention any amounts?" Scott asked.

"No. I just said 'a good bit of money.' She doesn't want it. She says it's blood money. It's cursed."

"Rebecca would gladly take it," Robert said. "Curse be damned."

"Now, now, Robert," I said. "That's your sister you're talking about."

"Who was ready to sleep with my cousin, Joseph, it appears. That's going to take some getting used to."

How could I tell him that Anna Maxwell was carrying his half-sibling?

Derrick poured us all some more tea. "What if you set up some kind of community foundation?" he said. "That way you could give the money back to the town it was taken from."

"Could I do that anonymously?"

"Sure," Derrick said. "It could be transferred directly from the Caymans' account to an account here. You wouldn't be involved, except maybe as a trustee of the foundation."

"I'm liking that idea more and more," I said. "It could be something to help drug addicts, you, know, a rehab program." An inspiration hit. "And I'll bet Artemisia could kick in something. Her brother is an addict."

"Are you okay with this, Scott?" Robert asked.

Scott shook his head. "I probably should not have been sitting here while this conversation was going on, but I'll pretend I didn't hear anything." He put his hands on his ears and said, in a funny, sort-of-German accent, "I hear nothing."

We all looked at him.

"Sgt. Schulz on *Hogan's Heroes*. How could you miss that?"

"Okay," Robert said.

I patted his arm. "Scott, darling, you need to work on some pop-culture references that come from this century."

"And that don't involve impersonations," Derrick said.

"Anyway," Robert said, "Derrick and I will start on the paperwork."

I wasn't sure where Artemisia was at the moment, so I called her early enough in the evening that I wasn't likely to wake her up. It turned out she was back home in Oklahoma between shows. I told her I knew an anonymous donor who wanted to start a drug rehab/prevention program for Lawrenceville with a $500,000 gift.

"Ms. Cooper, are you just being modest?"

"What? Oh, no. I don't have that kind of money. If I did and wanted to give it away, I'm sure my daughter would take me to court and try to have me declared incompetent."

"Well, at least Robert and Derrick are lawyers. I'm sure they'd take your case. I'll tell you what. A million is a nice round number. I'll add $500,000 to what your 'donor' is giving."

I was stunned. A sixteen-year-old who could drop that kind of money? "That's more than generous. I'm sure it will make the program very successful."

"Derrick can keep me informed. He told me all about what happened in your store. And that awful Dunmoore guy. I couldn't believe it. How is Dolores doing?"

"She's recovering nicely. I didn't realize you and Derrick were in contact. Of course, there's no reason I should have."

"Oh, yeah, we text and talk just about every day. He means so much to me, but don't you dare tell him I said that."

"It'll be just between us girls. How's your dad doing?"

"He's a lot better. They've made some adjustments to his prosthesis, and it's helping."

"I'm so glad to hear that. Well, remember you owe me some info about your childhood so I can get started on the book. I think I've pulled all I can get off the internet."

"And most of that's wrong. I don't have another concert until next week. I'll get out my diary and write up some stuff and send it to you."

"When did you start keeping a diary?"

"When I was six. There's a lot of printing in it at first."

The next day I stopped by my rental house to see how Dolores was doing. Her mother and Joseph were helping her clean out another room of Troy's old apartment. After examining everything in one room, I gave up and just told Dolores to use her judgment about what to toss. Because of her injury, she hadn't made any progress until the last couple of days. As I pulled up, Joseph was tossing two garbage bags into the dumpster in the driveway. Miz Maribelle met me at the back door.

"It's really nice of you, Ms. Cooper—I mean, Maureen—to set Dolores up here, but my family won't take handouts."

"This is no handout. Dolores is managing this building for me and saving me a lot of work by cleaning out this place. Joseph is going to be a big help at the store, especially with the website."

"Well, if they're doing honest work, that's fine. And I stress the 'honest' part."

Dolores rolled her eyes. "Mama, we've been all through that. I'm starting over. Everything's different now. Maureen's giving me a chance, and I'm going to grab it."

"I just want to do something to make up for what my grandfather did."

"Maureen, you can't atone for your ancestors' sins. Can you even atone for your own? That's not what they tell us in church. How could you know when you've done enough? What if you gave us a whole bunch of that money you found and then we said, 'That's not enough. We want more'? Rusty tried to make it right that we'd had a child. All that did was to get him into this drug business and that eventually got him killed."

Pepper was due to get his cast off. The vet wanted him for the afternoon to give him time to recover from the anesthetic. Rebecca and Wyatt had the store under control, so I decided to do something I'd been putting off for too long. I retrieved the little bear with the diaper from the desk in the office and walked across the square to Anna Maxwell's office.

Anna doesn't have a secretary. Her office is just one large room, with her desk and files on one side and a seating area on the other. There is a back room with file cabinets in it and a restroom. I waited just inside the door, with my hands behind my back, until she finished the phone call she was on.

I took the opportunity to compare the two of us again. I was wearing my typical jeans and loose-fitting shirt, with no make-up or jewelry. Whatever figure I had left was concealed. Anna, on the other hand, wore a navy skirt and jacket that hugged her waist and outlined her figure. The top two buttons of her white blouse were unfastened. Her make-up and earrings were complemented by a silver necklace that had an antique look to it. Had Troy given it to her? I wondered if I had just become too careless about my appearance. Was that why Troy lost interest?

Anna hung up the phone and said, "May I help you?" I hoped her tone with customers was less like an icicle through the heart.

I dropped the little bear on her desk, causing her to gasp.

"Where did you get that?"

"From the flowers you left on Troy's grave, with the note that said 'I wish I could have told you.'"

She kept her eyes on the bear and didn't say anything, but I saw tears starting.

"You're pregnant, aren't you? With Troy's child."

"What if I am?" She finally looked up. "It's none of your business."

"Rebecca says she's going to work with you on some more estate sales. Have you told her that she's going to have a half-sibling?"

"Not yet. Have you?"

"It's not my place to say anything about that. But I can say something about business ethics. I've told Rebecca that, if she expects to work for me in the store, she'd better not pull another scam like she did on Mrs. Boyd. I assume you were in on it."

Anna nodded. "Troy told me what they were going to do."

"And you were okay with that?"

"It was my first sale," she said defensively. "I needed Troy's help to pull it off and get myself established. The old biddy made a bundle from that sale—maybe not quite as much as she would have, but plenty."

I put my hands on her desk and leaned toward her. "Here's the deal. If I get the faintest whiff that you're scamming people on these sales, I will make sure word gets around that you're not to be trusted."

"I see." She stood up and folded her arms across her chest. "The Lawrenceville Old Guard will take a stand to crush the newcomer. Well, Ms. High-and-Mighty Cooper, if I hear that you've said one word against me or my business, you'll find yourself in court."

I straightened up and stepped back from her rather imposing figure. "Remember, my son is a lawyer, so that doesn't faze me. Can you afford the court costs?"

"I'll manage." She stepped from behind the desk and sat on one corner. "Troy and I took out life insurance policies on one another two years ago, for Valentine's Day. I'm not going to be rich, but I will survive."

"Is it enough money for you to leave Lawrenceville?"

"More than enough, but I won't give you the satisfaction." She picked up the little bear. "As I told you earlier, my girls like it here, for some reason. And I think Troy's child should grow up with his or her grandfather and half-siblings and their children. Oh, is everything okay with Robert and Derrick's surrogate?"

"She's fine." I slipped my hands into my pockets to lessen the temptation to punch Anna's face. "Didn't you take any precautions?"

Anna chuckled. "Oh, yes. Rebecca tells me you've been preaching safe sex since she was in high school." She drew a deep breath and turned more serious. "I thought if I got pregnant, Troy would marry me. He told me that was the only reason he married you."

Pepper and I were sitting in the porch swing as the sun went down. He seemed to need me now and lay with his head in my lap. His fur was matted where the cast had been, but he was walking pretty well. When Scott's car pulled into the driveway I looked up from scratching Pepper's head and sweet-talking him.

"Now that's an idyllic scene," Scott said as he came up the porch steps, carrying a small paper bag.

I tried to get Pepper to move enough for Scott to sit in the swing with us, but the dog was dead weight. "Sorry," I said. "Apparently getting the cast cut off was a little difficult for him. He hasn't let me get more than a couple of feet away from him since we got home."

"That's all right. I didn't mean to stay." Scott leaned against the

Albert A. Bell, Jr

porch banister. "I just wanted to give you this."

He handed me the bag, and I opened it see my gun. "Oh, have you finally decided that I can be trusted with it?" I had asked him about the gun a couple of times since the day he took it away from me. He said he was checking on permits.

"Maureen, I'm sorry I was over-protective and that I kind of creeped you out." He paused. "It's just that I care so much about you. If you could stop focusing on Troy and the past and look around you, maybe you could see more into the future." Before I could say anything he kissed me on the forehead and started down the steps to his car.

An inspiration hit me. I said, "Shane, come back!"

Albert **A. Bell, Jr** discovered his love for writing in high school, with his first publication in 1972. Although he considers himself a "shy person," he believes he is a storyteller more than a literary artist. He says, "When I read a book I'm more interested in one with a plot that keeps moving rather than long descriptive passages or philosophical reflection." He writes books he would enjoy reading himself.

A native of South Carolina, Dr. Bell has taught at Hope College in Holland, Michigan since 1978, and, from 1994 - 2004 served as Chair of the History Department. He holds a PhD from UNC-Chapel Hill, as well as an MA from Duke and an MDiv from Southeastern Baptist Theological Seminary. He is married to psychologist Bettye Jo Barnes Bell; they have four children and two grandsons

Bell is well-known for the historical mysteries of the series, **Cases from the Notebooks of Pliny the Younger.** *Corpus Conundrum,* third of the series, was a **Best Mystery of the year from Library Journal.** *The Secret of the Lonely Grave,* first in the series of **Steve and Kendra Mysteries** for young people, won a **Mom's Choice Silver Medal** and the **Evelyn Thurman Young Readers Award.**